ORDER OF

EDEN

A Novel by T.D. Orel

aBM

Published by:
A Book's Mind
PO Box 272847
Fort Collins, CO 80527

CHAPTER 1

ORIGINS OF WAR

"Again!" The one-armed grump shouted down from his perch, waving his stub in the air. The three boys looked up at their grandfather in disbelief. They had been training before the sun had risen above the stone towers behind their home; their stomachs growled with hunger and their throats were dry with thirst. The old man looked far too thick and gritty for his old age. His wrinkled chin and lips hid behind a dense and coarse gray beard. Despite his dotage, there was a heroic and powerful ring in his old voice. His natural girth and plentiful scars showed a fierce warrior once proudly wore the old man's skin.

"I said again!" The old man yelled once more, "You think the boys of Zaurak, who rely on their speed, haven't already run up the mountainside through the snow to strengthen their legs? Or the boys of Aldafar, who must always be keen and sharp, have not been studying by candlelight all night to strengthen their minds? I guarantee they have. So you, young Guardians, will train with your swords to strengthen your arms!"

All three boys responded in unison, "Yes, Grandfather!" Upon hearing their rival clan's names, more energy suddenly rushed to the boys. They looked around the training room and admired their clan's colors. The reds, golds, and other warm shades decorating the hall gave them strength. The masks and armor of fallen Guardians, which hung from the Eastern wall of the room, made them stir with anger. The clan crest of crimson and gold displayed on every banner and tapestry fueled their pride.

The fortress of Talitha sat cliff-side in a warm desert valley, completely isolated and hidden in an otherwise-barren land. No common road led to it and no ordinary man or woman new of its existence; a Celestial Cloud surrounded the city and hid the Guardians from both their enemies and human eyes. Great stone cliffs and orange rock formations encircled the home; it resided peacefully in a beautiful desert oasis. Patches of tall and sturdy palm trees sprouted wildly around the encampment, nourished by crystal blue streams and pools of water. The old stone towers and structures of the fortress were ruggedly handsome, forged from orange clay of the earth thousands of years ago. A variety of waterfalls spat from the clay cliffs around the fortress; the small city was a hidden paradise decorated with nature's finest desert plant life. Crimson banners embroidered with a bold and golden sun hung from every tower, gate, and bridge. Truly a beautiful estate, large and proud, just like the clan that found shelter there.

"Grandfather is right!" Eight-year-old Malachi cried out, "We will soon be the Guardians of Talitha, and we must have strength in our hearts and in our arms!" This brought a smile to the old man's bearded face. Malachi's cousins, motivated by his words, picked up their wooden swords from the ground and gripped them tightly. Dag was almost ten years old, and his brother Felix was now nine. Although older than Malachi, Dag and Felix always seemed to be far behind him in his training. Malachi was bred for battle; he feared nothing, and had a temper that was infamous within the house of Talitha. His dirty-blond hair was kept short on the sides and wavy on the top; a single braid dangled just off the side of his face. He was tall for his age and carried a strong chin and a stern brow; his green eyes were fierce and focused. The young boy's strength was unchallenged by any of the other boys in Talitha, and he often had to be reminded by his mother to show mercy in his training—unlike his father, who encouraged him to use his abilities to their full extent.

The sound of the boys's wooden swords cracking and slapping together filled the halls of the lower rooms of the fortress; they continued to train for at least two more hours. After their training was complete, their grandfather had a table, three chairs, and a large spread of food prepared for the three young warriors in the dining hall above them. With a mouth full of bread, Felix pleaded to the old man for a tale, "Please, Grandfather! Tell us of the Sun and the Moon again!" Malachi and Dag nodded in agreement.

"Ha ha!" The old king laughed deep and loud, "I have told you this story a hundred times! Yet you want to hear it again?" The boys, mouths all filled with food, nodded with excitement. "Very well then! As you know, Eden was once a perfect sanctuary. All things lived in harmony, and all creatures were safe and without fear. The Creator had done a marvelous job creating this place—as he does with all things—and He wanted to preserve it. So, he called upon the Moon and the Sun."

Malachi, getting too excited interrupted, "—and the Creator commanded them to make a Guardian stronger than any creature!"

"That is right Malachi, but you are getting ahead of yourself! Be patient!" The old man continued with his tale, "So, the Moon and the Sun created three creatures, much like man, but these were no ordinary humans. They wanted a creature that could see all things and have vast intelligence to help keep Eden protected. So, the Sun and the Moon took all of their combined knowledge and gave it to the first creature, whom they called *Aldafar*, the Knowledge Keeper, whom they dressed in elegant silvers and whites! His silver hair was woven in the wind and his spirit was plucked from the depths of the rivers. Next, they wanted a creature that could move through the shadows unseen with unchallenged speed. The Moon gave the power of stealth and haste to the creature known as *Zaurak*, who they cloaked in purple and shades of blue. His mind was born in a wild storm and his spine was sculpted from the icy frost of the mountains."

"The Shade Runners," said Dag with disgust.

"Correct, Dag. The Shade Runners of Zaurak." The boys began to squirm with excitement because they knew what came next. "Now, the Sun and the Moon needed a creature of great strength—one of courage and honor—a warrior fit to be the last line of defense against anything that may threaten the beautiful land of Eden! So, the Sun gave all of its burning strength to *Talitha*, the Fierce." An uproar filled the room; the boys cried out with prideful cheers as they pounded the table with their fists. The old king couldn't help but let out another deep laugh at the boys's excitement. "That's right, my young warriors. Talitha, clothed in shining gold, and ruby red, was the strongest creature to ever live. His breath was forged in the fires of the sun and his flesh was carved from the clays of the earth. Talitha was also the first warrior to receive the Savage Mark." Felix and Dag both awkwardly peered over at their cousin, Malachi. Malachi looked down at his right forearm, at this Savage Mark he knew so little about. Was it a blessing or a curse? Should Felix and Dag be envious they do not bare it, or praise the Creator they don't? The King suddenly furrowed his brow and his voice lost its cheer, "But what happened next, none of the three protectors were prepared for." Dag and Felix slouched in their seats and an uneasy churning began to shake in their bellies, but Malachi did not flinch. "One of the Creator's very own subjects turned against him."

"The Serpent," Malachi whispered with a stern face.

"Yes, the Serpent. The Serpent came to the Sun and the Moon and told them that he too wanted to be a protector of Eden, but he claimed he did not have the power to do so. You see boys, the Serpent is a deceiver, a trickster. He convinced the Sun and the Moon they should give him all of their intelligence, the Sun's strength, the Moon's mystique, and even a Savage Mark so he too could protect the land of Eden. The Sun and Moon gave him what he asked for, unaware of his wicked intentions. The Serpent came to Eden, and the most-epic battle of all time was fought against the protectors. Of course, Talitha was the only one that stood a chance," the boys all nodded in agreement unaware of their Grandfather's bias,

"But not even our great ancestor could stop him." Again, the King's gaze became focused and stern; he sat up straight with purpose. "The Serpent entered Eden and brought death and pain into the world. There was a time when the Serpent had so heavily corrupted the world, the Creator had to destroy it and start anew. But the Sun and the Moon had realized what they had done and took it upon themselves to stop the Serpent. They took seven spiritual relics, each more powerful than the last, and used them to seal the Serpent away. So, tell me boys, what is the purpose of our three clans today?"

"To locate, gather, and protect the Seven Scripture Seals!" Malachi shouted out the answer without hesitation.

"And who serves alongside us?"

"The other members of the Order of Eden, the warriors of Aldafar and Zaurak." Felix answered halfheartedly, he cringed his face and stuck out his tongue.

"Correct. A select few from each family keep the peace around the Earth still today."

"An easy task for the Guardians of Talitha." Felix said proudly.

"That is not always the case. As you know, a clan opposes the Order of Eden... The Immortals of Abaddon." The boys squirmed in their seats. "Before the Serpent was sealed away, he recruited six servants from all three families, and they still fight for him today. They search for the Seals with their undead minions and skilled warriors, led by the Serpent's general, Cain."

"Cain is the fiercest and most deadly Immortal," Malachi yelled out.

"Right. And that my boys, is why you train so vigorously. So, when you come face to face with a member of Abaddon, you will stand firm ready to fight, unafraid."

"It's a shame we have to fight alongside those other weaklings though—always protecting them, carrying their weight." Dag said with a smirk as he stabbed his fork into a chunk of ham.

"Boy, don't be such a fool." The King growled, "Just because they do not have our strength, does not mean they are not to be respected. We may be the strongest and the bravest warriors of the Order, but we too rely on the spies of the Zaurakian clan and the wisdom of the Aldafarian clan!"

"I understand Grandfather, forgive me." Dag said in embarrassment, his cheeks flush red.

"It's quite alright, my boy. You will learn all these things soon enough."

Malachi jumped in, "I am excited to fight alongside them. I read that Siren of Zaurak can run along walls like a spider, and that Shara of Aldafar can read another man's mind and even control his body. I cannot wait until I discover my abilities and fight the forces of Abaddon. Bring all the Vipers in the world. I will be ready." He raised his fork in the air like it was a mighty sword.

"Your time will come, Malachi. But know this: after a bloody battle with many fearsome foes, you will look back to days such as this, and wish you were simply playing with wooden swords in the safety of these halls." The old man looked down at his severed arm and thought back to a battle he wouldn't ever dismiss from his memory. "Be thankful for these days, my grandchildren. These are good days."

"Another story, Grandfather!" Yelled Dag, lightening the mood, "One of my father, the Great Tiger of Talitha!"

"Ha ha! Sure, I can tell another!" As the one-armed leader of the Talithan clan went on telling the stories within the corridors of the fortress, he couldn't help but watch Malachi's eyes light up at every heroic tale. Little did any of them know those stories would pale in comparison to the adventures and battles young Malachi would face.

CHAPTER 2

NEVER THE HUNTED

Ten Years Later

"Today is your day, my son; don't let anyone take that from you. Especially not some arrogant Zaurakian brat." Malachi blotted out the sounds of the horns and drums and focused closely on his father's words. "He will be fast. Do not let that throw you off balance. Keep your strikes clean and strong. If you land a blow, crush his skull with your next. Do not let him get back up." The crowd roared widely; this was the fight of the century. The pride of Talitha, Malachi, now eighteen, had surpassed everyone's expectations. His strength was terrifying. A well-placed punch could strike a hole straight through the chest of even the burliest of humans. He learned not simply to rely on his strength; his skill with a sword was just as intimidating as his fist.

Malachi was now truly handsome and fully grown into his body; he had a clean smile and a chiseled physique. His square jawline ran down into a stone pillar of a neck. The young warrior's nose was bumped and jagged, the result of being broken many a times during his training. Malachi's heroic brow and boxy forehead were ideal for delivering ruthless head-butts during close combat; a thin slice of his eyebrow was missing from a time he used that move against Dag—

and another larger *X*-shaped scar just below his hairline from when he tried it against a stonewall. His dirty-blond hair was shaved short on the sides, square and geometric Talithan designs cut into the right side of his head; on the top, his wavy locks were pushed back across his head and naturally swooped off to the left. Being over six feet tall, and built like a bull, he caught the eye of every girl he passed within the city walls of Talitha. With such admiration from his clan, naturally his pride had swelled as massively as his muscles. Every person waiting for the fight was nearly giddy with excitement, even if they did not show it. Malachi's grandfather had passed away some years back, and now his father, Tarjak, was head of the Talithan clan.

Tarjak appeared to be truly more grizzly bear than man. A fiery red beard covered his barbaric face and his rigid head sat upon a tree-trunk-like neck similar to his son's. Tarjak was the type of man that would take an arrow to the chest, casually finish his ale, then lumber over to rip the archer in half.

Because Tarjak led the Talithan clan, this meant Malachi was next in line to be the leader of Talitha. Malachi's opponent was the youngest son of Varden, the head of the Zaurakian clan. The crowd was calling it, the "Battle of the Princes."

On this night, their secret society—the Order of Eden—was wide-awake. No one, besides those involved and their enemies, knew of its existence: a secret task force trapped in the past, fighting for the future. Humans living a secular life were completely oblivious to their existence, blinded by worldly distractions and unaware that Shade Runners, Guardians, and Knowledge Keepers were the only thing standing between them and the savage and ancient forces of the Serpent, who would bring certain death and destruction.

If a young man was chosen to train as a Shade Runner or a Guardian, once the warrior turned eighteen, he must show his skill in battle in front of all three clans at the Tri-Family Feast. After his battle, the Elders of Aldafar would anoint him with an animal-inspired mask and armor, known as a totem. This mask would be a part of the warrior's life until the day he died. Every mission and every battle, the mask would hide his face and would become his identity.

Malachi and Zacharias had trained nearly ten years for this day, and they were ready.

"No one can stop you boy, prove it." Malachi's father believed these words, but he knew his opponent would not simply roll over. Zacharias of Zaurak, was not one to be trifled with himself. Although he was quite muscular, he was much sleeker than Malachi. Normally, his thick hair fell down past his shoulders, but for the fight, it was tied back neatly in a bun behind his head. His hair was a dense black, just like his cryptic eyes. A sharp scar ran down the left side of his face, courtesy of his loving father no doubt. His skin resembled dark-tanned leather, it contrasted the beautiful lavender markings that had been painted on his body. Looking at the boy, any man would fear him, but would not want to look away because of his mysterious swagger.

Clink clink, the iron gates in front of the boys slowly slid higher and higher. A heavy silence fell over the crowd.

"Come back a champion, or not at all." Varden said in his normal un-amused tone. Varden stood tall and dark. His cold and almost-lifeless eyes created a permanent glare of disapproval underneath sharp scowling eyebrows. Like his son, his hair ran dense and a shadowy black; it lay in thick black dreads, tied in a messy knot behind his head with a few strands running down over his shoulders. Zacharias nodded to his father and stepped out into the large circular pit, undistracted by the excited fans all around him. Zacharias would have been content if only his father spectated the brawl; he was the only person he cared to impress. He moved toward the center of the ring and heard a familiar voice he could not ignore; it came from behind him as the gate closed.

"Fear nothing, Zach. You are a wolf now," his older brother, Fenrir, whispered with a smirk from behind the closed gate. Zacharias instantly let his shoulders relax and he released a soft exhale. For a moment, he studied the arena around him. This could be the biggest day of Zacharias's young life: this day he must prove he is a warrior worthy of the Zaurakian name. The stone floor beneath his bare feet was marvelous. Each stone tile placed perfectly, decorated with simple and well-balanced colors. At the center of the pit, the family crest of each respective clan lay flat, carved deep into the stone. The war drums beat louder with fierce heavy thuds.

"Never the hunted," Tarjak said softly to Malachi as his gate began to creep upward.

"Always the hunter," Malachi replied as he moved toward the opening. With each step, the anticipation in the young warrior's heart rose. He had been bred for this very day—a child raised to fight, to kill, to win. Malachi's gate was now open, and he stepped down and moved closer to his opponent, Zacharias did not acknowledge him. Both boys were shirtless and painted with their clan's marks and symbols, Malachi in red and gold, Zacharias in black and purple. The symbols of Talitha were thick and bold, only straight lines and hard angles. Zaurak's symbols were thinner and more jagged designs as if they had been painted with claws and wild slashes. Neither boy seemed fazed by the situation; they kept their poise and continued to march forward in the direction of the center of the ring as the drumbeats grew faster and faster. Once they met at the middle, they locked eyes; the music and cheering ceased. They turned to the east side of the pit and kneeled before His Grace, the Lord of the Aldafarian clan.

The Leader of the Aldafarian clan and voice of the Order of Eden, was one of five men wearing their totem mask. The mask covered only the top half of his face and a thick white beard covered the rest. His age unknown, he was certainly the oldest member of the three clans and was respected as the wisest. Despite his old age, his mind was sharper than ever, a joyful and kind old man. His mask was a delightful sight; the stones and wood from which it had been forged were assembled with obvious precision. The silver designs swirled and seemed to dance around the contours of his face. A handsome and full rack, like that of a full-grown stag, sprung from the sides of his mask. Beads and jewels hung from the antlers, and a snowy-white hood hid the rest of his head. The elegant thin designs swirled down his robes and his thin armor all the way to his boots. The handle of a beautifully crafted short sword could be spotted peeking out from behind his silver robe. An ancient staff rested in his wrinkled palms. He rose to his feet, everyone else in the coliseum did the same, except Malachi and Zacharias.

Everyone was dressed in their best, looking quite dashing. The crowd was split into three sections. The men of Talitha wore all black with small gold pins on their chests and crimson undershirts. The women were in their finest ruby dresses—sleek, yet modest, complimented by classic Talithinan gold jewelry. Valor, courage, and respect were characteristics the people of Talitha held dearly in their hearts. The red colors they wore represented passion, and the golds stood for honor and trust. The men who were not chosen at birth to become a Guardian often became talented forgers and blacksmiths. They used heavy, and almost indestructible metals, to craft priceless weapons for the warriors.

Zaurakian men bore all-black garments as well, but wrapped, tucked, or hung a violet scarf around their necks. The woman of Zaurak wore sapphire dresses, usually with a black or gray fur scarf; stone jewelry hung from their ears and necks. The people of Zaurak valued discipline, pride, and success at all cost. They were a rather rough and mysterious people, not often comfortable in social settings. Some men in the clan who would not become Shade Runners would master working with pelts and leather. They designed very practical and handsome clothing from furs and hides for all the warriors.

Only the five Elders of Aldafar were in the crowd; the other men and women of Aldafar were down below preparing their healing chambers in case of an injury. All five Elders bore their totem masks: the stag at the center, accompanied by the Bear, Elephant, Crane, and Lynx. The people of Aldafar were truly gifted healers and physicians; they practiced perfection in everything they did. Intelligence, skill, and precision were often the main qualities of a member of Aldafar. A few of them could be quite snobby. Their silver and white clothing screamed elegance and sophistication, and their silver hair always looked as if it took hours to complete the braiding and beading. Although the other members of the Order often viewed them as uptight, they could be particularly nurturing and gentle—and in battle, remarkably dangerous.

"Welcome members of the Order of Eden!" The whole arena bowed slightly to their elder. "Pray with me, my friends." The old Stag's voice was soft and soothing, yet authoritative. "Creator, we thank you for these two young men who are about to do battle; they have trained since they could walk so that they may serve you and protect those who cannot protect themselves. We ask for no injuries that our healers could not heal, and no foul play be afoot. Creator, we thank you for the breath in our lungs and this divine purpose you have tasked us with. I pray that all the members of the clans grow closer on this day, especially these two young warriors below us."

"I would rather die here in this pit." Zacharias whispered to himself just loud enough for Malachi to hear as he rolled his dark eyes.

"Careful what you wish for, sweetheart." Malachi replied with a snicker as he clenched his fist and flexed his body. Zacharias was taken aback; no one had ever spoken back to him before. He had been told his whole life that he was a king amongst simple servants; he had never faced verbal confrontation. Zacharias was quite embarrassed by the comment, but mostly consumed with rage.

The old man continued the prayer unaware of the squabbling below him, "Continue to protect us, and guide my hand tonight when presenting these young men with their new identities. We live to serve you and keep evil forces at bay. Give us the strength, haste, and knowledge to do so. In Your great name, we live to serve You." The crowd sat back down and prepared for the battle.

"You better pray that the old man picked their best healers today." The normally reserved Zacharias said with a stern face, never actually looking at his opponent.

"My only prayer is that they will be able to sew your jaw back into your face." Malachi snapped with a smile. Malachi loved banter; he and his cousins were masters at it. Zach's breaths became short and choppy as he began to pant in anger. Tempers were beginning to flare; the fight could not start any sooner for either one of the boys. They rose and headed back to their gates, turned, and faced each other. Again, a dramatic and powerful ambience spewed from the drums and horns, the crowd was on the edge of their seats.

Meanwhile, in the back of the arena, Fenrir was heading toward an enemy of his own. "Ah, takes me back." He said in a sarcastic tone, flipping his dark hair out of his face as crept behind Dag. Fenrir had scurried to the top of the stands so he could sit behind Dag and Felix, Malachi's cousins. Dag rolled his eyes and pretended not to hear him. "Takes me back to when the mighty Dag and I battled only two years ago, and Dag crushed me with his mighty strength!" Fenrir chuckled to himself knowing well he had bested Dag in their fight.

"Leave Fenrir; no one wants to hear your boasting." Felix said, uneasy with Fenrir's presence.

"The great Leopard of Talitha brought to his knees by the young much-more-handsome Wolf of Zaurak! It was too easy." Fenrir said proudly. He was similar to Zacharias in appearance, but much different in character. He was cocky, arrogant, and awfully troublesome. The only people he seemed to care for were his siblings; everyone else was simply a peasant—surely an idea inspired by his father. He was deviously good-looking like his brother, but he knew it. His thick black hair sat around his shoulders and parted at the center of his scalp; his violet scarf was draped underneath, and his sleeves rolled up to his elbows. His eyes carried a mystery; they were two completely different colors and rumors spread that he could seduce any woman with them. Obviously, Zacharias and a few others close to him knew it was an outrageous tale, but he milked it anyway. His left eye was an icy blue, and the other was a crisp gray. They seemed to be able to trace his enemies every movement and were a perfect fit for such a zealous young man.

"If I remember correctly, you simply got lucky. It was a very close fight." Dag finally spoke up, nodding his head to reassure himself.

"Ha! Then your memory is as weak as your skill in battle." Fenrir leaned in close. Dag shot out of his seat and was ready for a rematch. Thankfully for Dag, Varden snapped his fingers getting both the boys's attention from down below. With a look of sheer frustration, he signaled to his son to return to his seat.

"Ah, maybe next time boys. Enjoy the show." He walked away, chest puffed out; he had all the talk in the world, and he could back it up.

Dag, frustrated as ever, looked down at Malachi. "Come on cousin, show them that Talitha is the heart of the Order of Eden." Dag's hair was shaved, except a single thick stripe down the middle. Dag, with his Mohawk and large build was quite intimidating, and he loved to accessorize. He had four piercings on one ear and two on the other; he always sported a large stone necklace of Talithan colors around his thick neck. After his Tri-Family feast, was given the mask of the leopard for his skills as a tracker and hunter; he now used large heavy spears in combat. Dag obsessed about the idea of a rematch against Fenrir; he felt his skills had doubled since their last fight. This was true, but Fenrir's had tripled. For now, though, he would have to let Malachi do the fighting.

Dag and Felix, now twenty-one and twenty, had become fine warriors. Both large men like their cousin, and both proud new Guardians of Talitha. Unlike his brother, Felix had let his brow hair grow long and wild. The mane fell over his shoulders and was decorated with an assortment of red and gold beads. Felix, a versatile and powerful hunter, was awarded the mask of the eagle. Felix had mastered the twin-sword technique, and used two heavy straight blades.

Just as the intense music met its climax, the Great Elder spoke once more, "Let us begin!" He lifted his brittle wooden staff into the air and the very ground beneath Malachi and Zach's feet began to shift. Many of the stone tiles erected from the floor and created pillars all around the battleground, some over fifteen feet tall. A collection of the stones created walls, others created steps, and others simply rose straight in the air. "It is rare that a Guardian or Shade Runner will ever battle on flat ground; adapt to your environment, gentlemen." Neither boy was caught off guard. They had trained for this. The time for talk had ceased. The entire arena fell silent. The boys locked eyes; it was time to see who was the better warrior.

Both young men dashed toward each other. Zacharias threw the first punch. Malachi blocked it with his forearm and sent his own fist slamming into his opponent's gut. The punch lifted Zach straight into the air; he had never felt such strength. A croaky groan shot from Zach's lungs. Just as Zacharias' feet touched the ground, he spotted another punch coming straight for his chin. The wind knocked from his chest, but he knew he needed to move. A quick dodge! Malachi's fist struck nothing but air as he swung his arm, the miss threw him off balance and left him vulnerable. Zacharias sent two fierce blows at Malachi; the first caught him in the throat and the second in the collarbone. As he stumbled backward, Zacharias jabbed three more times at his face; all three were direct hits. Malachi had never seen such speed.

Zacharias became over confident and threw two more quick jabs. Malachi swatted them both away with ease. Malachi answered with a huge right hook; Zacharias leaned back and flipped out of the way with impressive agility. Malachi drove after him, throwing another heavy punch at his torso. Zacharias was now pinned, his back against a stone pillar and a raging bull charging at his front. Zacharias flipped off the pillar behind him using all of his acrobatic skills and speed. The punch drove into the granite pillar and crushed it into pieces as if it was made of glass. The crowd gasped in admiration. Tarjak sent a smug smirk in Varden's direction; Varden was un-amused.

Zacharias leaped upon one of the twelve-foot walls landing with much grace and ease, hoping to escape his attacker. Despite his efforts, Malachi was pursuing him relentlessly. Malachi jumped high in the air and tried to hammer Zach from above with both his fists clenched together. In a blur, Zacharias vanished from atop the wall, once again showcasing his quickness. The crowd blinked rapidly, thinking maybe something was wrong with their eyesight, but it was truly just the young boy's speed.

When Malachi brought his fist down where his opponent once was, it turned the wall to rubble. Shrapnel and dust sprayed the crowd sitting nearest to the action. With wicked speed, Zacharias attacked from the rear, throwing rapid jabs into Malachi's spine. Zacharias moved so quickly, not even Malachi could tell how many strikes his attacker landed. Mumbled grunts rolled from Malachi's lips as each punch drove into his back. Malachi twisted to the side and caught Zach with a heavy backhand to his torso. Zach nearly crumpled under the force and the hit sent him flying straight through one of the stone pillars! The spectators winced in pain at the heavy blow.

Zacharias quickly staggered to his feet; he would show no weakness. He spit blood from his lips onto the ground. Dust filled the air, and more excitement filled the room. Each boy bled either from his lips or face. Their war paint had become smeared and messy. Neither warrior showed signs of quitting; actually, they seemed to be just getting started.

Zacharias sprung forward, dust and gravel flew up behind him. Like an arrow shot from a long bow, Zach ripped through the air, staying low to the ground. Anyone in the stands who blinked would have missed the attack. Malachi was struck hard in the face; he spun and fell to the ground in a daze. Zacharias went to strike him again while he was on the ground, but Malachi was not going to take another hard hit. He threw his legs back over his head and flipped off the ground, just dodging Zach's attack. Now they were face to face in the middle of the arena. They snarled as they drove after each other.

Both warriors unloaded, holding nothing back. Zach was blocking, dipping, and dodging like a small bird avoiding a hawk. Malachi blocked and swung like a ferocious grizzly protecting its young. They slid and flipped over the stone obstacles with speed and grace, all while trying to land a blow on their opponent.

Malachi used his massive forearms to smash away Zach's attacks; he waited for an opening, ducking under a jab, and came up with all the fury of a Talithan warrior! He crushed Zach's jaw with a brutal uppercut. This first strike knocked Zacharias off balance; he followed it with a heavy right elbow across his cheek, then a quick cross to the chin. The rattling shock waves and sheer force of each attack was strong enough to crush the skull of any average man. Zacharias's eyes spun in his head as he struggled to stay conscious. Most people would have given up after such a terrible combination of punches, but as crimson blood rolled down his lips, he could only think of the shame and disappointment in his father's eyes if he were to lose.

Malachi threw his meaty fist once more from the left, but Zacharias spun beneath his attack and jabbed twice at his throat on his way out. Malachi gasped for air, but instead of receiving oxygen to his lungs, he received a swift kick to the side of the head. He stayed on his feet and shook his head to try and awaken himself the brutal kick. Malachi's mind spun and he blinked rapidly; he struggled to stay focused as blood ran over his right eye, hindering his vision. Despite the damage, he refused to fall to the stone beneath him.

The crowd was astonished. Malachi was keeping pace with the Shade Runner's speed, and Zacharias was taking devastating punches from the hands of a Guardian. No one knew who would win; it was like watching two bucks lock horns and fight vigorously for the heart of an admiring doe.

"The boy from Talitha fights like a blubbering troll, and the boy from Zaurak throws his offensive strikes like a blind cave bat." A soft whisper came from behind the seats of the Elders of Aldafar. The young voice spoke casually, as if he meant no offense by his negative commentary.

"I thought I asked you to stay down below with the healers, Cyrus." The Crane of Aldafar said without looking back at his son. Shara, or the Crane, was one of the most respected Elders of the Order, and he expected that his son would follow his path and become an Elder.

"I know all that there is to know about healing; I grew bored of their talk of minerals and herbs. I wanted to spectate the combat." He paused for a moment as he watched Malachi and Zach flip and dive in the arena. "I could defeat both these warriors with six strikes, father." The hooded boy stayed close behind his father as he watched intently at the action below. His cloak was gorgeous, as his clothes always were, trimmed with silver and all the beautiful markings of Aldafar. A dignified and handsome face lay hidden beneath his cloak, with flawless skin and thin dark lips. His snow-white hair could just barely be seen from under his gray hood; it was lengthy, but very neatly kept with an assortment of braids that ran all the way down his spine. His eyes were a sharp sky blue that popped against his powder-white skin.

"I'm aware your technique in battle is superior, but the Knowledge Keepers do not partake in such trivial competitions. You will be recognized tonight at the ceremony, be patient."

"Very well, may I stay and continue to observe the competition?"

"You may not. Return to the healers, Cyrus." Shara ordered sharply from under his beaked mask. Cyrus bowed respectfully and snuck away the same way he came, his eyes filled with disappointment. He was now eighteen and still trapped under his father's tyrannical rule. He felt strongly that he was much more intelligent and gifted than the two young men in the arena and he was confused why is father wanted to continue to keep his existence a secret until the ceremony. He was sleek and not as muscular as Malachi and Zacharias, but just as tall. His face was thin and had been seen by few; most people of the Order did not know he even existed. He always looked presentable; some had even said pretty—not a hair out of place on his head, and his clothing always very dashing. As he headed back toward the healing chambers, he took one last glance at the young warriors in the pit battling for their clan's honor and love. He observed everyone in the stands; he watched the people cheering on their comrades and being merry with those around them. A swirling anxiousness rolled in his chest; loneliness gripped his heart.

CHAPTER 3

ALWAYS THE HUNTER

Frustration and anger spread in Malachi like a wildfire; in his mind, he had let Zacharias challenge him for far too long. He forced back his fatigue, pain, and soreness and refused to let up. Pushing forward, he moved at a speed even the people of the Zaurkian clan were impressed by. Malachi drove the inside of his arm into Zacharias's neck, sending him to the stone floor. Malachi grabbed him off the ground by the neck and pinned him against a nearby pillar, the people of Talitha were on their feet bellowing with pride. Zacharias attempted to break free from the chokehold and thrashed about wildly, but Malachi was too strong. He decided if he could not release Malachi's arm, he would break it. Zacharias started unloading punches with his right hand into Malachi's shoulder. His hand moved so viciously no one could count how many strikes he landed, each blow weakening Malachi's grip. Finally, Malachi's collarbone shattered beneath Zach's fist, and the ligaments in his shoulder were torn like threads. He cried out in pain, but only for a split second as he fell to one knee. Now the people of Zaurak were on their feet cheering, except for Varden, who sat with an expressionless glare across his face—as usual.

"Damn! He's hurt." Dag looked down at his cousin with concern.

"Ha! Please, if I know Malachi, this will only piss him off. That Zaurakian boy is in trouble." Felix was right; a new fire was lit inside Malachi. Zacharias looked into his opponent's eyes and saw no pain, only ferocity.

"Run, Shade Runner." Malachi said as he looked up at Zacharias. The crowd fell silent; Malachi's confidence shook the whole arena.

Zacharias scoffed as he sent a punch straight at Malachi's face. Instead of dodging the blow, Malachi caught him by the wrist with his good arm. He slowly rose from where he knelt, squeezing Zacharias's arm tighter and tighter. *SNAP!* Even the healers below the arena heard the snap of the bone. Zach yelped in agony; in the stands, Fenrir had to look away as his little brother tried frantically to free his broken arm. Malachi released his wrist and palmed Zach's entire face; he slowly began to raise him by nothing but his muzzle. This battle was over. Malachi heaved him high in the air, straight above his own head, and then smashed him violently into the ground with a heavy *thud*. The ground cracked beneath Zach's limp body.

The coliseum shook from the attack, and the crowd fell silent in awe of Malachi's brute strength. After a long silence, the Great Stag rose from his seat, lifted his staff, and slammed it into the ground. Just as the staff hit, huge banners of Talitha fell from the ceiling and the drums and horns began to play once more. Sparks and confetti in red and gold filled the room, followed by joyful cries from the people of Talitha. Malachi held his head high and smirked heroically at his clan members, hiding a childlike excitement stirring within him.

"Well done, my boy!" The old man shouted as he shot his staff in the air. The healers scurried out to take Zacharias out of the arena and encouraged Malachi to follow. Zacharias, barely conscious, refused to take his eye off Malachi as they carried him away; anger swelled through his body. Zacharias furrowed his brow and bit his lower lip in frustration. A hate he had never known came over him as he stared at the prince of Talitha, standing triumphantly at the center of the arena enjoying the splendors of his victory.

Down beneath the arena, the two healers immediately went to work on Zacharias. Thin laces of light swirled around the healers's hands and danced down his broken body. Zach moaned in pain as the healers reset his bones and the radiance burned his cuts closed. A sleek spider web of light seemed to be spun with great speed from the healer's hands and covered his wrist, back, and head. As they worked on their patient, simple white stones framed by silver rings on the healers's fingers shined dimly.

In the room just down the hall, Malachi was also being attended to, but by the head Elder himself. The Great Stag removed his mask and set it down beside Malachi; he leaned his staff against the stone table where Malachi sat. Beneath the mask, the old man had two very soft gray eyes surrounded by wrinkles. A swirling silver Aldafarian design was tattooed above his right eye and continued down the side of his face. The signs of Aldafar seemed almost angelic, thin, delicate, and without fault.

"Amazing job, my boy. You truly impressed the lot of us this evening." The old man said in a genuinely pleased voice. Malachi simply smiled and nodded, trying not to show how exhausted he was. The excitement of the battle and his victory was starting to fade, and his many wounds began to release the agonizing pains of battle. Malachi shifted his position on the table, then cringed as a terrible burning shot through his shoulder and up his neck.

"Here, let me see that," the Great Stag said as he stretched out his thin arm and gently placed his hand on Malachi's still-dislocated shoulder. A white stone, set in a silver ring, began to shine; it released a legion of luminous strands. The threads of light covered his shoulder in all directions, quickly healing his injury, reattaching the ligaments, and mending his shattered collarbone. A recovery that would normally take a few months was being completed in a few minutes.

After about ten minutes of treatment, the old man spoke up again, "Well how do you feel?"

Malachi moved his arm back and forth. "Great, actually," he said, sounding rather surprised. "Thank you, your Grace."

"It was my pleasure to help such a promising young warrior," the old man said with a wink.

"Is that a Healing Stone you're using? I've never seen one used in person." Malachi studied the old man's ring and its elegant Aldafarian design. The white stone on the ring shone and the metallic band seemed to move as if it were alive while its abilities were in use. The Great Stag had a Legacy Ring on each one of his fingers, each with a different color stone, and hosting a unique ability.

"Good eye, Malachi. Yes, it is; your father will probably give you a few rings later after the festivities." The Great Stag said with a joyful grin, smooshing the wrinkles around his face.

"Tell me, are you nervous for the ceremony this evening?" The old man asked.

He thought about his answer for a moment. "I would be lying if I said I wasn't a little nervous." Malachi said with a chuckle as he moved his nearly healed arm up and down. "But I am more excited than nervous. I just hope I receive a totem that makes my father, and my clan, proud. So, don't give me a butterfly or a dolphin." They both laughed and imagined Tarjak's face, the great Lion of Talitha, seeing his son being assigned such an adorable creature.

The Great Stag was very surprised by Malachi's sense of humor; he ran his fingers through his snow-white beard.

"Do not worry about that my boy; I think the Creator has something exceptional planned for you. You must not worry about pleasing your father. Eventually, the cub always leaves the den and must hunt his own prey." The old man paused and looked Malachi straight in the eyes. "No matter what you do, as long as you serve this Order, your father will be proud of you. And the cub will return to the den a king, and one day lead the pride." Malachi nodded to show his understanding; he let a tiny grin sneak across his lips.

"I see great things in your future boy, but you have a difficult road ahead. A road that no one else would have the strength to follow— everyone else would turn back. At times, even you will wish to turn back..." Malachi cocked his head to the side in confusion. The Stag paused and took a deep breath; he studied one of the white jewels on his ring. "Do you know how to get a mineral to its purest form, Malachi? It must first be exposed to extreme pressure and heat. After undergoing an intense treatment, the mineral will be presented in its most beautiful and true form."

Malachi looked confused, and thought to himself, "Does the old man tell this to everyone before their coronations?" Malachi said, almost comically, still confused by the Stag's words, "All warriors of our Order face challenges, right?"

"Of course they do! But I warn you now, no one's trials thus far will compare to the burden that falls upon you. I fear the weight of the world will come down on you and that Savage Mark of yours." Malachi's eyes widened, and he puffed out his chest a little as he ran his hand over the mark on his forearm. Malachi was used to hearing how important he was, but not from the head of the Order of Eden. He ignored the obvious caution in the old man's voice. "But I promise you, you will not face this alone. And Za—"

Malachi interrupted, "I do not fear whatever lies ahead, your Grace. I will be ready. I promise you." Malachi said with an arrogant smirk, confused why the Great Stag seemed so concerned.

"Apologies, Malachi, I am getting ahead of myself," the Stag said with a hearty chuckle as he patted Malachi on the leg. "Relax and wash up for the ceremony." He rose to his feet and grabbed his staff from its resting place. He nodded at the confused young warrior, then gently placed the head of his staff against Malachi's chest. "Many have fought in this war, only some can change it. And no one can change it alone." The old man emphasized the word *alone* greatly, and tilted his head; he then scurried from the room without warning.

"Wait, what?" Malachi had a million questions, but the old man was gone. "Silly old kook. What the hell was he talking about?" Malachi got to his feet and followed him. The great stone hall was empty; the old man was nowhere in sight. Malachi continued down the hall, moving quicker and quicker, hoping to catch up. He came around the corner leading to a marble staircase and his heart nearly stopped.

He had never feared battle, giants, or Vipers, but in this moment, he froze in nervousness. He had never seen anything like this before—his jaw seemed to become unhinged. At the top of the stairs was a girl descending the steps toward him.

Obviously, Malachi had seen girls before, but this mysterious creature was different. She walked with a confidence that could scare off any man—as if she owned the entire coliseum. Her hair was as black as the fur she wore around her neck. It was long and thick, bouncing and flowing weightlessly with each movement she took upon the stone steps. Her eyes were moon-like, but brown, like rich caramel over a chocolate candy. An icy-sapphire eyeliner ran across her eyelids, contrasted by dark and long lashes. Malachi was so mesmerized by her tan skin, beautiful face, and stunning physique that he did not realize she was clearly of the Zaurakian clan. A single braid ran behind her head, purple beads woven in with two black raven feathers. A violet flower sat behind her right ear and a handsome charcoal fox pendant, with sapphire markings, was pinned to the strap of her dress. A layered stone necklace of Zaurakian colors hung from her neck and sat on her chest. Complex earrings and rings accessorized her small ears and fingers. If she had a flaw, Malachi could not see it.

He felt sweaty; his stomach turned and twisted. He fought for words; he tried to think of anything smooth or funny, but nothing came out. Before he knew it, she had walked right by him. Practically buzzed from her intoxicating presence, Malachi thought to himself, "Did she even know I was here? She didn't even look at me." He watched as she strutted away through the hall, still amazed by her beauty. His eyes wandered down and looked at her rear, as any weak-willed eighteen-year-old would do. He quickly looked away in embarrassment, his face candy-apple red. He was happy his father was not there, because he knew he would have been whacked across the back of the head with terrible force. "Be respectful, you idiot," he thought to himself. "That could be your wife... Actually no... That will be your wife. Yes, I'm going to marry that girl." Again, Malachi ignored that she was of Zaurak. Obviously, overconfident, he bolted after her.

"Um, hi," all the muscles and skill in battle could not help Malachi here; he was off to a poor start.

The mystery girl said nothing and continued on her way. Malachi skipped after her, his eyebrows raised in surprise and confusion. But the setback did not defer young Malachi; it only motivated him; the hunt was on.

"Excuse me. I... um..." Malachi ran his hand threw his hair awkwardly; she continued along the stone corridor. "I have never seen you before. What's your name?" The girl did not answer. She rolled her eyes a little and continued on her path. She walked with purpose and poise. Malachi did not seem to peak her interest at all. The young warrior noticed the purple flower in her hair, "Fine, I will call you... *Violet*."

"Violet?" She whipped back at him, "That's awful!" She said in disgust with an un-amused chuckle. Every word she said melted Malachi's heart; she was unbearably fierce.

Malachi cleared his throat and tried to answer with confidence this time. "Um... Yes. Yes Violet. That is your name until you tell me what your actual name is." Malachi cracked a smile, now feeling more confident.

"Ha! Fine, I will call you Brainless Meathead then." She responded with an ice-cold glare. Malachi smiled again, amused by her sass. This was no damsel in distress; Malachi was infatuated.

"I like it, Violet. Where you heading?"

The girl squinted her dark eyes, apparently impressed by how well he took her insult, but she still seemed annoyed with his persistence. She no longer seemed to be in such a hurry though. She was still walking, but moving a little slower. Simply swaying back and forth across the hallway now, to Malachi she was like a weightless leaf floating in the breeze.

"So, where are you heading?" Malachi pried, thinking maybe she did not hear him, but there was still no response. "Violet, you're killing me. Come on, give me something here." He pleaded. She just kept walking, enjoying the little game she was playing. He gently grabbed her wrist. "Listen, you should come riding with me one day." Malachi asked, promise in his voice.

She finally stopped moving, then pulled her wrist free from his grasp with surprising force. "Riding?" She asked, sounding rather confused.

"Yes, like on a hors…"

"I know what riding is, Meathead." She interrupted. The girl before him stepped forward and scowled, blinking wildly as if she were trying to clear her eyes of Malachi's annoyance. "Everyone's been riding. There's nothing exciting about riding." Malachi's eyes widened, he was shocked, and a little scared that the idea of riding offended her so greatly.

"I just saw you turn a stone wall into ruble with your bare hands. I saw Zacharias move faster than the human eye could follow, and you think riding some miserable pack mule through some daisies would entertain me?"

"So, you saw the fight?" Malachi asked with a cocky and oafish grin, ignoring what they were originally talking about. She released a frustrated groan and rolled her eyes as she turned away, slinging her raven hair over her shoulder with ferocity.

Malachi realized his own stupidity and again darted after her. Once more, he gently grabbed her shoulder from behind. With a chuckle he said, "Please, Violet, I'm sorry." Malachi moved a little closer, his voice was serious and steady this time, "Go on then. What does entertain you?"

To Malachi's surprise, she advanced nearer as well. His heart began to race. She put her hand on his chest and inched her face closer to his. Her presence nearly made Malachi shake; for the first time in the young warrior's life, he felt intimidated—outmatched even. Her lips were now alongside his ear; he could feel her breath on his neck.

She whispered softly, "A good chase..."

"Hell of a fight, cousin." Dag and Felix were running through the corridor toward them. Malachi spun around to face them, his face redder than Dag's crimson shirt.

"Best fight I've ever seen!" Felix yelled.

"Ya, except mine." Dag barked, and smiled at his brother. Felix shook his head and laughed. Dag and Malachi grabbed each other's forearms and touched foreheads, "You are a true champion, cousin."

"Um, thank you, cousin." Malachi said, clearly distracted and a little frustrated by his cousin's timing. He turned around to return to his conversation with the mystery girl, but she had vanished into the shadows. Malachi looked in every direction in a panic.

"Everything okay? What's wrong?" Felix asked, very concerned for his cousin.

"Crap." Malachi ran his hands through his dirty-blond hair and sighed. "Eh, it's nothing. Forget about it."

Dag and Felix looked at each other, confused by their cousin's odd behavior. "Whatever, let's get you ready for the ceremony." Dag put his hand on Malachi's shoulder.

"I'm sure you would like that, but I think I can get dressed by myself!" Malachi gave Dag a concerned and disgusted look. Dag shook his head and fought back a snicker. Felix leaned up against the wall to brace himself as he roared out in laughter. Dag slung his beefy arm around Malachi's neck and playfully threw some quick jabs into Malachi's ribs. Malachi launched his cousin off and began to head down the hall, still chuckling at his own joke.

"Truly Malachi, you were amazing." Felix said proudly.

"Ya, you really shut up Fenrir and his father." Dag scoffed. "Everyone is talking up there, Malachi. They say you're the best anyone has seen in a long time. Besides me—but that goes without saying." They all chuckled.

"You sound surprised." Malachi said with a flex of his chest.

Just then, Fenrir and Varden came around the corner, heading toward the room where Zacharias was being treated. The three boys of Talitha puffed out their chests and marched with their heads up, hoping to avoid having to talk to either of them. Varden walked with the authority of a conquering warlord; Fenrir did not look much different.

"Be thankful you didn't fight a real warrior, boy." Varden said in an unimpressed tone.

"Excuse me?" Malachi said as a vein bulged from his neck and forehead. Varden kept moving as if he had not heard Malachi. Malachi stepped toward him, fist clenched, hoping Varden would stop and face him.

Felix grabbed him, "Come on. Let's go." Malachi hesitated; Felix turned him and gave him a reassuring look. He knew it would be foolish to start something. Malachi agreed, and they headed back toward their room. Fenrir looked over his shoulder and winked at the boys, very pleased with himself and his father. That boiled Dag and Malachi's blood; they couldn't stand Fenrir, and he knew it.

Varden and Fenrir entered Zach's room. The healers were just now finishing up his wounds.

"Leave us," Varden said coldly. The healers all hurried out of the room keeping their heads down. "I told you he would be strong, and you underestimated him. You made me look like a fool today. Try not to ruin the ceremony this evening." He turned and walked out before Zacharias could say anything. All the wounds he had received from Malachi combined did not hurt as deeply as his father's words. He laid down on his back and stared at the ceiling. Fenrir sat in a wooden chair next to the stone table where his brother lay and threw his feet up.

"I thought you did great, brother." Fenrir said with confidence and pride. "Honestly, don't let him get to you; he just expects perfection."

"Like you?" Zacharias said quietly, as if he were just mumbling to himself. "You dominated your fight. You always impress him."

"Ha!" Fenrir flipped his thick black hair back out of his face. "You know what he said to me after my fight? 'You could have ended it faster.' Not 'good job,' or a pat on the back. We will never please him, little brother." They sat in silence for just a moment, then he spoke very dramatically using his hands, "You may not be as handsome as me, or as tall, Zachy. But you are a great fighter, and if you had that bow of yours, you wouldn't have lost. Come on now, let's get dressed.

There's a party to celebrate your glory upstairs, little brother." He threw another charming wink with his icy-blue eye.

"What if I get a Crow or Raven totem?" Zacharias growled, his voice was filled with anger; he pulled and tore at his own hair.

"Oh, stop with this foolishness. You fought well. You will be a Wolf of Zaurak like father and I. You are no spy. You are a warrior, a hunter, an assassin... a Wolf." Fenrir said as he sprung to his feet and checked his reflection in a mirror hanging from the wall.

Zacharias prayed he was right, he feared nothing more. If he was not assigned Wolf, his father would surely disown him. The Crows and Ravens of Zaurak were spies and messengers; the Wolfs were the warriors. The Wolfs were the strongest of the Shade Runners, and both Varden and Fenrir wore the mask of the Wolf.

"Boy," a deep voice said from the hall. Zacharias sat up from the table. Fenrir stopped fixing his hair and spun around. A large bearded man, the Lion of Talitha, was standing in the doorway. His brother, the Tiger of Talitha accompanied him. His voice was heavy and strong, "You fought a great fight. I am honored that you gave my son such a challenge. You are a true warrior and will make a great Wolf of Zaurak." Both boys nodded at Tarjak and said nothing. Zacharias was confused by the kind words from the leader of his rival clan. Tarjak nodded and made his way toward his son's room. Zach stared down at his feet in confusion, his wild and long hair falling freely over his face.

Tarjak burst into his son's room, "Malachi the Invincible!" He bellowed. Dag and Felix jumped up from their chairs terrified by their uncle's entrance. "What's wrong girls, did I startle you?" He grabbed both his nephews and squeezed them against each other.

"Uncle, please. Father, tell him to get off us." Dag yelped as he gasped for air. They both squirmed away looking more like frightened schoolgirls than brave warriors of Talitha. Roman, Dag, and Felix's father, laughed boldly as he entered.

"There's my boy!" Malachi, embarrassed by his father's praise rolled his eyes and continued to get dressed. "Come here, son." He pulled Malachi over; they locked forearms and touched foreheads.

"Ha ha, the Creator has blessed me with a real lion heart for a son. What do you think boys? Could he be the next warrior to bare the lion's mane?" He lifted his son's arm straight in the air, triumphantly.

"No, he will be a tiger like his uncle. He definitely fights more like me. Did you see him out there?" Roman yelled proudly as he whacked his nephew on the back. Roman was always excessively loud.

"Ha! You are a fool, brother." Tarjak said as he pulled Malachi away from his brother.

"With his strength, Uncle, he could get an Ox or a Bull totem." Felix declared as he rose to his feet with excitement.

"No. Are you saying he's slow?" Tarjak said defensively in a deep growl. The Ox or Bull was often given to a warrior of great strength, but they moved slower because of their mammoth-like build.

"Maybe in the head," Dag jested as he leaned forward from his seat. The uproar from the room was tremendous; every person in the arena could hear their laughter. It was an hour of triumph and joy for the people of Talitha, but Malachi could not free his mind from the beautiful goddess who was somewhere in these halls. She haunted his every thought, and he didn't even know her name. She had won his heart in that brief encounter, and he would win hers even if it took an eternity.

CHAPTER 4

THREE TOTEMS

Upstairs, the ceremony was almost ready, and the two boys sat anxiously alone in their rooms. The drums above them were like a pounding heartbeat of a gigantic creature—deep thuds filled every hall and room as if the stone coliseum were alive. Each boy was dressed in their best, looking much more presentable than during their fight. They were both in traditional Talithan and Zaurakian warrior garments, a surprisingly handsome sight. Sleek hooded cloaks draped over their shoulders; Malachi's was a dark crimson with gold stitching. Zach's was black with violet detail. As the drumming picked up its pace, the boys knew it was time for them to present themselves. They both left their rooms and met each other at the bottom of the stairwell.

"Hell of a fight, Zacharias." Malachi reached out his arm, hoping Zach would grab his forearm. Zacharias said nothing; he stared straight ahead, motionless. His black eyes filled with pain and annoyance. He dawned his hood, stepped forward, and began to head up the stairs, leaving Malachi at the bottom still holding his arm out. Malachi chuckled and soon followed him. He pulled his crimson hood over his head.

The stairs led to a long straight hallway with a vaulted ceiling. There were members of the three clans on both sides cheering enthusiastically. Girls giggled and swooned at the two young warriors as they passed. Malachi sported a childlike grin as he winked and waved at the cheering crowd; Zacharias remained stoic and stern as if he we were attending a funeral. Lining the hallway was a row of massive twisting and dead trees. They hung upside down from overhead, covered in priceless and ancient decorations that dangled and swayed from the barren branches. At the end of the hall, the Great Stag sat behind a large stone table. Behind him was a ginormous tiled wall of stone. At the center of the wall, each clan's respective mark was beautifully displayed. Each symbol was fifteen-feet wide and elegantly carved into the stone. Banners and flags were draped across the pillars; purple and black, red and gold, white and silver filled the hall. Malachi and Zacharias made their way past their adoring clan members, all the way to the end of the hall where the leaders of Aldafar, Talitha, and Zaurak were waiting. All three men were fully armored as if they were prepared for battle. Despite their differences, all three clans used their own talents in collaboration to create the flawless armors and masks worn by the warriors of the Order.

Malachi's father, Tarjak, was in his notorious lion armor. His nose to his chin was covered in a mask that resembled a lion's snout and snarling fangs. Made from rare metals, stones, and other materials, the mask was a masterpiece. It was bold and looked like a person would break every bone in their hand if they tried to strike it. His eyes and brow were uncovered, but a dark hood rested over the top of his head. On the black hood was a thick golden mane. Red feathers and beads were braided all throughout the huge mane that ran down to his burly shoulder blades. The leather armor was plentiful around his arms and chest, reinforced with stones and thin metals. Unlike the dangly and frayed accessories of a Shade Runner, the Guardians wore solid heavy objects around their limbs. His right hand bore a heavy gauntlet; its materials matched those of his mask. It started at his elbow and went all the way down to his clawed fingertips. The same golden fur used for the mane padded the gauntlet and poked out in random places all over his armor. A long claymore was strapped to his back. It ran parallel to his body. The large two-handed sword's handle was stone gray, with a leather grip. Red and gold beads and jewels ran from the very end of the handle. BLOOD HUNTER was inscribed on the blade in an ancient angelic script only the people of the Order could read. The Lion of Talitha led his people with strength and honor; he stood proudly in his crimson and gold armor at the end of the hall.

To Tarjak's left, stood the Great Stag. The antlers on his mask were tall and beautiful; they were truly the perfect centerpieces for the room. Even the old man was in his armor, which was rare to see because of his age. He wore a black hooded cloak, embroidered with silver Aldafarian designs. His armor was thin and looked like it was more for show than for battle, as most things of Aldafar did. He leaned on his staff for support and grinned through his beard at the fast-approaching boys.

On the far left, stood Varden, the head Wolf of Zaurak. His mask was the opposite of Tarjak's; it left his mouth uncovered instead of his eyes. The top half of Varden's face was replaced by an intricate and angry scowling wolf. The mask was a dark violet and charcoal black. Its scowl was dark and fierce; it struck fear into anyone who caught it's gaze. The ears perked straight in the air; the right one had two piercings that dangled and flicked as he moved. Out of the mask came thick black fur; it covered the top of his head down to his back. Similar to Tarjak's mane, black feathers and beads had been woven into the fur. Varden's left arm was noticeably more armored than his right and had many more accessories as well. The warriors of Zaurak—more so than the other clans—had many beads, tassels, feathers, and other dangling objects they loved to sport on their armor. Besides sharp claws at the tip of each one of his fingers, his wrist and hands were unarmored. Although one could not see them, Varden had many knives and blades hidden within his armor and fur cloak. A bow and quiver were fastened to his back, accompanied by beads and other accessories. He was a warrior of few words, respected by all, and he looked fierce as ever standing at the front of the room awaiting his son.

On top of the great stone table were three wooden boxes, long and thin. Each rustic box had the clans' symbol hand-painted on the lid. Malachi and Zacharias knew what was in those boxes. Although on the outside they appeared relaxed, they were about to burst with either nervousness or excitement on the inside. Malachi fought back a joyful grin; Zacharias fought back a sickening nausea in his gut. Both boys were so fixated on their own box they had not noticed that there was a third sitting in the middle.

The Great Stag raised his staff straight in the air; not a peep was heard from the crowd. "This is a great day—an amazing day, my friends." He announced to the whole room, even through his mask, everyone could see the joy on his face. "A day where three boys will become men!" The crowd looked around in confusion.

"Three boys? There are only two?" The crowd whispered back and forth. Malachi and Zacharias looked at their fathers in confusion.

"From the time these warriors are born, we pray for their journey. We pray that the Creator would guide our hand in picking their totem. These masks that will soon be presented to these young men are a reflection of their skill and character, a piece of them until the day they return to the soil from which they came. Although each mask is different, depending on their family and clan, they are a sign of unity within our Order, for all three clans worked together to forge these relics." The old man paused and surveyed the room, "Now, some of you may be confused why there are three boxes on this table. It is my pleasure to present the newest Knowledge Keeper of Aldafar: Cyrus, son of Shara."

The crowd was on their feet once again; they applauded the boy as he made his way toward the front table. Cyrus was the first child of Aldafar to be chosen as a warrior in nearly thirty years; the announcement was quite shocking for everyone. His long white hair draped over his shoulders as he strutted down the hall like a handsome peacock displaying his feathers for the first time.

"Who's the pretty boy?" Malachi whispered to his father. Tarjak swiftly knocked Malachi across the back of the head. No one noticed; everyone's eyes were on Cyrus.

Cyrus reached the table and stood in-between the two other boys. He bowed respectfully to the three leaders of each clan. He then greeted both Malachi and Zacharias in a very respectable manner; he then turned again to the Stag.

"Very well, now that we are all here, we shall begin. Malachi, Cyrus, please kneel. We shall start with the boy of Zaurak." Both young men did as they were told and waited patiently for their turn. "Zacharias, you have proven that you are a dangerous warrior and loyal to your family. You are quiet, fierce, and always seize an open opportunity to strike. Your speed is unchallenged, as is your skill with a bow. You have always been reserved and respectful to those around you, and I believe you will serve the Order of Eden well in the times to come."

It was time. Zacharias took a deep breath and closed his eyes. The other members of Zaurak were on the edge of their seats—except Fenrir, who felt he already knew which totem he would receive. "Therefore, Zacharias, son of Varden, I am honored to present to you the totem mask of the Wolf." The Great Stag opened the wooden box revealing the mask to Zach. Zacharias felt a great peace rush over him; Fenrir was right all along. Unlike his father's violet and black mask, Zach's was a dark matte-gray with sapphire accents. "Because you are loyal to your pack, and a keen predator, you are now a fully realized Shade Runner, Zacharias." Zacharias bowed in respect, the members of Zaurak behind him clapped quietly in admiration, and Varden gave a simple nod. Dag, hidden in the crowd, rolled his eyes and gave Felix a look of disgust.

"Now, your clan leader will present to you your new arsenal." Varden removed from under the table the most beautiful bow Zacharias had ever seen. The wood was pitch-black, like burnt charcoal. The sky-blue designs that danced around the curves of the bow matched his new mask. Two raven feathers dangled from the top limb of the bow.

Varden also presented a pair of short hatchets with jagged sapphire markings across the blades. The twin set of identical single-sided axes were both crafted from black steel. They were truly primitive-looking weapons ideal for slashing and tearing at great speeds. Zacharias did not show even the slightest sign of excitement; he simply gave a quick glance to his brother in the crowd.

"Praise the Creator. How great." The old man said with a joyous cry; he was truly enjoying himself. "Next, Cyrus. Please stand." The crowd was quiet once again. "Sadly, not many of these people have come to know you as I have, Cyrus. They soon will! Cyrus, you are overwhelmingly intelligent, shockingly observant, and always hungry for more knowledge. It has been a pleasure to watch you grow into the young man that stands before me. Your knowledge and mental abilities have far surpassed anyone your age, and you will one day make a wise Elder. You are cold and calculated in combat, deciphering and predicting every movement of your opponent; you mastered our healing techniques at age ten, and have a very gentle and nurturing soul when need be." Cyrus seemed relaxed, as if he knew exactly what was going to happen next. "Therefore, Cyrus son of Shara, I am honored to present to you the totem mask of the Owl." The box was opened, and Cyrus bowed to his elder.

Malachi peaked over the box from where he was kneeling, "Incredible," he thought to himself as he admired the beautiful artisanship of the mask.

Malachi heard a voice resounding, like it came deep from within his own mind, "I agree, Malachi of Talitha." Cyrus looked down at him and nodded, unaware Malachi was oblivious to Cyrus's ability to use telepathic communication. Malachi's eyes were huge; he had no idea what was happening. The Stag chuckled seeing Malachi's expression, knowing that Cyrus must have contacted him.

The mask was white and black but shining platinum accents truly made it pop. A petite sharp beak was in the center of two large, black circular eyes. A *feathered* look had been carved into the edge of the mask and around the eyes.

"And we cannot forget your new weapons, my boy!" The old man reached beneath the table and pulled out another box and a sword. Inside the box were long thin throwing daggers, handcrafted to resemble silver feathers. Cyrus pulled one out and examined the knife looking pleased as he twirled it between his fingers. The sword was also long and thin, straight until the very end of the blade where it curved slightly. A one-sided, one-piece sword, elegant designs, resembling harsh winds swirled down the blade. Definitely not a defensive weapon, this was made for precise slashes. The handle was long as well; it was big enough to be wielded by two hands, but it was light enough for one. Cyrus smiled at his clan leader and bowed. "Ha! Congratulations to our newest Keeper. Cyrus, the Owl." Again, the people were on their feet shouting and celebrating, except the members of Zaurak who now seemed bored with the festivities.

"Now, I believe we have one more." The old Stag said trying to get Malachi's attention. He was still looking at Cyrus, confused how he entered his mind. Malachi realized he was being summoned and jumped to his feet with a tiny grin. "Malachi, what a performance today!" The crowd agreed. "You have shown you are a fearless and strong young man." Varden was rolling his eyes under his black totem mask. "You are a joy to be around, and a weapon to fear. Your strength will be respected even by the Immortals; you are truly a fierce warrior, my boy. And you even bear the Savage Mark. I pray you never have to use its power, but I fear you will. But you must never fear its strength, for it is a part of you and we trust you will use it wisely when the time comes. I have known you since you were a small boy and you have always wanted to defend those who could not defend themselves, and that is your greatest quality." Malachi's heart was pounding. He so deeply wanted the mask of the lion to be in that box, so he could make his father proud. All other noise seemed to cancel out except the Great Stag's voice; he clenched his fist in anticipation. "Picking your totem mask was surprisingly difficult Malachi. It took a lot of prayer and patience to find what was right for you. But we know we chose wisely. Therefore, Malachi, son of Tarjak..." Malachi became worried;

what did he mean it was difficult to pick his mask? He wanted to rip the box open and see what was inside. "I am honored to present to you the mask of the Sabertooth." It felt like all the air had been sucked out of the room. This news silenced the crowd—even Varden peered over in dismay.

Malachi, looking terribly worried, whispered "Um, what does this mean? I didn't even know Sabertooth was an option."

"It is a great honor, my son." Tarjak whispered back in disbelief as he motioned at him to be quiet.

"Your father is right, Malachi." The Great Stag explained. "The only other Guardian to have received this totem was the eldest son of Talitha himself, the first Guardian. For some reason, the Creator guided us to this decision; we know you will make us proud." Malachi stood in silence, but he was not terribly surprised he received such a great honor.

The mask was similar to his father's; it started at the bridge of his nose and covered everything below his eyes. The growling face of a tiger covered where his mouth would be, two huge sabertooth fangs ran all the way down to the chin of the mask. The mask was dark red, bronze, and gold. It wasn't a solid piece; it was many pieces of stone and metal forged together. It looked rugged and fierce. The fangs were clenched as if it was snarling at its prey. Malachi wanted to throw it on right then and there.

Tarjak removed a sword from beneath the table. A thick, single-sided, square-cut blade. The handle was gold and bronze with a red tassel at the end. The words TIGER FANG were carved into the blade in the ancient angelic script of the Order. The sword was heavy; Malachi realized as he picked it up off the table. Very few warriors could swing that blade—especially not with one hand, as Malachi was doing. After Malachi had examined the blade, his father handed him a beautiful gauntlet made of tan fur and leather, coated in stone and metal—solid crimson and gold decorated the armor. The gauntlet would make Malachi's arm look two times as massive as it already was, and the giant tiger-like claws at the fingertips could tear through any man with ease.

"You could rip through steel with those claws, Malachi." Tarjak whispered to his son who was not listening; he was far too excited to hear his father's words. Malachi was swooning over his new weapons and gear; he almost forgot where he was.

"Clans of the Order of Eden, please join me in congratulating our newest Guardian, Shade Runner, and Knowledge Keeper. The Wolf of Zaurak, the Owl of Aldafar, and the Sabertooth of Talitha!" The building rattled with excitement; the Talithan clan members shook the whole building with their pride, cheering and stomping. All three were truly proud with their assigned totems; Zacharias was the only one who did not express it.

Malachi noticed, "Look at that angry fool over there, too tough to even show a smile for his clan." He thought to himself.

"It is strange how he refrains from displaying emotion." Cyrus answered back through the mental link. Malachi again peered straight at Cyrus, wide-eyed and startled. He wanted to confront Cyrus and figure out how he was performing such an impressive feat, but family members and friends were rushing toward the boys to congratulate them. Malachi accepted thank yous, handshakes, and forearm grabs from what seemed like hundreds of people. Then, through the swarm of people, he saw her. She was even more beautiful than when he saw her down below in the healing chambers.

"Congrats, Malachi." Dag jumped in front of Malachi to embrace him.

"Not again. Move, Dag!" Malachi almost pushed Dag over trying to get past him. The swarm of people was overwhelming; it was almost like they were trying to keep him from his target. He could see her heading in the opposite direction, exiting the great hall. He burst through the crowd, now moving almost at a full sprint—desperate to talk to her once more. She had snuck up the southern stairs and was now on a balcony overlooking the hall where they just had the ceremony. She stood alone watching all the people from overhead, enjoying the privacy. After a few minutes of tireless searching, Malachi stumbled upon her.

"How's the view?" He asked quietly as he stepped out on the balcony, nearly panting from running up and down the stairs of the building. She didn't turn around; she knew exactly who it was. She had a small leather-bound journal in her hands, and she quickly closed it, putting it aside.

"Fine. Some ceremony, huh?" She said, almost sarcastically.

"Ya, I guess so." Malachi said humbly, still carrying his new sword in a leather sheath.

"Do I have to call you the great Sabertooth of Talitha now? Or can I stick to Brainless Meathead?" Skye scoffed.

"Ha ha! How about Malachi?"

"No, no. Brainless Meathead will do just fine." She said as she continued to peer down at the people below. Malachi laughed and shook his head.

"Ha, fine. Well, can I know your name now?"

She sighed a long breath; she now realized Malachi was not going to give up until she gave in. "You can call me Skye." She continued to peer over the balcony.

Malachi's eyes grew, and his stomach sank a little. "S-Skye?" He stuttered a little and asked in disbelief. "Skye of Zaurak? Like the same Skye that the Order ha—".

"Yes, that Skye." She said sharply. Malachi fumbled for words; he did not know what to say. The Sabertooth cleared his throat and leaned against the balcony next to her.

"Well Skye, it's a pleasure to meet you." She didn't respond. She continued to gaze out at all of the people below them. "I have to be honest—you are not at all what I expected. All the stories make you seem kind of…"

"Evil?" Skye interrupted. "Dark? Twisted?"

Malachi could tell it was a sensitive subject. "No. Rebellious, that's all."

"To the people of Zaurak, they are one in the same." She said in cold frustration as she glared down at all the people below.

"Well, that explains why you're up here on your own." Malachi said cautiously. They sat in silence for a while until Malachi mustered up the courage to ask another question. He studied her for a moment, this new mystery and strength made her even more beautiful to Malachi. "Well, is it true?"

"Is what true?" Skye said with a sharp exhale knowing that Malachi, and everyone else in the Order, had heard many whispers and rumors about Skye of Zaurak.

"That you kill people. *Humans*, I mean." Malachi asked quietly, his body tensed as he anxiously awaited her response. The music and chatter of the banquet seemed to fade, her eyes ran across the crowd, and her raven hair covered her face.

"We claim to be the protectors of this world. That without us, corruption and chaos would consume humanity." She paused, and for the first time she looked straight into Malachi's eyes. "It already has, Malachi." Her caramel-brown eyes seemed as if they were about to burst from pent-up anger and pain. "As we throw our parties and banquets behind our fortress walls, there are people being murdered, raped, sold, beaten, and torn from their families—but we drink and dance and glorify three new *protectors* of the human world. You three won't protect anything. You won't change anything." Malachi peered straight back into her eyes, his eyes shaking. "So, no. It's not true. I've never killed humans. I've killed rapist, murderers, and slave traders, but never humans. Never people... only monsters."

They sat in silence for what felt like an eternity. Skye waited anxiously for Malachi to walk away and never speak with her again, but he stayed by her side.

"You lost someone didn't you." Malachi asked gently. Skye stared down at her feet and said nothing. "Well, you're wrong about one thing." Malachi said with a smile as he looked down at his family enjoying the party...large loud people dressed in reds and golds stomping, drinking, and singing merrily. Skye slyly shifted her head so she could see him. "I am going to change this world." Malachi said proudly as he stood up straight. "Yes, this world is broken and wicked, but I'm gonna defend it. It is my purpose to fight for those who can't. Whether they deserve it or not; I will always fight for them."

Skye scoffed. She did not know how to respond. She brushed her hair behind her ear and faced the Sabertooth of Talitha once more. The contrasting black feathers and turquoise beads wrapped in her braids danced and dangled as she spoke. "Well Malachi, the Sabertooth of Tailitha, I hope you do." She allowed a thin hopeful smirk to slide across her rosy lips.

A dorky grin sprung upon Malachi's face as he ran his hand through his hair; the gorgeous girl made him feel weak. "W-Well, Skye. It's truly been a pleasure, I hope we..." Malachi stopped, noticing something odd below them. "Oh gosh, what's his problem now?" Malachi growled. Varden, no longer wearing his mask, was staring up at the two on the balcony.

Skye looked down to see what Malachi was talking about, "Oh. Who knows, my father is always upset about something." Those words were like a dagger to Malachi's chest. His stomach dropped, and fear swept over his face.

Panicked, he looked at Skye and thought to himself, "Did she say *father*? No. Anyone but him. Of course, the most perfect angel on the face of the Earth is the daughter of *that* prick. Please be joking." Malachi was starting to feel sick; his lips were nearly quivering. Out loud, he said, "When were you going to mention that? So that means today I fought your..."

"I thought you knew. I thought everyone knew. And yes, today you fought my brother, Zacharias." Skye exclaimed in amusement, enjoying the terrified look on Malachi's face; she could not help but giggle.

Malachi looked down at the floor of the hall again but didn't see Varden. He turned back again to face Skye. Varden was standing in-between them. He moved like a shadow in the dark, unseen, and unheard. His speed was even more impressive than his son's. A cold, strong voice spoke up, "Skye, it's time to go. Now." Varden said as he stared straight at Malachi. Skye rolled her eyes. Varden leaned in close to Malachi and whispered, "Talk to her again, and I will carve your tongue out with a spoon, child."

It took every ounce of Malachi's strength not to thrust his fist into Varden's scowling face. They just glared intensely at each other, Skye casually fiddled with her nails. Malachi started to open his mouth, without a doubt to say something that would escalate the situation. Malachi took a step closer, feeling rash and a little over confident. All of the sudden, the silence was broken with a terrible shriek.

"Ahhhhhhhhh!" A woman downstairs was screaming in terror. All three of them dashed for the edge of the balcony to investigate the source of the noise—it was utter chaos. The creatures were filling in the main hall from all directions, crashing through windows, and breaking down doors.

CHAPTER 5

THE SERPENT SHALL RISE AGAIN

"Vipers!" Felix cried out, trying to warn the rest of the people who were still confused in all the commotion; he kicked one of the monsters in the chest and sent it flying across the room.

Vipers were awful-looking creatures. Their skin was pasty white, as if they had never seen the light of day. Their hair was unkept, long, and greasy. Green veins ran through their white necks and arms—green from the Serpent's Venom coursing through their bodies. They were fast; their limbs swung and whipped like a snake's tail, as if they had no bones in their bodies. They wore filthy, green bandages and cloths around their eyes; their eyesight had decayed from the venom injected into their corpses. Their bodies randomly lost control as they seized and shook while crying out and squealing like demon swine. They attacked as crazed animals, twitching and snarling uncontrollably. The Vipers' snake-like tongues allowed them to smell and taste everything around them. Their mouths dripped with toxins, and their undead bodies flooded frantically into the room. The once-human creatures varied in size and shape, their armor worn and splintered. Primitive knives, swords, hatchets, and clubs filled their rotting hands. Their weapons were not only made from iron and stone, but from the bones of animal carcasses. These creatures had been created for one task: to butcher anything that crossed their path, and they were quite gifted at it.

In order to create such a vial creature, the Immortals of Abaddon drench the Blade of Isaac in the Serpent's Venom. They then plunge the infected knife into the corpse of a fallen warrior. Upon removal of the Seal the body is reanimated into a mindless and undead savage.

"How the hell did Vipers get in here?" Malachi said frantically as he gripped the handle of his new sword a little tighter.

Varden looked at Skye. "Stay hidden," he said in a surprisingly calm voice. He drew a short sword with a shadowy black blade from under his thick cloak, and in a great flurry of fur and speed, he dropped down to the battlefield from the balcony.

"I have to go to." Malachi said hesitantly, he questioned if he should leave Skye alone.

"I know. Go!" Malachi nodded and darted for the edge of the balcony. Malachi stopped abruptly when he heard a strange hiss behind him. He turned around; three Vipers were diving right for Skye.

"Run!" Malachi commanded Skye.

"Not likely." She muttered as she stepped toward the monsters.

He unsheathed Tiger Fang from its leather scabbard and dove into action. Despite its tremendous weight, the sword was perfectly balanced. The first Viper snarled and swung his jagged sword directly at Skye. It crashed into Malachi's blade. As he blocked the attack, he forced the creature back, away from her. A new anger flushed over Malachi as his face turned red with ferocity, no one would get past him. With his free hand, he sandwiched the creature's head in-between the wall and his fist; with a heavy punch, he felt its skull crack beneath the force. The monster released an empty *croak* before falling limp at his feet, the body still shaking on the ground. Malachi ducked under an attack from the next Viper and ripped his sword through his attacker's torso. Although the creature's chest was split open and spewing a black liquid, it kept attacking; these monsters could feel no pain. Now, two Vipers attacked Malachi; Skye drew a small dagger from a sheath hidden on her thigh, but Malachi needed no assistance. Malachi flung his blade diagonally and carved through both the Vipers with ease. It looked as if he had trained with that sword for years—he and Tiger Fang were a deadly duo.

"Are you all right, Skye?" Malachi asked, truly concerned, the blood of his victims trailing down his face.

Another Viper sprung from behind him, catching a distracted Malachi off guard. It squealed and whined as it brought a hatchet down toward Malachi's neck. Skye, without hesitation, blocked the Viper's attack with her dagger. With impressive speed and grace, she twirled past the pale creature, her dress spinning around her, and she drove her blade into its spine. It reared its neck back and screamed, revealing its toxin-covered fangs. Malachi's blade slid through the beast's neck and across the top of its shoulders, relieving the creature of its head. The head fell to the ground, but continued to snarl and snap its fangs. Malachi stared at Skye, baffled by her performance.

"Um, wow. You... you are incredible. I-I mean you looked really good... Not you. The way you fought. Well, I mean you do look good. But I—" Malachi awkwardly fiddled with his sword in his hand. Skye peered at him in confusion. "Um, good job." He finally managed to say.

She rolled her eyes once again. "Focus, Brainless Meathead. Go, I will be fine." He was reluctant to leave her, but this woman needed no protecting.

"Right," Malachi said as he refocused. Suddenly his face shifted back to that of a stoic warrior, his brow narrowed and his shoulders pushed back. Instead of dancing and twirling over the balcony railing like Varden did, Malachi lowered his shoulder and barreled straight through it. Pieces of the balcony rail showered the people and Vipers beneath him; he landed with a heavy crash that shook the whole battle-field. Hundreds of Vipers filled the main hall; Malachi fought his way back to the stone table where the ceremony had been held. Dag and Felix joined him there, fully armored in their Guardian gear.

"Ah! The Leopard and Eagle of Talitha have come to watch me in action. Glad you gentlemen had time to change." Malachi said as he punched a Viper in the chest, crushing its torso.

"Just try not to get in my way, cousin." Dag said confidently, smiling under his mask as he spun a spear in his hands. He was in a black hood, and the scraggly pelt of a leopard draped over his back and shoulders. He carried a mighty spear in his hand that he wielded like a bow staff. He had four more spears strapped to his back.

"Did you bring enough spears, cousin?" Malachi teased.

"Oh please, Malachi. You know Dag loves to accessorize." Felix laughed.

"Do you two hens ever stop cackling?" Dag asked as he plunged one of his many spears straight through the chest of a Viper.

"I'm honored to be present for your first fight as a true Guardian, Malachi." Felix said through the golden beak on his face. He always spoke warmly to Malachi, even as his sword removed a Viper's head from its shoulders. His mask sat just like the rest of the Guardians's, but instead of snarling fangs, the fierce beak of an eagle covered his face. His leather cloak was feathered from his hood all the way down his spine with golden and crimson feathers pinned throughout.

Malachi could not help but admire the tactic Zacharias and Fenrir were using across the room. Fenrir too now dawned his full armor, fighting back-to-back with his brother. His wolf armor was a navy blue and onyx black; a thick gray pelt covered his hood and back. Although he wielded a thin sword, he also had a bow strung to his back—there if he was needed for his archery skills. The two warriors mesmerized Malachi as he watched them. Zacharias struck down many Vipers from a great distance using his bow; well-placed shots tore through the skulls and throats of the wild creatures. If any Vipers got too close, Fenrir would cut them down with terrible speed using his long straight sword. Despite the length of the two-handed blade, Fenrir wielded the thin sword as if it were made of feathers. They spun back-to-back and flipped over and beneath each other like a well-rehearsed dance.

Anyone that came near their radius of blades and arrows would surely perish.

Cyrus too spun in the heat of the battle. Casually, as if it were a training exercise, he calmly walked through the center of the war zone on the tips of his toes. His attacks were so precise and well-placed that Vipers collapsed all around him. He jabbed at their throats and limbs with just his fingertips severing vital ligaments and tendons. Any enemy that Cyrus could not reach with his fingertips would get to meet the steel of his white sword. He danced like a leaf in the wind, elegantly avoiding enemies and strategically slashing at them with his new blade, all while keeping one arm comfortably behind his back. Each attack perfectly placed, never a sloppy movement.

"There must be over a hundred of these things!" Dag yelled out, looking a little overwhelmed as he threw a creature across the room.

"Actually, two hundred and forty-seven to be exact." Cyrus said calmly, as he passed the three Guardians. He sliced through two enemies, showcasing his skill, "Excuse me, two hundred and forty-five." The Guardians were annoyed, but had no time to show it; they too were fighting vigorously.

Soon all the Crows and Ravens of the Zaurakian clan were up in the balconies of the room picking off Vipers with their archery skills. Arrows descended like deadly black rainfall from above, pinning Vipers to the ground. Malachi, Dag, and Felix pushed forward, leaving terrible carnage in their path. Cyrus, Zach, and Fenrir were controlling the sides of the hall, pushing the Vipers toward the Guardians. Varden and other leaders were busy escorting non-warriors out of harm's way. The warriors finally seemed to be taking control of the battle. Suddenly, there was a bone rattling crash; debris fell from above, as a large part of the ceiling was torn open.

CHAPTER 6

THE IMMORTAL

W arriors dove and scattered in an effort to avoid the falling debris. Brainless Vipers were crushed and flattened as a section of the roof collapsed upon them. There was now a large hole in the dome-like ceiling; the commotion brought a cease to the fighting as dust rolled over everyone in the great hall. The Vipers stood motionless as if their minds had been turned off, their weapons brought straight down to their sides. A shrill voice came from the hole above them—every warrior froze. The voice was terribly smooth, yet shrill and disturbing. It sent chills down Varden's spine. The Great Stag emerged into the center of the room looking up at the gaping hole.

"Death," a whisper filled the whole room and echoed off each wall. It snickered to itself, then continued, "Death to all who deny the Serpent. The Serpent shall rise again." The voice rolled across the room like a chilling wind. "As you throw your parties, his strength grows. Every new warrior you train is just another corpse for the Serpent to feast on." It quietly laughed to itself in-between each sentence. The soft, whispering voice slithered down every hall.

Malachi gripped his sword tighter and tighter; he feared he knew whom this demonic voice belonged to. He had heard story after story, warning after warning. He knew who this demon was.

It showed itself. Cloaked in all black, it stepped to the edge of the chasm, its clothing was ripped and torn, flapping in the frigid wind. The creature was silhouetted dramatically from the dim moonlight above. It wore a mask made from a boar's skull and shattered white stones. The mask covered his entire face, a thick green stripe of war paint, faded and weathered, ran down the right side of the mask. Flesh and other rotting things hung from the sharp tusks on his face; death seemed to swirl around him. He was large. Bone armor covered his broad shoulders; black steel chains ran across his body, clanking and chiming in the breeze. The green mark of the Serpent was on his left breast for all to see. That mark brought death; he wore it like a badge of honor.

Another figure, even larger than the Boar, lurked from the distance. A black cloak and hood covered the creature's body as it stood brooding over the hole. Malachi assumed this creature had created the massive aperture in the ceiling… and with a single strike.

"Your woman and children will be his slaves," the Boar hissed with confidence. "You men will not die honorable deaths; your lifeless bodies will be fed to the Vipers of Abaddon. Your homes will burn and the people of Talitha, Zaurak, and Aldafar will be forgotten. The world will be his for the taking. For the first time, in hundreds of years, the Seals are revealing themselves—they wish to set the Serpent free from his prison. This is your final warning." He slowly moved his head, surveying the room. "Surrender and your deaths will be painless. Resist—" it was as if the whole room could feel him grinning joyfully under his mask, "and you will suffer a long and cruel demise." He pointed at the Great Stag's staff, "And the forces of Abaddon will pry that Seal from your cold, dead fingers, old man."

A strong, confident voice came from behind the Great Stag, "Then come and get it you undead piece of filth." Tarjak emerged from behind the Stag, his boots and heavy armor shaking the surrounding area with his every step. He then stood proudly next to the old Knowledge Keeper.

"Yes, please come down here so I can remove your head," Tarjak's brother, Roman, appeared on the other side of the Stag. The room seemed to feel brighter; the looming terror was being washed away. Malachi, Dag, and Felix looked at one another and exchanged reassuring glances after seeing their fathers's lack of angst. Tarjak and Roman did not seem to fear the Immortal in the slightest.

The deathly laugher of the Immortal filled the room once more. He lifted his two axe-and club-like weapons and pointed them at the Guardians. Weapons straight out of an awful nightmare—made of bones and steel—they were jagged, rusted, and crusty with the blood of his unlucky victims. "Ah, the Lion and Tiger of Talitha. Stay out of my way, or I will sever each one of your limbs from your bodies, like I did to your father." The warriors of Talitha snarled at the comment.

Roman growled under his mask. The Tiger of Talitha was a bloodthirsty warrior. He had fought this Immortal before. He was thick and sturdy as a stone pillar like his brother. A gorgeous tiger pelt was draped over his right shoulder and arm, while his left was heavily armored. He carried a massive, seven-foot single-bladed axe, and like his son Dag, he loved to accessorize. He had smaller axes strapped to his waist and his back; they were mainly for show, because his principal axe usually required two hands. "How dare you!" Roman grumbled through the teeth of his mask.

The Boar snorted and laughed at his frustration.

"I'm going to shred you to pieces, Pig!" Tarjak stripped off a piece of his armor, revealing the Savage Mark on his shoulder. Everyone in the room gasped. Malachi could not help but notice how unafraid the Immortal seemed—the strongest warrior of Talitha was about to come after him, and the Boar seemed unshaken, almost excited. Could the Immortals truly be as strong as the legends? Did the Immortal truly not fear Malachi's father or his Savage Mark?

"Malachi, you and your cousins finish off the Vipers here and protect our people." Tarjak said, drawing the gigantic sword from his back. The song of steel rang loud through the hall as the massive sword was freed from its leather sheath. The Boar stepped away from the hole in the ceiling, as if he were taunting the hunters, just before he vanished into the surrounding wilderness. The second cloaked creature began to fade in an emerald cloud of smoke. Then he too disappeared into the wind.

"No. I'm fighting with you, Father."

"No. This is too dangerous. I need you here."

"But—" before Malachi could finish, his father and uncle took off for the exit with a ravenous fury. As soon as the Immortal vanished, the Vipers were alive once more and attacked.

"They will need me!" Malachi shouted as he dove for the stone table, dodging the blade of a Viper.

"What are you doing, Malachi?" Felix yelled in confusion.

Malachi grabbed his huge clawed gauntlet and slid his hand in up to his elbow, "I'm going to help them." Vipers swarmed Malachi; he felt the weight of his armored forearm and grinned. He threw a catastrophic punch with his new gauntlet; it rattled the whole building. The force of the punch nearly obliterated the Viper in front of him and sent the rest flying back—as if they weighed nothing at all—screeching and squealing as they were launched across the room. Malachi was already a brute, and now he was a heavily armored war machine. Another Viper slashed an axe at him; he blocked it with his sword, then in one powerful swing of his arm, he ripped the creature in half with his knife-like claws. Like a rampaging bull, Malachi made his way down the center of the battlefield and out of the great hall after his father and uncle.

Felix and Dag tried to follow, but the old Stag stopped them, "We need you here, gentlemen. There are still many Vipers to slay."

"Dammit. Yes, your Grace." The brothers reluctantly dove back into battle, knowing well not to disobey a direct order from the Great Stag.

Malachi was confident when he first followed his father's trail into the woods, but as he gained on them, he recalled his grandfather's stories about the Immortals of Abaddon—horror stories to be exact. Terrifying stories of non-living creatures with unimaginable power, the poison that ran through their blood made them virtually unstoppable. They had skills greater than any single warrior and were gifted with the ability to heal from nearly any wound, almost instantly. Maybe most troublesome: they had a wild lust for killing. They were the six most feared creatures on the entire earth, and Malachi was blindly running after one of them. As he drew deeper into the woods, he could no longer hear the battle going on at the coliseum. An uneasy silence filled the forest. Nothing but dim moonlight lit his path in the dark woods; the trees towered high over his head.

He ripped through branches and shrubbery, never breaking stride. He was getting closer and closer, pushing his fears aside as he kept moving forward. His eyes adjusted to the darkness around him. Deeper and deeper into the blackness of the woods he ran, an awful maze of trees and shadows. As Malachi flipped over a fallen tree, he heard a weak voice come from the bushes.

"Stop, Malachi!" The voice startled him, and he raised Tiger Fang as he attempted to slow his momentum and slide through the mud.

"Uncle? Are you all right?" Malachi looked upon a sight he never thought he would see: the great Tiger of Talitha lay beaten and bloody in the dirt. His cloak was ripped from his body and there was a large gash in his forehead; the blood ran down and over his beaten face.

"Turn back, Malachi. You are going to get yourself killed." He coughed and gasped under his mask. "You have never faced power like this." Malachi looked around in a panic, no longer fearing for his own safety, but for his father's.

"Stay here, Uncle. I will be back."

"Malachi, no!" Roman tried to get up, but his wounds sent him crashing back to the ground. He watched helplessly as Malachi disappeared into the woods.

With a great leap, Malachi busted out of the tree line into an open clearing. As he landed, he was forced to stop dead in his tracks. Not twenty yards away, the Immortal stood as if he had been waiting for Malachi. Malachi, frozen with fear, looked around, but his father was nowhere in sight. It felt as if the very breath was ripped from his chest as he stared over at the demon across from him. The Immortal watched Malachi curiously. He cocked his head to the side and took an interest in his new victim. His black, tattered clothing swayed in the wind. He stood proudly in the empty quietness of the night, like a phantom silently haunting its prey. The silence was maddening for Malachi; all he could hear was his own heavy breathing. The creature's primitive bone weapons dripped with fresh blood.

"Come, boy. Face your death." The words slithered off the Immortal's tongue with a cold whisper.

"I d-don't fear you, Boar." Malachi said unconvincingly, with a slight stutter.

"You should, boy. I am death. The Serpent is all around you, in every shadow. Can't you feel his eyes always watching? His breath on the back of your neck?" Malachi flinched nervously as a chilling breeze ran across him.

Malachi raised his sword and pointed it at the demon, "You and your master don't scare me, Immortal. You will be a simple message." He could not believe the words that were flowing from his mouth. He desperately wanted to shut up, but youth and stupidity had taken over. "A message that if you threaten a Guardian, all the wrath of Talitha will fall upon you!" Arrogance and pride were forcing him toward the creature. He leaped at the Immortal with a thunderous battle cry. Every rational thought told him to run the other way, but battle called to Malachi like a lustful mistress. He was hardwired for war—it was in his blood.

Malachi swung his blade wildly at the Immortal, not landing a single blow. He charged harder, thrashing his new blade across the sky with ferocity. The two warriors danced and spun as silhouettes against the star-filled night sky in the open field. As Malachi brought his sword above his head, in one swift movement his chest was ripped open by the Immortal's demonic weapon. Malachi fell to his knees, his body shaking as he tried to stay upright. He felt the warm blood run down the front of his torso and soak his clothing. The bottom of the Immortal's foot slammed into Malachi's face; with an empty *thud*, he was sent sliding through the mud into a nearby tree. He released a muffled grunt as he slapped into the trunk of the tree; blood and spit sprayed from his lips.

Before he had any chance to react, the Boar was upon him once more, "I'll be sure to deliver that message for you, boy. Ha ha!" His laugh was as sinister and cold as ever; he lifted one blade in the air and pushed his other club into Malachi's open wound. The steel chains around his body clanked and scratched together as he lifted his weapon to deliver the final blow. In less than two moves, the Immortal had bested Malachi. He was trapped in the chains of humility and disbelief.

Just as the Immortal's weapon fell, a massive creature rammed its shoulder into the Boar, sending him ripping through the woods like a poorly aimed cannonball. Malachi had no idea what was unfolding before him; the creature looked over its shoulder at him. Fiery-red eyes, burning with ferocity, stared at Malachi as the creature panted wildly. Malachi's eyes widened from both terror and confusion; he was completely dumbfounded by what stood towering in front of him.

"Father?" He asked in disbelief, his voice shaking. The monster before him was surely once Tarjak, but now it was some sort of crazed and furious beast. The creature was probably seven foot, but hunched over like a lion stalking its prey. Every muscle on Tarjak's body was now shredded and thicker than ever, twice the size as before. His body was steaming; it looked as if his totem mask and armor had been welded into his flesh. Malachi could feel the heat radiating off his father. The totem mask was now a part of his face; the jaw and teeth moved with Tarjak's every breath. Both his hands now had razor-sharp claws, and his forearms and thighs were the size of tree trunks. The Savage Mark was burning and sizzling; it spread further down his arm and up his neck, like hot magma rolling down the side of a volcano.

His hair had grown like a wild fire—it wasn't clear where his hair started and the mane on his hood ended. He and his totem were no longer separate creatures; they had fused together to form a single entity, a savage force of nature.

Tarjak took his glowing crimson eyes off Malachi and whipped his thick neck back toward the Immortal. He took off after his prey with an earth-shattering roar. Dirt and debris shot up from beneath him, as he moved like a lumbering hulk with immense speed. The Immortal did not stand a chance; the monster held nothing back. Malachi watched in horror as his father kept his word from earlier—he literally shredded him to pieces with his mighty claws. His power was unexplainable; Malachi did not know if he should be amazed or petrified. Malachi could no longer see the battle as the two fought deeper into the forest, but he could hear the awful sounds of the slaughter. Claws slashed, and teeth snarled as the Boar tried desperately to free itself from the superior predator. Groans of agony and muffled grunts came from the Immortal's bloody lips as he struggled to free himself from the burning monstrosity.

Suddenly, across the open field, movement caught Malachi's eye. Emerald smoke began to swirl across the moonlit field. Malachi watched as the cloud formed into a man, and Malachi realized it was the dark hooded creature from back at the arena. The smoke cleared, replaced by the demonic figure, and Malachi's heart sank. The creature's empty eyes were locked on Malachi... it stepped forward.

Out of the forest, a hand grabbed Malachi's shoulder; the other covered his mouth. "We need to move *now*." His uncle's voice was quiet and weak. "Stay quiet, Malachi, but hurry up." Both wounded, they hobbled together through the woods, leaning on each other for support.

"What about Father? We can't just leave him." Malachi struggled to speak; his chest ached with pain.

"He can handle himself, obviously."

"What was wrong with him? How did he turn into that monster?"

"That was the power of the Savage Mark." Malachi was amazed. He looked down at his own mark on his forearm that was now covered in his own blood from his wound.

"Why has he never used it before? It was incredible."

"It gives the user amazing power, but at a cost. One can't control it. After he is done with the Immortal, he will look for something else to kill. He is not your father right now, Malachi. He is very dangerous." The two, bloody and exhausted, hurried through the forest—nervous that the monster could be hot on their trail. The woods once again seemed oddly quiet. Back at the ceremony hall, the fighting had ceased, and silence filled the air. It was not a pleasant silence, even though this battle had been won. Little did the members of the Order of Eden know—this was simply the quiet before the storm.

None of them would be ready for the wave of chaos that would soon be upon them.

CHAPTER 7

A PHOENIX CHARM

Sunlight trickled in through Malachi's bedroom window—just enough to wake him from his sleep.

"How you feelin'?" Felix was sitting at the edge of Malachi's bed and Dag was next to him in a chair. The bags under their red eyes and the bear-like yawn released from Dag were clear signs they had stayed up all night beside their cousin. Malachi lifted his head slowly with a groan and observed the room, confused on how he had made it home. He was in his own bedroom—a large room chiseled from clay and stone. His new armor and blade were displayed neatly on a wooden manikin's head and torso across the room; a crimson and gold tapestry hung proudly behind his arsenal. From one of his many windows, he could see the great canyon walls where his fortress hid.

"What happened? How did we get here?" Before Felix could answer, Malachi remembered the battle in the forest as he winced from his soreness. His torso was wrapped tightly in gray bandages, he could still feel the sting of the Immortal's spiked club across his chest. Suddenly, he sat up frantic; his eyes widened with worry. "Is my father back? How is he?"

"Uncle Tarjak is fine. I promise."

"What about your father? How's Uncle Roman?"

"He is resting too. They are both fine, Malachi. Everyone is fine."

Malachi laid back down as he released a sigh of relief. He pulled away at some of the bandages wrapped around his chest to look at his wound. To his surprise, only a jagged scar running from his left shoulder all the way across his chest remained.

"Those healers do a hell of a job, huh Malachi?" Dag said, examining his cousin's scar from across the room.

"Sure do," he said with a groan as he ran his fingers down the long gash on his chest. "But seriously, how did we get home?"

"When you and Father were returning from the forest, you blacked out. After the healers patched you both up, the Great Stag used his staff to port us all here. Your father just came in this morning." Dag leaned toward Malachi. "Well, go on, tell us what happened? Did you fight the Immortal? Were you scared?"

Malachi sat up once again, "Ha! Please." Malachi said smugly. "Outmatched? Yes." He muttered quietly. "But scared? Never." Malachi said, in an effort to mask his true terror; he lied straight through his teeth.

"Ha ha! You coward. You were terrified, I bet. I wouldn't have been afraid; you should have let me go." Dag crossed his arms and sat back in his chair with a smug look as he threw his feet up onto the edge of the bed.

"You fool!" Roman barged in, his face redder and angrier than usual. "A foolish, stubborn child. You could have been killed. Just be thankful that Cain wasn't with him, or you would surely be dead." Roman was standing in the doorway, not amused by the boys's jokes. All three boys hung their heads and averted their eyes from their furious elder. He too was bandaged and moving stiffly, "I told you to turn back; you are lucky to be alive."

"My father was still out there. I couldn't just leave him." Malachi growled, he continued to look down at his lap.

Roman slammed a punch into the doorframe; it cracked beneath the force of his burly fist. His voice rolled like thunder, "Yes a lot of help you were, boy. He never would have forgiven me if you were killed. I would never forgive myself…you arrogant brat." He struck the wall again and stomped out of the room.

An uneasy silence filled the chamber and the boys could only peer down at the ground or ceiling. Eventually, once Roman was far enough away, Dag spoke up.

"That's just his way of saying he loves you." The boys all tried desperately to keep their laughter down, scared Roman would hear and come back in. Malachi curled and winced with every giggle; a fiery pain shot through his chest each time he laughed. He laid back down again.

"You're a fool, brother." Felix said as he shook his head, still chuckling. "But he has a point, ya know? You shouldn't have chased off after them like that. They can handle themselves."

Malachi ran both his hands through his hair, then gripped his pillow, "I know, I know. I wasn't thinking. I just…reacted." He became silent and stared at the ceiling for a while again. "I've never seen power like that."

"So, the legends are true then? The Immortals are as deadly as everyone says?" Dag asked curiously.

"Well, yes, but I wasn't talking about them. I meant my father." He stayed on his back and lifted his arm above his head; all three boys studied his Savage Mark.

"I wish I could have been there," Felix said, sadly.

Malachi's voice lost his normal charm and he spoke coldly, "No, you don't."

"How did they find the arena anyway?" Dag asked. "I thought the whole point of the Celestial Cloud was to conceal our location from humans and the members of Abaddon?"

"It is. I don't know."

"You think they have someone on the inside?" Felix asked, looking out the window.

"A traitor? In the Order? I doubt it." Malachi said, sounding unsure of himself.

"Then how the hell did they find us?" Tarjak's stoic voice interrupted. "Excuse me gentlemen, may I have the room?" Tarjak entered, his wife close behind him.

"Thank you for staying with him, boys." Malachi's mother said sincerely, her auburn hair pulled back tightly behind her head.

"Of course, Aunt Rosy." Felix said with a smile.

"Come on boys, let's give them a minute." She said gently, motioning them to follow her. Dag and Felix got up from their seats and headed toward their smiling aunt; she sent a quick reassuring wink at Malachi before leaving the room.

Tarjak patted both Felix and Dag on the back as they passed him and made their way out of the hall. He pulled up a sturdy wooden chair next to Malachi, "Are you all right, son?"

Malachi stayed laying down, anxious for the lecture he knew was coming. "I'm a little sore, but honestly, I'm fine. Are you all right?"

"Good. Yes, I'm fine." The huge man ran his grizzly hand through his reddish beard and seemed to have lost his train of thought. He peered straight down at his feet for a while before erupting, his voice crashing like boulders. "That was idiotic! You disobeyed a direct order. I should kill you myself and feed you to the dogs." Malachi averted his eyes, ashamed of his actions. "But, you did show great courage, son. You followed your heart and did what you felt was right to protect the people you care about. It was arrogant and foolish... but courageous." Tarjak nodded his head as if he were reassuring his own words as he spoke; pride rang in his voice. Malachi still did not look in his father's direction, but he let a small smile sneak across his lips.

Finally glancing at his father, he whispered, "What is it like? Using the Savage Mark?" Malachi's voice grew quiet; he knew it was a delicate subject.

"Terrifying." Malachi had never seen Tarjak—the great Lion of Talitha—speak with such vulnerability. "Well, terrifying at first. It feels like scalding, hot lava is running through your veins and your flesh is being ripped from your bones." He paused for a moment and stared straight ahead, "But then, after the transformation is complete, then..." He was quiet once more; it was like his mind was in another place. "Then, you feel the power. You feel as if you could rip through the heart of a mountain with a single blow. You feel like you could slaughter an entire legion of foes with the flex of your arm. You feel as if all the forces of heaven and earth would kneel before your claws, and they would cry out for mercy at the sound of your roar," inspired just thinking about the sensation—Tarjak's voice burgeoned, louder and louder. Malachi's eyes grew bigger and bigger; just the thought of such power made him squirm with excitement. Tarjak saw the lust in his son's eyes, "But, when you release the power of the Savage Mark, you no longer have control of your own mind. An animalistic force takes over, and a fierce anger runs through your blood. It is nearly impossible to pick out friend from foe. We must only use this power in dire situations—it is extremely dangerous. Do you understand?"

"Yes, Father." Malachi answered, but his mind was clearly dissecting the advantages the mark could provide in battle.

Tarjak handed him a wooden box, "Here, these are for you."

Malachi knew exactly what was inside, "My rings." He said with a grin as he lifted his sore arm to grab the box from his father. He swung his burly legs off the side of the bed. Malachi opened the box. He gazed at the four beautifully displayed rings. Each more handsome than the last, the intricate and complicated gold jewelry appeared thick and square. "Thank you, Father. They are amazing."

"Well, they are not amazing *yet*. Legacy Rings are simply just rings; the stones give them their power. We can go get one today if you feel up for it."

"Yes, please." Malachi said with a nod. He tried to hide his aches and pains. "Maybe a Nova Stone? Or a Scorch Stone?"

"Ha! You wish, boy. Those are *very* rare stones." Tarjak looked down at his own Scorch Stone and thought back to how long it took him to earn it. "We will have to start with a more common stone, like the Solar Stone." He raised his hand and activated his Solar Stone; the pieces of the ring lifted and separated as if they were never connected.

The stone emanated a great light that filled the whole room; Malachi squinted and shielded his eyes.

"Fine," Malachi said, unenthusiastically. He sounded a little disappointed. He had seen the Solar Stone a hundred times and now viewed it as a glorified flashlight. He thought back to the awesome stones the Old Stag had at the ceremony, and he remembered something. "Father?" Malachi asked. Tarjak grunted in response. "Is there a stone the Keepers use to communicate telepathically? I think Cyrus used one on me." Malachi asked.

"I wouldn't be surprised; those fairies have a stone for just about everything." Tarjak hid a smug grin beneath his dense beard. Malachi grabbed at his chest once more as he laughed. Malachi glanced over at his armor fiercely displayed to the side of his room.

"When is my first mission?" Malachi asked with anticipation gleaning in his eyes; he had waited his whole life for his first mission.

"You will go on your first mission when I tell you you can." Tarjak said sternly. Malachi fought back the urge to roll his eyes.

"Do you really think there could be a spy in the Order?" Malachi asked cautiously.

"I'd be lying if I said it hadn't happened before." Tarjak said with an uneasy scowl. Malachi stared straight ahead, thinking about who it could have been. "All right boy, get dressed. We will head to Aldafar and get you a stone and a Phoenix Charm."

"I'm getting a Phoenix Charm too?" Malachi asked, his eyes shaking with excitement as he leaned forward.

"Well, how else are you going to port back and forth for your missions?" Tarjak said with a nod as he got up from his chair. The muscular young man looked like a child as he sprung out of bed to get ready. He was grinning from ear to ear. He ignored the pain of his injuries as he frantically reached for a shirt. As Tarjak headed out of his room, he looked back at him, "I am proud of you, Malachi. I don't think I would have challenged an Immortal at your age." Malachi tried to hold back his smile and be stoic like his father. "Never the hunted..." Tarjak said.

"Always the hunter." Malachi finished the statement proudly with a nod as his father left the room. A trip to the home of the Aldafarian people was always a treat. Similar to the isolated fortresses of Talitha and Zaurak, it was a full and lively city, and the center of trade for all three clans; a wide assortment of relics and artifacts could be found there. Aldafar was a gorgeous ancient civilization surrounded by lush forests and woods. The only thing Malachi enjoyed more was visiting actual modern communities and observing their strange human behaviors. He hurried to get ready, then raced down the halls of his home to find Tarjak. They ported straight from their home to the center courtyard of Aldafar.

Malachi spun around in amazement and looked at all the shops and vendors that were carved from the marble cliffs. The courtyard was tidy and clean; the gray stone paths led off in any direction to a variety of shops and temples. The pearl-white city sat handsomely within the emerald-green forest surrounding it. The civilization was chiseled from marble mountains and hidden in every direction by massive redwoods and pines. The smell of pine and aspen was carried through the city by a crisp mountain breeze. Each building and wall had intricate designs and artwork all inspired by the Aldafarian culture. Sleek silver banners floated in the wind above the buildings; wild goats and sheep made their homes around the cliffs and often wandered into the courtyards. This kingdom's architecture and elegance would have made even ancient Rome turn green with jealousy. It all seemed as if it had been flawlessly painted, by a truly talented artist, across the towering cliff-side.

Tarjak handed Malachi a small leather bag of coins, "Listen, go to Lady Winslow's shop. You know where it is." Malachi nodded. "Tell her you need a Phoenix Charm and a Solar Stone."

"Ya, ya, ya, I know!" He said confidently, too excited to focus.

"All right, I'm glad the mighty Sabertooth of Talitha feels comfortable shopping on his own." Tarjak said sarcastically. "I need to go meet with the Elders about last night. I will find you when we are done."

"Yes sir." Malachi took off toward Lady Winslow's and Tarjak headed toward the main temple where the members of the Order of Eden often held meetings of importance. Malachi passed under beautiful willows that hung over the paths of the courtyard. Every tree blossomed with hundreds of snow-white flowers year-round. Shops and Aldafarian banners filled the town square; the little town buzzed with life. As he rounded the corner, he saw a rather unpleasant sight.

"Well, it is good to see you alive, Malachi! We thought for sure the great Sabertooth of Talitha was a goner." Fenrir laughed as he approached Malachi who was clearly limping and still sore from last evening. Zacharias strutted with pride next to his brother. Malachi just shook his head and grinded his teeth, doing his best to keep his temper at bay. "Is it true you pissed your pants when you faced the Immortal, Malachi? Zacharias and I would have slain the pig, with ease. I hear you barely got out alive."

"Ha! You would have zipped away with your tail between your legs, Fenrir. You're a coward who hides in the shadows, and shoots arrows from the dark." Malachi growled with a grin; he certainly did not fear Fenrir after facing an Immortal.

"You brainless Guardians are all the same—quick to jump in a fight but can never finish it." Fenrir said with a devilish smirk as he inched closer, his black shirt unbuttoned inappropriately low. He flipped his dark hair out of his face.

"I'd be happy to start—and finish—one right now if you are, princess." Malachi stepped closer. Zacharias was un-amused by their pointless conflict. He just stood back and scowled at Malachi with his arms crossed. Fenrir's ego, versus Malachi's pride—it would be a fierce battle.

"Hm, maybe later. Zach and I have some more shopping to do." He held up an artfully crafted charm, a black pendant with a spiral made of sparkling stones at the center; he handed it to Zacharias.

"What is that?" Malachi asked observing the pendant.

"You are as brilliant as they say, aren't you?" Fenrir giggled to himself. "It's a Ghost Charm. It's how Shade Runners port from long distances, just as you rock heads use Phoenix Charms." Malachi nodded curiously. Fenrir continued, "As fun as this has been, I have a mission to prepare for." Fenrir gestured to his brother to follow.

"A mission?" Malachi said in jealously, "What kind of mission?"

"A simple surveillance mission. It seems a few Seals have resurfaced around the globe and the Great Stag wants us to investigate. He briefed all the Shade Runners on possible locations this morning. We Shade Runners do all the research and hard work so we can pass it on to you ill-informed oafs." Fenrir said dramatically as he flipped his raven hair back out of his face again. Malachi ignored the insult; he just scrunched his face and thought about how desperately he wanted to go on a mission himself. Fenrir winked his gray eye at Malachi and continued past him. Malachi realized they were leaving. He respectfully nodded at Zach, who naturally ignored him. Malachi was honestly a little jealous of Zacharias's mystique. He was always calm and acted like nothing interested nor bothered him. Malachi, on the other hand, was brash and short-tempered. He studied the two as they walked away, their noses high in the air as if they owned the entire marketplace.

Malachi continued down the path under the willows; it seemed as if every person was watching him. "That's the boy who fought the Immortal last night." He heard whispered in the crowds.

"That's the Sabertooth of Talitha. He beat Varden's boy." Another voice slipped from the crowd. Word traveled fast throughout the Order; all of these shopkeepers and farmers in the town were not even at the ceremony last night.

"Our Cyrus could beat him." Malachi bit at his own lip and clenched his fist, but he just put his head down and kept moving.

He walked until he reached a small stone building. An old wooden sign—chipped and in need of a new paint job—hung above the door. It read: WINSLOW'S CHARMS. The stones of the building were a faded gray and covered in emerald vines; it had been there for hundreds of years, and it showed. The battered wooden door was heavy and weathered; the iron hinges creaked and moaned as Malachi opened it. The inside of the shop was much different. The walls were decorated with charms, artifacts, and other mysterious objects. There was not a blank space on any wall or in any corner; Winslow's was always fully stocked. Stones of every color were neatly displayed in cases all around the store. Each stone had its respective name inscribed under it, written in ancient angelic text.

"Um, Lady Winslow? Are you in here?" Malachi asked cautiously. He looked around; she was nowhere in sight. He decided to walk about the shop and browse some of the items. The selection of Talithan items appeared rather limited; the Guardians relied more on their strength then they did stones and charms. There were about three times as many Legacy Stones for the Knowledge Keepers as there were for the Guardians. Malachi made his way into a smaller room hidden in the corner of the shop. There was a mix of items from every clan—daggers, charms, stones, and jewelry cluttered the display cases.

Within the mess of hundreds of miscellaneous objects, a dark piece of jewelry could be seen suspended in the center of the wall surrounded by other elaborate pieces; it caught Malachi's eye. A thin black chain hung from a hook; a dainty necklace shimmered from its resting place. Malachi took the necklace in his hand and examined it closely; a small stone pendant hung at the center of the chain—Ancient Persian writing encircled a lilac stone at the heart of the pendant.

"Good eye, Malachi!" An elderly woman sprung out from behind him. Malachi nearly leapt through the ceiling and fumbled with the necklace. She threw her head back and laughed hysterically; she remained overly energetic for her age. She stood short and plump; her hair was as white as the Aldafarian banners out in the yard. She was always cheerful, warm and happy to see a customer.

"Ha! Lady Winslow." Malachi said happily; he gave her a big hug after regaining his breath. "It's great to see you. Did you miss me?" Malachi said in a flirty voice as he bounced his eyebrows up and down.

"Oh Malachi, you fool. It has been too long." She gave him another hug. Malachi had been visiting the Winslow's shop since he was a young boy. He loved seeing the crazy old shopkeeper. "I heard you gave that Zaurakian boy quite the whoopin' last night." Again, she cackled uncontrollably, grabbing on to Malachi for balance.

Malachi laughed with her, "I only won for you. I had to make my favorite lady proud."

"*Favorite lady*, my fanny!" She said as she nodded at the necklace. Malachi's face turned blood red.

"W-What do you mean? I was just looking around, waiting for you." He said defensively; Lady Winslow's eyes grew bigger behind her thin wire glasses.

"My God, Malachi, Son of Tarjak. A girl has a hold of your heart. And a Zaurakian one at that." His face got redder; he shook his head frantically and hung the necklace back on its hook. "I don't need a Sight Stone to see you're in love, sweetheart." Again, her chuckles shook the old rickety shop. This time, she grabbed a hold of Malachi and shook him wildly as she joyfully bellowed.

"L-Love?" Malachi scoffed in embarrassment. "I barely know the girl." His hands were now running through his wavy-blond hair nervously; he kept looking around, making sure no one else was in the store.

"You barely know her, huh?" She removed the necklace from the hook and put it in a small wooden box after wrapping it carefully in a thin navy cloth. She handed it to Malachi. "Well, go get to know her then, you big fool."

Malachi smiled and laughed; he looked down at the ground, "You're crazy. You know that?" He reluctantly took the box from her frail, wrinkled fingers.

She howled again, as merry and loud as ever. "People have been telling me that for years, Malachi. Now, what else do you need? A Phoenix Charm, maybe?"

"Yes, ma'am. And a Solar Stone as well."

"Okay, this way, sweetheart." The old lady waddled back into the front room and gestured Malachi to follow.

"How's business been?" Malachi asked politely.

"Oh, just wonderful!" She said as she threw her hands in the air; she shuffled around in a circle, admiring her own shop.

"That's always your response." Malachi replied, shaking his head. "This place could burn to the ground and that would still be your response."

"Well, of course. Then I could have a huge sale on ashes." She said with a bellowing laugh. Malachi slapped his face deep into his palm. "Okay, okay. Enough foolin' around. Come here."

She showed him to a display case with about twenty Talithan clan stones of red, yellow, and orange. The majority of the stones were simple yellow Solar Stones, the least rare of the Legacy Stones. Lady Winslow lifted the glass and picked one out. "The miners of Talitha do just a splendid job of bringing me stones, don't they?" Malachi nodded in agreement, surveying her collection. "Did you bring a Legacy Ring?" Malachi nodded again and reached into the pocket of his leather vest; he removed a single gold ring. She brought the stone right in front of the ring, as close as she could get it without touching them. The geometrically shaped ring shifted and separated—countless pieces sliding to create an opening for the stone. Once she released the smooth stone, it fell into place, as did the other pieces around it. Lady Winslow handed it back to Malachi.

"Thank you," he exclaimed with a smile, sliding it onto his finger.

"Now that ring and stone are linked together. You can never use that ring with another stone, or that stone with another ring. To activate a stone's power, you need to really concentrate. It will take some practice, but you will get it. The rarer the stone, the more concentration needed to master it." Malachi was barely paying attention; he was still browsing the other stones, wishing he could have something more exciting than just the Solar Stone. She grabbed him by the ear, "Hello? Malachi, are you in there? Are you listening?" She asked as she playfully knocked on his massive head.

"Ow! What? Oh, yes, I'm sorry. I am." She laughed at him and pulled him away from the other stones.

"You are not ready for those stones, sweetie. All right, let's go get a Phoenix Charm!" She said as she guided him into another room. Malachi was focused once more. She took him to a wall across the shop where a variety of small golden birds were displayed. The elaborate and complex birds seemed to be made out of the same materials the Legacy Rings were crafted from—forged of metal and jewels. "No one Phoenix is the same," she grabbed a magenta one off the wall first. It was a bright red, almost pink, and had black tail feathers.

"Okay, Malachi, let's try this one. Take the charm in your hand." She handed it to him and moved behind him. "Now raise your arm like you're throwing a spear." Malachi did as she said. "Now, I want you to think about the room you found the necklace in, think hard! Now, throw it!" Malachi threw it with all his might; the metal Phoenix was like a lethal dart cutting through the air. It slammed into a nearby shelf; objects and relics went flying through the air. The bird fell to the ground, thankfully unbroken. Lady Winslow was laughing wildly again, shaking Malachi's body with all her might.

"Why didn't it work?" Malachi asked in frustration as he tried to free himself from the old woman's grip. "I did everything you said."

"Ha ha! It's all right sweetheart. We just have to find one that works for you. Your cousin Dag did the same thing his first try. Every Phoenix is different, just like every Guardian is different. Let us try again." She grabbed a yellow bird off the wall this time; it had white wings and a white beak. She handed it to Malachi, who looked at it nervously. "Well, go on then."

Malachi reared his arm back, and he thought about his destination hard. This time, the bird began to smolder and spark; he could feel it getting hot in his hand. Malachi released it with a mighty throw, and the bird burst into flames. It shot into the same wall just as the other bird did and began to consume the wall in flames. Malachi froze, unsure of what to do. Lady Winslow lifted her hand, the ring on her pointer finger shifted and separated, the gray stone in the middle shined dimly.

What looked like a wave of light pushed out from her hands, and like a strong gust of wind, it extinguished the flames. Malachi was in awe of the awesome power.

"What? What stone is that? How did you do that?" Malachi asked in amazement, his mouth flopped open. She slapped him on the arm. "Never mind that. Focus, Malachi, and quit destroying my shop." She laughed at how hard he was struggling. "That Shade Runner boy you whooped did it first try with his Ghost Charm. He and his brother were just in here."

Malachi's eyes suddenly squinted and focused, his voice now deep and stern, "Give me another one." She was impressed with his sudden determination. She handed him a charcoal black Phoenix with gold feathers. He took a strong stance and readied the tiny metal bird in his hands with confidence. With his arm back, he closed his eyes, and took a deep breath. He slowly opened his hand, the bird levitated above his open palm. It gently began to be engulfed in flames; in a quick snap, he threw it. As it left his hand, he too began to catch fire. The bird vanished in a puff of flame and the flames from his body chased after it. He vanished in the blink of an eye and a flash of fire.

Lady Winslow had a joyous grin on her wrinkled face as Malachi emerged from the other room, looking rather serious. "Well done, sweetheart. I knew you could do it. Now remember, just focus hard on your destination and you can go almost anywhere. Some things to remember though: you can't port outside if you are inside, and you can't port into a building if you're outside. These charms are the only thing allowing us to port in and out of the Celestial Cloud that surrounds our homes—so don't lose it. Without the charm, you cannot enter the dimensional pocket that the cloud creates, which allows our civilizations to exist hidden from the human world…" She looked up at Malachi, who had cocked his head and furrowed his brow in confusion. "Oh, listen to me, rambling like some sort of Knowledge Keeper. Never mind any of that. But, now you are a full-fledged Guardian, ready for any mission!"

Malachi grinned cheerfully and puffed out his chest, quite pleased with himself. "Thank you, Lady Winslow. And I'm sorry about the damage I caused." He helped clean up the best he could and left a few extra coins with her. "I will come back and visit soon." He made his way out of the shop.

"You better. You big old hunk." Everyone in the town could hear her laugh from the open door of her shop as Malachi headed back toward the center of the courtyard to find his father.

Malachi did not see Tarjak anywhere once he reached their meeting place, and Malachi did not want to interrupt their meeting, so he decided to rest for a while under the shade of a tree just outside the main courtyard. He observed his new trinkets and lay in the grass until he fell asleep under a white bark tree with a lush green blossom. He napped for about an hour and was then awoken by a swift tapping on his arm. Malachi looked up and saw Cyrus standing above him.

"Oh, hey. Cyrus, right?" Malachi said, still only half awake; he blinked rapidly to clear his eyesight.

"Correct, I am Cyrus of Aldafar. And you are Malachi of Talitha, son of Tarjak."

"Yes? Did you need something?" Malachi rubbed his own face and squinted.

"Your father, Tarjak of Talitha, asked me to deliver a message to you." Malachi sat up, now very interested in what he had to say.

"Is everything all right, what is it?"

"He wanted me to inform you that his meeting with the Elders of Aldafar will not cease in any approaching hour, and he recommends that you return to the fortress of Talitha without him." Cyrus stared expressionless; his long white hair was pulled back neatly as usual. His new thin sword strapped to his hip, and Malachi could not help but notice that he had about six rings on his hands. "I hope this information proves useful to you. Would you like me to convey a message back to your father, Malachi of Talitha?

"No, no. That's okay. Um, thank you, I guess?"

"You are welcome." He turned away and headed back toward the temple.

"Hey, Cyrus. Wait up. Can I ask you something?" Malachi jumped from his spot.

"I suppose that would be all right. What is it?"

"How were you talking with me the other night at the ceremony? I mean, you weren't talking, but you were in my head somehow..." Cyrus raised his hand and Malachi stopped talking.

"I was using the Echo Stone." Cyrus's voice was in Malachi's head once more. One of the rings on Cyrus's fingers was shifting and moving. "That is how I created a telepathic link between us."

"Wow," Malachi thought to himself, but also to Cyrus. "All I have is a Solar Stone, and you have so many."

They continued communicating telepathically, "As a Knowledge Keeper, my mental capacity allows me to have many Legacy Stones. They can be useful tools. You too should gather more stones; you will surely need them."

"Why do you say that?" Malachi asked, his head slightly tilted to one side.

"Since your skills as a warrior are inferior to mine, you should acquire all the assistance you can from stones and charms." Cyrus thought this and smiled. He believed he had just given helpful advice.

"Inferior?" Malachi was no longer using the mental link and shouted aloud as a new vein seemed to bulge from his neck. Cyrus stepped back, his icy-blue eyes wide with concern.

"Is there an issue? I was simply stating a fact."

"Fact? I would snap you like a twig!" He said, obviously commenting on Cyrus's thin figure.

"Impossible. I am much thicker than the average twig. You would need to use exactly thirty-six times the amount of force in order to snap me. Well, depending on the type of wood the twig originated from." Cyrus clearly did not understand the threat. Malachi clenched his fist tightly; he was truly annoyed. "I am simply observing the fact that you are a slow and undisciplined warrior who I would easily defeat." Cyrus said softly. He was confused why Malachi was reacting the way he was.

Malachi slammed his fists together with a heavy smack that shook their immediate area; Cyrus's long hair flew back from the force. "Prove it!" Malachi cursed as he winded up and threw a fierce punch right at Cyrus's face. Cyrus leaned back, almost becoming parallel with the ground; Malachi's attack barely missed. Cyrus jabbed twice at his attacker's bicep with just his fingertips; Malachi's arm fell limply to his side. It dangled by his hip, unable to move. Malachi looked down at his lifeless arm in shock, "What did you do to me?"

"I momentarily disabled the nerves in your arm by striking multiple pressure poi—" Before Cyrus could finish, Malachi spun and kicked him square in the chest. Cyrus flew back and slid across the grass. Cyrus was amazed; Malachi was unpredictable and did not allow him a chance to calculate a defensive maneuver.

"You little rat. Get out of here before I show you what I can really do." Malachi had fierce anger in his eyes; he clenched his disabled limb.

Cyrus was still lost, his blue eyes drooped in sadness, and he held his head low. "Very well. I am truly sorry if I offended you, Malachi of Talitha, son of Tarjak." He bowed respectfully and turned away—still curious as to what went wrong. Cyrus had spent his whole life studying and being mentored by the Elders of Aldafar; he had very little contact with anyone else. He was just now learning basic social protocols, and he knew nothing of interacting with people his age.

"What the hell?" Malachi thought to himself, trying to decipher the Keeper's strange behavior and figure out how to fix his limp noodle of an arm. He started to get the feeling back into his bicep. He wiggled his fingers. Once Cyrus reached the stairs of the temple, he turned back and watched Malachi use his Phoenix Charm to port home in a quick flash of flames. Cyrus shook his head and fought the tears that were beginning to swell in his eyes. He was unaware why Malachi showed no interest in being friends. After clearing his throat and brushing himself off, he fixed his hair, which had fallen out of place from their bout—a Knowledge Keeper must always look his best. The silver Owl of Aldafar slowly headed back into the quiet temple to study on his own, his head held low.

CHAPTER 8

NO BLADE AND NO ARROW

Malachi ported into the Talithan training yard just outside the mansion. He burst out of the flames and crashed into his cousin Dag; they both fell to the red dirt beneath them. They were in a large square courtyard; the area was flat and great for training. It was at one of the highest peaks of the fortress and it overlooked the canyon. Five identical statues of a warrior holding up the sun surrounded the training area, in-between each statue sat a row of towering king palm trees.

"Malachi? You idiot." Dag, sweaty and sore from his day of training, barked at Malachi. Dag pushed Malachi off himself in a fuss.

"Sorry. Sorry. I still haven't really figured out how to use this thing." He said with a chuckle as he flipped the small antique in his hand.

"No worries, it just takes some practice." Felix said as he extended his hand to help Malachi off the ground.

"Sorry to interrupt your training session, boys. Were you sparing?"

"Ya, right. Felix isn't much of a sparring partner, more of a punching bag." Dag said confidently as he jumped back to his feet. Felix put his wooden sword to Dag's chest and pushed him back.

"Then let us go again, brother. So Malachi can watch me crush you."

"I'm ready when you are, little brother." Dag picked up his bow staff off the ground; he spun it back and forth in his hands. He put the end of his staff in Felix's face, "And I won't hold back this time." Dag spun and whipped his bow staff toward Felix's torso; Felix blocked it easily with his two wooden swords. Malachi did a backhand spring out of the way of the action; he sat down off to the side. Felix threw a quick combo; the right sword attacked high—the left sword went low. Dag blocked both the attacks as he twirled his weapon with impressive control.

"I got my Solar Stone today," Malachi said as he watched his cousins battle. "I really need some other stones. That Cyrus guy has a bunch."

"Ya, those Keeper pretty boys always have the best stones." Dag said as he ducked under an attack, Felix's sword brushing the top of his Mohawk.

"The miners of the Order only seem to find rare stones for the Knowledge Keepers, and all they bring us are Solar Ston—" Dag landed a blow on Felix's shoulder interrupting him, he answered with a kick to his brother's ribs. They were both skilled martial artists like their cousin.

"If I wasn't a Guardian, I would be a great miner. I would go to the most isolated places in the world and bring back the rarest of stones." Malachi said theatrically as he raised an open palm toward the sky. "Keep your elbow up Felix." Malachi barked. Felix raised his arm and blocked Dag's next attack. The following strike was too fast to be blocked; he punched Felix right in the gut. He cringed and leaned into Dag's fist; the punch sent him to the ground.

"You should become a miner Malachi, 'cause you're gonna be a terrible Guardian." Dag jested as Felix rolled across the dirt from the punch. Felix kicked up off the ground; he went after his brother with a flurry of attacks. Their wooden weapons whacked together, and Felix drove his brother back. This time, Felix threw his older brother to the ground; he put his swords to Dag's neck.

"Well if you become a miner, you better bring me all your best finds, Malachi." Felix said as he pressed his sparring blades against Dag's neck.

"You got it, Felix."

"And if you do become a miner, don't worry about the clan. I can lead it after Tarjak is done." Felix said with a cheeky grin. Dag and Malachi exchanged confused glances.

"What are you talking about?" Dag said with a chuckle, still sitting in the dirt.

"Well, I've been thinking… I am of the royal bloodline and I could challenge Malachi for rule of the clan." Felix stated as he nodded his head. Malachi and Dag broke out in an uproar. "I'm serious!" Felix barked. They both fell silent.

"Truly?" Malachi asked, sounding a little offended.

"Truly," Felix said, pushing his long sweaty hair from his face. "I think I would make a great clan leader."

Malachi nodded with a grin. "Honestly, so do I." Malachi said sincerely, "But you better keep training, 'cause that's going to be the fight of your life."

"I wouldn't want it any other way, cousin."

"What is happening?" Dag asked, shaking his head.

Malachi got up and proudly grabbed Felix by the forearm. "I look forward to our fight, cousin." Felix nodded confidently.

Malachi glanced down at his new ring after releasing Felix's forearm; it reminded him of the necklace he had stored in his pocket. His pupils dilated, and he blushed a little just thinking about his Zaurakian crush. "All right Guardians, I will see you later." Malachi said suspiciously.

"Where you off to, cousin?" Dag said, still on the ground, as he swept Felix's feet from beneath him with his staff. Felix hit the ground with a thud and his hair flopped in his face.

"N-Nowhere. Just inside. I will be back." His answer seemed rushed and frantic. Felix and Dag looked at each other confused by their cousin's sudden awkwardness.

"Whatever," Dag lost interest, returning to his training. "Come, let us battle, oh sovereign ruler of the Talithan clan!" Dag said as he humbly and dramatically bowed to his brother. Felix rolled his eyes, and they continued to spar as Malachi hurried away. Once he was out of view from his cousins, he pulled out his Phoenix Charm.

"Well, now is as good a time as any." Malachi thought to himself; he felt now was an opportune time to deliver the necklace to Skye. He lifted the charm in his hand; it again levitated above his palm. It gracefully ignited, and he threw it straight in front of him. Before he knew it, he was knee deep in snow, and icy wilderness surrounded him. Just like the Talithinan estate, the Zaurakian fortress was completely isolated within its own Celestial Cloud. It's harsh surrounding environments and freezing temperatures made it the perfect environment for the mysterious and cold people of Zaurak.

Malachi had ported in alongside a frozen cliff side about a mile from his destination; he clearly still did not have full control of his new ability. He threw on his dark crimson hood, that he grabbed before leaving, and accepted he would have to hike the rest of the way. He trudged through the snow until he reached the tall outer wall of the Zaurakian home—a gothic castle surrounded by black stone towers. Black banners with crystal blue or violet crescents hung from the fortress walls. Seven different towers, staggering in height and width, sprung upward from the massive fortress; a spiderweb of swaying iron-forged bridges connected the towers to one another—a frosted, treacherous maze in the sky.

As Malachi looked up at the towering fortress, nearly hidden in the night sky, he recalled the stories about a test the young Zaurakian boys had to complete if they wished to become a warrior. Guards would be posted in each tower and scattered all around the estate, a single young Zaurakian boy would have to sneak through the courtyard, then scale the highest tower and retrieve a flag pinned at the very top without being seen—supposedly a grueling test that very few pass on their first attempt. It was a true testament to a Zaurakian warrior; could they disappear into the faintest of shadows? Could they move at inhuman speeds in order to avoid detection? Rumor had it that Fenrir, at only age fourteen, held the record for the fastest flag retrieval in the history of the clan. After studying the height and treacherousness of the climb, Malachi was quite impressed.

The stones of the outer wall of the estate were a charcoal black and frosted with ice; Malachi flipped over it with ease. He was now in the outer yard of the Zaurakian fortress, and Malachi soon realized he was not dressed for such cold weather. His teeth were chattering as he made his way to their home; he was much more accustomed to his desert climate. A thick white puff of cloud slid from his mouth with every frigid breath he took. He was quick, careful not to be seen by anyone as he hurried across the empty courtyard.

Malachi's heart raced at the thought of seeing Skye; his breaths became quick and choppy, and despite the terrible cold, he could feel himself begin to sweat. He watched patiently for a while, hoping to see her pass by the frosted window where he was now perched. Instead of Skye, he saw Zacharias sending off Fenrir on his mission. Malachi clenched his jaw in a jealous scowl; he hoped that Fenrir would have an uneventful mission. Fenrir was in his full armor and escorted by two Crows—both skilled spies and archers—who followed close behind him in a rhythmic march. Their feathered black cloaks draped all the way to the floor, and their beaked masks left only their mouths and chins exposed. Both of the spies were tall and lean, their quiver of arrows strapped firmly to their backs. Zach and Fenrir grabbed the back of each other's necks and touched foreheads, Zacharias then handed his brother his mask and bow.

"No blade..." Fenrir said to Zach.

"No arrow..." Zacharias replied.

"...can match the fang of the wolf." They both said together in unison. As children, they would recite this to each other before combat training. Now as men, they recited it when they left for a mission.

To Fenrir and Zacharias, it was a reminder that no man could challenge them; they were the world's deadliest weapons. Fenrir dawned his Wolf mask and threw a heavy black fur cloak over his shoulders. Malachi watched as all three Shade Runners, decorated in Zaurakian designs and armors, dashed away into the night.

Zacharias closed the heavy stone doors behind them and began to head out of the center lobby of the mansion. Just before reaching the next hallway, he stopped, as if time had frozen. Malachi watched him, very confused by why he had so suddenly halted. Zacharias new someone was watching him. He could feel Malachi's stare through the glass, but he had no idea who it was. Zacharias whipped around with fierce speed and bolted up to the window like a bullet. Malachi, shocked by Zach's sudden actions, dove out of the view of the window. He had nearly fallen off the wall in the process, and was clinging to a ledge with his fingertips—just low enough that Zach could not see him. Zacharias leaned up against the window, his breath fogging up the glass.

"What are you doing up there, brother?" A confused voice came from down below Zacharias.

"Skye? Oh, I thought I saw something." Zacharias responded as he frantically looked through the glass.

"Well, get down from there." She laughed at her brother clinging to the windowpane. Zacharias nodded and took one last look; he now realized he was probably being paranoid. He saw nothing; so he squatted down and pushed off the window. He performed an impressive backflip from the wall and landed with grace. His thick dark hair danced wildly as he landed next to his sister. She could see the concern in his eyes. "What's wrong with you, Zach?" Zacharias ignored her and kept staring at the window. "Hello? Zach?" He continued to look at the window, his dark eyes reflecting the moonlight that trickled through the glass. His fists were clenched and he seemed almost angry. Skye put her hand on his shoulder, "Seriously, what has gotten into you, Zach?"

"Something's wrong. I should have gone with him."

Skye raised her thin eyebrow and shook her head; she knew that Fenrir was a talented warrior and that he did not need protecting. "What do you mean? Fenrir is fine, and he has two other Shade Runners with him."

"I don't know. I just have a bad feeling." He said in his usual cold, dark tone. Zacharias was still looking out the window, wishing he were out in the field with his brother. He turned quickly, his hair and cloak thrown around him dramatically before he stomped out of the room.

"It is just a simple scouting mission. He will be back in a few hours." She watched him march out; she too now felt uneasy about the mission. She glanced out the window to try and see what Zach was so concerned with, she gasped and covered her mouth. Malachi, sporting a huge grin, was waving at her through the glass like an excited toddler. She looked around the room in a panic to make sure no one else saw him or her reaction—then frantically gestured for him to meet her upstairs. Malachi was confused why she looked so angry, but he scaled the wall up another story to meet her anyway.

On the next floor, Skye flung the windows to her bedroom open in anger, "Are you crazy?" She whispered violently. "Why would you come here?" She looked distraught, constantly surveying the room.

"I had to see you again." Malachi said loudly; she shushed him and whacked him in the arm a few times.

"Keep it down. Malachi, what were you thinking? My father will kill you." She ran her hands through her raven hair, nearly ripping it from her head; the stress was almost unbearable. Malachi climbed through the window and took her hands. "I'm serious Malachi; he will kill you if he finds you with me."

"Then my last few moments would be well spent." She rolled her eyes and made an exaggerated gagging noise as she ripped her hands away from him. Malachi just chuckled and shook his head.

"I'm serious though, Malachi. I am not worth the trouble."

"Trouble?" Malachi scoffed. "Skye, I would have fought off every last member of Abaddon just to see you once more. I had to see you. I needed to see you." Again, she tried not to react to his adoring words. "You are a fool, Malachi." She said with a smile as she shook her head. Then suddenly she remembered where she was. "But I'm serious, if my father finds you here he will release the wrath of the Creator on you. You need to go."

"I do not fear Varden."

"Ha! The Sabertooth of Talitha—so courageous," she said, sarcastically. "You are too sweet Malachi, but I don't want you to get in trouble with my family, and definitely not with yours. You should go." Her voice was surprisingly soft, but still anxious; Malachi knew she was being genuine.

"Okay, fine I will, but first I have something for you." Malachi pulled out the necklace he got her from Lady Winslow. Skye froze and tilted her head to one side.

"Malachi. I couldn't." Again, she rolled her eyes and shook her head. He ignored her and went behind her to put it on, the small trinket sat right above her chest. "Malachi, I couldn't." She said as she gently ran her dainty fingers across the pendant.

"Please, keep it." Malachi gave a reassuring glance.

"It's beautiful, thank you." She said reluctantly, realizing that Malachi would not take no for an answer.

"Do you really like it?"

"Yes, not bad for a brainless meathead." They both laughed, but quickly became silent when they heard Varden scolding one of the house maidens downstairs.

"Man, I'm glad he isn't my father. I don't know how you do it." Malachi said with a chuckle while he listened to him hound the unlucky woman down below.

"He wasn't always like that." Skye pushed her raven hair out of her face as she sat down on the floor beside her bed. "When my mother died, something died in him as well. She meant the world to him. He put all of his focus and frustration into training Fenrir and Zach after she passed... and he forgot about his daughter." She looked down and fumbled with her new necklace.

"How did she die?" Malachi asked gently, he knelt down and sat next to her. She did not raise her eyes from the necklace. "I'm sorry, you don't have t..."

"She used to take me places." Skye said to Malachi's surprise. "She had this leather journal where she wrote down all the places she wanted me to see. Anywhere in the world: Paris, Tokyo, Africa—she wanted me to see it all." She smiled and squeezed the necklace tightly in her hands. The smile quickly left her face and dread soon filled her hazel eyes, "But we did not always go to safe places. Although she wanted me to see the beauty of the world, she also wanted me to see the darkness: war, poverty, ruin." Her eyes shook as if she was there now; strands of raven hair fell in her face. "One day, we went to a... bad place. Men took her. They hurt her in front of me. She threw me the Ghost Charm and screamed at me to port home. I couldn't do anything. I was so young. Helpless. Worthless. Weak." A single tear ran down her face. "I will never feel that way again."

Malachi nodded and gently placed his hand on her shoulder. "I'm so sorry." He said under his breath.

"I never told my father where it happened. I knew he would go there and slaughter them all." She pushed her hair back and adjusted her posture, a fierce and strong woman sat before Malachi. "I never told him...because I wanted to do it."

Chills ran down Malachi's spine. He had never experienced such pain or torment; his heart hurt just simply listening to her story.

"Once I started, I wanted to save more women from having to go through what I did; I wanted to save them all. That's why the Elders took away my Ghost Charm. That's why they forbid me from traveling on my own. That's why everyone in the Order keeps their distance from me. They only see a murderer, a monster." The hallway where they sat felt cold and without life, dark and empty. "Some reason, I thought it would bring her back." More tears ran down her face, but her voice remained steady and strong. She pulled out her mother's leather journal, flipping through the pages. Location after location was listed on page after page. "Now, the only time I feel her presence is when I visit the places she had planned for us to go to together. I'm going to go to them all, for her."

Malachi wiped away her tears with his thumbs and smiled a reassuring grin; she pulled her face away. "She's so proud of you, Skye." Malachi whispered quietly. She glared off straight ahead, as if Malachi were not even the room.

"You don't need to do this."

"Do what?"

"This." She gestured to the necklace and to Malachi who still sat beside her on the floor. She brushed away the rest of her tears on her wrist. "The last thing I need is a…"

"Friend?" Malachi interrupted, finally sounding irritated. "Look, I'm just trying…"

"I know what you're trying to do." She cut him off coldly and slid away from him. "Just go." She got to her feet and pointed to the window as she fiercely pulled off the necklace. Malachi slowly rose to his feet, biting his lower lip in frustration.

"I'm sorry if I…" Malachi attempted to apologize.

"Now." She pushed the necklace into his burly chest and forced a small grunt from his lips. Malachi reared his head back in disbelief and scoffed; his face turned red and his blood began to boil.

"Well, I get it now, why everyone thinks you're insane!" Malachi growled as he headed toward the window.

"Another mystery solved by Malachi the wise. Are you sure you're not a Knowledge Keeper?" Malachi may have tossed a dagger, but she was throwing spears.

He fumbled for words. "Y-You ungrateful, heartless…"

"Ugh. Just send it in a letter, Malachi. I don't have time for you to try and think of a substantial insult." Skye said casually with one hand on her hip, looking terribly un-amused. Malachi's face was cherry red, and a vein bulged across his forehead as he turned to throw himself from the window.

Suddenly, they heard the front door downstairs crash open; commotion filled the halls. They could both here Varden yelling and people from all over the estate heading for the main door. Malachi turned back to Skye who was already darting from the room. He slammed his fist together and scowled, then placed his foot on the window seal. Peering out at the quiet beauty of the snow-covered fortress, the young warrior paused for a moment and began to control his wild breathing. Malachi closed his eyes and rubbed at them fiercely with his meaty fingers. After a long, regret-filled sigh, he walked to her bed and gently placed the necklace on her pillow. He then lowered himself from her window.

Malachi was watching once again from the same spot as earlier, trying to see what all the excitement was about. Both the Crows of Zaurak hobbled into the center of the room, followed by a trail of blood. Grisly wounds, drenched in blood, ran across their bodies; their armor was split and beaten. Fenrir was nowhere to be seen. Skye hurried down the stairs to meet Zacharias who stood behind their father. Malachi watched as the Crows explained the tragic news to Varden; his eyes filled with disbelief and rage. Skye fell to her knees and wept behind him. Zacharias kneeled beside her and wrapped her up in his arms. Malachi sat quietly out in the snow; a bitter chill ran over him as he watched the family morn through the frosted window. The house of Zaurak was broken.

CHAPTER 9

THE SABERTOOTH, WOLF, AND OWL

Nearly a year had passed since the night Malachi gave Skye the necklace. The chasm between the three clans of the Order had grown even wider.

After Fenrir's death, the Zaurakian clan had become consumed with bitterness and no longer bothered to attend the Order's meetings or affairs. Varden blamed the other clans for his son's untimely death; he believed that the Elders of Aldafar were using Fenrir and the other members of the Zaurakian clan to lure the Immortals out from hiding. When Varden accused the Elders of purposely endangering his son, Tarjak and Roman defended the Knowledge Keepers, so Varden shunned the Guardians as well.

The Shade Runners were now running secret missions of their own and no longer sought the wisdom of Aldafar, nor the strength of Talitha. Zacharias, heart broken by the death of his closest friend, was now hell-bent on revenge. Nearly every night, Zach ventured off on his own—hoping to track down the forces of Abaddon. He had nothing to show for his tireless efforts. His cold and reserved anger increased as it continued to consume his heart. Skye had not communicated with Malachi since that night, despite his many attempts.

Malachi was no longer seen as a rookie Guardian. He had earned his name as the Sabertooth of Talitha. After multiple successful missions, fighting alongside Dag and Felix, Malachi's fame and prestige as a Guardian grew. Malachi's sword, Tiger Fang, had slain many Vipers and his skill in battle grew every day. Not a day went by that he did not think about Skye of Zaurak—no mission or training could distract him from what his heart truly desired.

The three clans, Talitha, Zaurak, and Aldafar had not met since that fateful night nearly a year ago. The Great Stag grew tired of the division within the Order. He called a mandatory meeting; all three clan's warriors were to meet at the temple of Aldafar. Tarjak, Roman, Malachi, Dag, Felix, and even Ravor came to represent Talitha. Ravor, the Bull of Talitha, was a hardened warrior. He came from a family of Talithinan miners—a massive bald man of very few words who preferred to work alone. His head was tattooed with Talithan markings all the way across his boulder-like skull. His unbelievably burly torso made other men—even Malachi—look average. The six Guardians all took their seats to the right of the five Knowledge Keepers. The Great Stag and Tarjak sat at the front of the two clans and waited for the Shade Runners to arrive and complete the triangle. Cyrus stood behind the Elders, dressed as sleek and elegant as ever.

"Of course, the Shade Runners are late," Dag whispered in a disapproving tone. "They are the whole reason we are having this meeting. They could at least be on time." He slouched in his chair and picked at his teeth in boredom.

"They have been through a lot; they can be as late as they please." Felix said as he nudged his brother to sit up straight.

"Warriors die," Malachi said sternly. "It's an occupational hazard. It's not an excuse to go rogue and dismiss from the Order." Malachi sat up with perfect posture, his dark-blond wavy hair pushed back handsomely.

"You're just mad 'cause your girlfriend doesn't talk to you anymore." Dag teased his cousin. Felix held back a snicker. Malachi jabbed a punch at Dag's ribs, wondering why he ever told his cousins about Skye. Malachi was about to say something, but the heavy doors of the temple swung open. The Shade Runners had arrived. They walked in—in perfect unison, not a step out of place. All of them dressed fully in black cloaks and fur, each of them was hooded, except Varden. He exuded the air of terrifying drill sergeant as they marched into the main hall. Malachi felt like the Shade Runners seemed more sinister than before. He watched Zacharias carefully. A heavy awkwardness fell over the room—no one said a word. Varden, Zacharias, seven Crows, and five Ravens all made their way to their seats. They greeted no one.

"Welcome, my brothers." The Great Stag stood and greeted the Shade Runners. He held his arms open with a hospitable bow. Varden did not acknowledge him. "Thank you all for coming; let us get started." The old man leisurely strolled to the center of the meeting hall, using his staff to lean on and resting his free hand on the hilt of his silver short sword. "As all of you are aware, the Seven Seals have the ability to mask their supernatural properties and remain hidden if they wish. For unknown reasons, some of the missing Seals have revealed themselves. Consequently, the Immortals have had a serious spike in activity during this last year. Almost a year ago today, we sent three Shade Runners to spy on an archeologist in Southern Africa who we believed had discovered a Seal. We were right." Everyone tried not to look at Varden or Zach; they knew what came next. "Unfortunately, the Immortals were also aware of the Seal's whereabouts, and engaged three of our brothers: Zane, Siren, and Fenrir." The air in the room felt heavy; Malachi looked down at his feet. "Fenrir gave his life to ensure his comrades escaped." He paused for a moment and took a deep breath, "But we mustn't mourn over this loss my friends, for to die is to gain. Fenrir now rests in paradise, and his sacrifice will never be forgotten."

Varden stared back at the Lord of Aldafar expressionless. Zach's eyes rested on his own feet. "We cannot let anything steal our joy, and we mustn't be consumed with anger or ideas of revenge. The enemy will take those feelings and twist them against us. We must stand strong—unified as one body—in order to protect this fallen world." Varden finally looked away, aware he was no longer serving the Order of Eden as he had sworn to.

"Which brings me to why I have asked you all here. The Immortals are on the move. They have three of the Seals: the Blade of Isaac, the Coins of Judas, and the Club of Cain. At the moment, we are in possession of only the Staff of Exodus. The Chains of Sampson, Pendant of Esther, and Spear of Golgotha's whereabouts have yet to reveal themselves. The time for watching from the shadows is over—it is time we push back."

Everyone was now sitting straight up in their seats; a new energy filled the room. "It is time we take the fight to them and defend this world as we have been anointed to do." The Guardians shouted, hollered, and pounded their chest in approval. Tarjak raised a stern fist to silence his warriors. "We are given a spirit of power and we mustn't live in fear. The Serpent and his minions must be destroyed." The Stag activated a Legacy Ring on his finger and thrusted his wrinkled palm against the stone floor beneath him. The angelic signs of Aldafar, in blinding threads of light, spread out across the ground. The illuminated strands revealed a detailed map of the earth drawn in Aldafarian designs. The old man raised his hand from the floor – suddenly the lights formed terrain and mountains as the map became three-dimensional.

"This world," The Stag ran his hand over the glowing display, "has been placed under our protection. They have no comprehension of the evil that hunts them. Serve them. Fight for them. Defend them just as you would defend your brothers who sit beside you now." The Guardians could hardly contain the fire burning in their chest. Again, the men of Talitha howled and roared.

"No one stronger, cousins." Malachi looked to his comrades and held out his fist.

"No one." Dag and Felix responded in unison as they pounded their knuckles into Malachi's.

"Again, thank you all for coming," the Great Stag said with a soft smile across his wrinkled lips. "I have no doubt it my heart that *together* we can protect those who cannot protect themselves. It is an honor to serve alongside you. May the Creator be with you all."

"And with you," everyone replied.

As the order dispersed, the Great Stag made one last announcement: "Malachi, Zacharias, a moment please." Both boys looked at their fathers, both men gestured to follow the Stag. They followed him into a secluded room—the Stag's private study—where Cyrus was waiting for them.

"Is there something wrong, your Grace?" Malachi asked, terribly confused by the dynamic of the group.

"No, not at all," he reassured the young warriors. "I have a mission for you." Ah, music to Malachi's ears; he puffed out his chest and fought back a grin.

"Beautiful," Malachi replied. "When can I leave? I will tell Dag and Felix." Malachi said, almost leaving the Stag's study and heading out the door.

"Actually..." the Great Stag announced, making Malachi stop in his tracks. "Your cousins will not be joining you on this quest, my boy." The old man gestured at both Cyrus and Zacharias. Malachi's jaw fell unhinged. He shook his head hysterically. He ran his fingers through his hair in a nervous brush and gritted his teeth.

"What? These two?" Malachi said with a slight giggle.

Even Zacharias looked concerned, "Is this a joke?" He asked with a cold piercing gaze.

"I, too, am quite perplexed by this decision, your Grace." Cyrus chimed in, "Would it not be more effective to simply send me?"

"Hush. All of you." He raised his staff and pointed it in all their faces, "You three will be my elite task force. Together..." He put an aggressive amount of stress on the word *together*, "I think you three are our best chance against the Immortals." All three boys were speechless. It was unheard of to send members of different clans out on a mission together—not to mention three that did not particularly like each other. "We believe we found another Seal. We are sending the three of you to retrieve it. Our spies tell us that a human by the name of David Leilani is in possession of it."

"Who the hell is David Leilani?" Malachi crossed his arms and grunted.

"David Leilani is a forty-five-year-old Caucasian male—a popular bachelor in human culture. He is a respected businessman, and has a net worth of exactly fifty-six million dollars. He collects ancient relics and came in possession of one of the Seals at an auction. We believe he is keeping the Seal in one of his vaults at his main office in Los Angeles, California. Obviously, he has no idea how priceless the Seal truly is." Cyrus said casually, as if that were common knowledge. "Unknown to the humans, most of his fortune comes from the trafficking of young females." Cyrus said somberly; he twiddled with his own thumbs.

"Oh, I'm going to enjoy this," Malachi said as he smashed his fists together.

"Precisely, thank you Cyrus. So, it is crucial for the three of you to recover the Seal."

"Please, your Grace, with all due respect, just send Dag, Felix, and me. We would be perfect for this mission. We will bring the whole building down. He deserves—" Malachi pleaded to the Elder, but was interrupted by a fierce glare from the Great Stag. Malachi bit his lower lip and looked down at his feet.

"This is not up for debate. Hurry home and gather your things. Meet back here in an hour; you leave tonight." He walked out of the room. All three boys stood in disbelief. Zacharias growled an angry scoff as he turned to leave the room, bumping into Malachi's bulky shoulder. Malachi looked to the ceiling and exhaled a heated snarl before leaving the Stag's study. Cyrus glided majestically close behind them.

"If you both follow every single one of my orders, there is a ninety-six percent chance we will be successful." Cyrus yelled after them with a friendly smile, feeling very sure of himself.

"*Shut up*," Zacharias and Malachi both said in unison as they exited the hall.

The sun made its daily descent behind the trees, night fell over the city of Aldafar. Zacharias placed his Ghost Charm against his chest as he knelt down in the snow outside his home. The Charm's wide variety of stones and metals separated, then released a smoke of pure darkness. The smoke quickly spun around Zacharias like a murder of crows swarming a corpse—then he disappeared into the night.

The assassin appeared kneeling in the courtyard of the Aldafarian city. His charcoal bow and quiver were strapped firmly to his back, his black claws freshly sharpened, and his gray and sapphire wolf mask hid the anger in his eyes. He slid his knife-like claws across the stone walkway beneath him; a jagged screech filled the air. A jet-black fur pelt was draped over his shoulders and back. The same color fur fanned out from his mask in every direction and covered his head. His left bracer had the ancient Zaurakian writing: "NO BLADE AND NO ARROW CAN MATCH THE FANG OF THE WOLF," etched into the armor on his forearm. His two hatchets were slung low on his back, just above his hips. He was an assassin of darkness—the young Wolf of Zaurak.

A flash of flame smoldered behind him; the Sabertooth of Talitha emerged from the blaze. The colossal, well-built warrior slammed his barbaric fists together with a deep *thud*. Malachi then stretched his arms and neck as he approached Zacharias. From Malachi's tan fur pelts to his heavy armor, he resembled a savage Titan. The fangs of his mask snarled. His brow hid just under his hood, which was engraved with gold Talithan markings. Tiger Fang hung from his back, her handle riding just off his right shoulder. His clawed gauntlet clung snuggly around his chiseled left forearm as he swayed its heavy weight to and fro. The crimson and gold of his armor shined with pride, and his leather chest plate could not hide the definition of his iron-forged pectorals. He walked with a swaggering confidence; the clanking of metal and stone armor rang rhythmically with each step. Malachi was a warrior bred for battle. He looked terribly comfortable in his armor.

Cyrus awaited them at the top of the stairs of the temple. He too looked quite intimidating; although he was much sleeker than the other two. A black hood, with thin swirling silver designs, covered his head; his snowy-white totem mask covered his entire face. The black eyes of the Owl seemed vacant, yet omniscient. His arms were thin and precisely wrapped in white leather straps from his forearms to the palm of his hands. He, too, had clawed talons at his fingertips—that looked as if they were made from roughly cut diamonds. His throwing knives were pinned all the way across his chest with a few across his left bicep. A long silver cloak was feathered and winged across his shoulders and back, his elegant and lengthy blade strapped to his hip. Once Malachi and Zacharias reached him, he turned in a graceful pivot; his silver cloak cascaded around him as he followed his new allies. The Sabertooth, Owl, and Wolf looked like mythic gods of war as they stomped up the stairs of the Temple.

Malachi pushed the heavy gates open by himself, while Zacharias and Cyrus followed close behind him. The Great Stag waited for them in the center of the hall. "Greetings, gentlemen." The three nodded. "Remember, obtaining the Seal is of the highest priority, but you will only succeed if you work together. The Order of Eden is counting on you. The world is counting on you. May the Creator be with you."

"*And with you,*" all three warriors responded from under their totem masks. The Great Stag lifted his staff in the air and slammed it to the ground. Three distinct lines of blinding light shot out straight across the ground from the impact point of the staff and created a circle around each boy, accompanied by a variety of ancient markings. In a great flash of light, the warriors vanished; the old man stood alone in the hall.

CHAPTER 10

A BLOODY MESS

The warriors appeared on a high rooftop in downtown Los Angeles. Despite it being deep into the night, the city below them buzzed with life. Malachi and Zacharias marched to the edge of the building and examined the city beneath them. Zacharias crouched at the lip of the structure like a brooding gargoyle; Malachi stood tall and crossed his arms as he looked out over the busy streets below. They had never seen so many people.

"Look at all of them," Malachi said as cars and people scurried in a hurry from one street to the next. "They have no idea we even exist."

"Why do we have to defend such incompetent and blind people?" Zacharias said to himself in disgust.

"It is our duty to defend those who cannot defend themselves." Malachi grunted through the teeth of his mask. Zacharias ignored Malachi's answer. "How many people are down there? There must be millions."

"Actually, there are 3.5 million people in this human civilization." Cyrus informed the other two warriors. They both glared at him unimpressed by his seemingly endless knowledge.

"Whatever. Where is he?" Malachi asked.

"The structure directly beneath us." Cyrus gestured toward a tower about fifty feet away, four stories down from where they stood. Without saying a word, Zacharias dashed toward their destination; dust and wind kicked up as the Wolf darted away. Malachi chased after him; the Sabertooth wanted to lead.

"Wait! You need to listen to my strategy," Cyrus pleaded as Malachi and Zach hurried away. Zacharias flipped off the rooftop and zoomed down to the next building; he slid across the roof like a bolt of lightning. Next, Malachi crashed on to the roof; he dropped like a ton of bricks and came down with a heavy *thud*. He rolled out of the landing and sprinted hard after Zacharias. Cyrus daintily twirled off the rooftop and fell on his tiptoes without making a sound—as light as a feather. They all raced for the iron door on the rooftop.

Malachi yelled out, "Cyrus, scan the structure." Cyrus raised his hand and one of his rings shifted and glowed. He used his Sight Stone to locate their target.

"Leilani is two floors down with two guards—five watchmen in the room east of his and six to the west. There are multiple unarmed females in the room to the west. Two men are in the floor directly below us working some sort of surveillance room."

"Zacharias, take the room to the east. I will clear the one to the west. Cyrus take out the men in the surveillance room."

"You will not give me orders, Guardian," Zacharias scowled. "I will take the room to the west; stay out of my way." He zipped toward the door leading into the building and left a massive dent, but it did not open.

"Move!" Malachi came crashing through the door like a runaway freight train; it crumpled under Malachi's weight and was ripped from its hinges. "No. *You* will stay out of my way, Shade Runner." The Sabertooth turned and was now muzzle to muzzle with the Wolf—they both shook with rage.

"I think it would be more effective if I cleared a room with more hostil—"

"Shut up," Malachi and Zacharias both interrupted Cyrus, breaking the tension between the two. All three warriors went their separate ways. Cyrus headed for the camera room, entering it without a sound as he cartwheeled in. The two men were oblivious to his presence as he snuck behind them and jabbed at both their jugulars. They both became stiff and fell to the ground, motionless. He activated his Echo Stone and created a mental link between himself, Malachi, and Zacharias.

"The guards in the surveillance room are incapacitated. I am disabling the cameras now."

"Get out of my head, you snob," Zacharias was not happy with Cyrus's intrusion.

"Both of you shut up. Just clear your room, Zacharias." Malachi grumbled through the telepathic link.

"Stop giving me orders, you oaf." Zacharias killed the lights to the west room and snuck in unseen.

One of the females in the room yelled in surprise as the lights fell off and she spilled her drink all over her ruby dress. She was met by a swift backhand across the face from one of the guards. "Quiet," the man hissed at her as she hit the ground, holding her swollen cheek.

The hired guns spun around in confusion, curious as to why the lights suddenly went off. Zacharias used his Predator Stone, activating night vision so he could see his prey in the dark. He removed his bow from his back and took position. Three men dropped one after another, arrows deeply embedded in each one's chest. Blood gargled from their lips as they tried to warn their fellow guards of the hidden assassin.

"What the hell? What is it?" One of the men yelled as he popped off some wild rounds from his pistol into the dark. The flash from his barrel lit the room just enough for him to see the dark wolf-like creature pouncing toward him. He did not even have time to scream before Zach's hatchet was drawn deep across the man's gut with a hurricane-like slash. The next two guards panicked and shot wildly into the dark, terrified by the monster hunting them. The women in the room screamed in horror and huddled together—bullets, and what seemed to be a monster, flew past them.

"What do we do?" One of the men yelled.

"Run!" The other answered in a panic. Before they got more than a step away, Zach sliced one of them across the back with his claws, sending his lifeless body to the ground. The last of Zacharias's prey reached the door, and frantically fumbled to open it. Like a hawk darting down upon its prey, an arrow shot into the man's spine and he slowly slid to the floor. The smell of blood and death filled the room.

"My room is clear." Zach informed the Owl and Sabertooth. Both Cyrus and Malachi were astounded; it only took the Shade Runner thirty seconds. He was a ghost in the darkness, blood thirsty, and driven by rage. Malachi was now determined to crush his enemies as fast as possible; he growled under his mask. He put his ear to the wall; he could hear an overweight guard's deep breathing on the opposite side. Malachi punched straight through the wall with his gauntlet and pulled the chunky man to his side. The other guards froze in terror. Malachi crashed through the wall himself like a wrecking ball and headed straight for the next unlucky victim who was screaming in confusion. He kicked the terrified man in the torso, sending him flying across the corridor like a rag doll. Malachi tore through the room like a tornado. Gunfire and groans of agony swept around the room as the Sabertooth wreaked havoc upon any armed creature in his path. He swatted bullets away with his gauntlet and sliced their guns and limbs in half with Tiger Fang. The Sabertooth of Talitha crushed their bodies and struck fear into their hearts.

"Mine is clear. Move to the target." Malachi tore down the wall that separated himself from David Leilani's main office. Once in, the Sabertooth ruthlessly elbowed one guard in the side of the head. Now only David Leilani and one last hired gun remained. The Owl of Aldafar slightly rolled into the room just as the final guard raised his pistol at Malachi. Cyrus darted a throwing knife straight into the guard's underarm, forcing him to bring the gun back down as he pulled the trigger. He squawked in pain while his bullets tore only into the office floor. The next flying dagger stung into his back, his entire body syn-ched as vital nerves had been severed and he fell to the ground.

"I had that one!" Malachi yelled at Cyrus.

"By my calculations, he would have gotten off at least two rounds from his firearm in your direction before you reached him." Cyrus rebutted; Malachi growled back. David Leilani squirmed and squealed as the monsters entered his office. He nearly pissed his custom navy suit. His black hair was cut high and tight, a sky-blue tie hung around his neck. He pulled out a revolver from under his massive oak desk and fired three shots. Zacharias emerged from the darkness; he sliced the three shots out of the air with his hatchets and drew his bow in one swift movement. An arrow ripped through David's wrist and made him drop the revolver. Before the gun hit the ground, Zacharias already had another arrow drawn back. David Leilani moaned in pain. Warm blood trickled from his arm and onto his desk. He gasped for air, but the pain had stolen it from his lungs.

"The next one goes through your throat." The Wolf of Zaurak growled with ferocity, he hoped Leilani would give him a reason to finish him.

"I'm only going to ask once..." Malachi stepped forward; he dragged one of the guards by the leg behind him. "Where is the Seal?" His voice was like a roaring lion; he threw the limp body savagely across the room to show his inhuman strength.

"The what? I don't know." David yelled frantically. Blood was splattered across his suit; he was sweating profusely. The three monsters before him made his heart race and his stomach churn.

"The spear. Where is it?" His voice was even louder this time; he snarled under his totem mask.

"You don't understand. It cost me a fortune. My partners will kill me if I lose it." His whole arm shook in pain, and his suit was now drenched in a thick coat of his own sweat.

"Ha!" Malachi gawked. "I will do much worse than that," Malachi leaped across the room; he pounded his gauntlet into the giant wooden desk. It split down the middle and Malachi threw the pieces to the side as if they were made of Styrofoam. He leaned in close and stared straight into his eyes.

Leilani screeched and shook frantically. "All right! All right. It's there." He pointed with his good hand at a large painting on the wall. Malachi nodded at Zach and Cyrus; they went over and took down the painting. An iron safe was hiding behind the artwork.

"Mr. Leilani, if you could be so kind as to give us the combination that will unlock the safe?" Cyrus asked politely. Zacharias rolled his eyes under his mask.

"Eleven, twelve, five" David replied hesitantly, his voice shaking. Cyrus spun the dial and opened the vault; the top half of an ancient spear was neatly displayed in the center of the vault alongside what appeared to be covered containers of assorted drugs.

"The spear of Golgotha." Cyrus said amazed at the relic. "This Seal has the ability to pierce any material."

"Looks like a rusted piece of crap to me." Malachi said from across the room.

"What an arrogant fool," a cold, shrill voice came from the shadows. It echoed throughout the room. A throwing knife, chiseled from bone, spun through the air and sliced into David's chest—a perfect kill shot. His head fell; he sat dead in his chair. The voice sent chills down their spines; they dove to the other side of the room and drew their weapons. Suddenly the room felt smaller as if it had been consumed by a living darkness.

"Damn. An Immortal." Malachi cursed to himself.

"No, two." Cyrus corrected him, as he spun his sword in his hand.

"One Guardian, 230 pounds, nineteen years old, heavy sword technique. One Shade Runner, 185 pounds, nineteen years old, archer. One Knowledge Keeper, 165 pounds, nineteen years old, single sword technique." A creature with a bat totem mask emerged from the shadows with an arrogant sway. The skull mask had tall thin ears, chiseled fangs, and disgusting patchy fur around the edges. The green sign of the Immortals was carved into the forehead of the mask. Two thin hatchets made of bone and iron, with long curved handles, hung from his hands. He dragged them across the floor as he inched closer, creating a noise far more vile than nails across a chalkboard. His cloak resembled tattered bat wings strung with chains.

Behind him was a mountain of a man, more than twice his size. He even made Malachi look petite. He wore an Ox totem mask, clearly an ex-Guardian. Beads and bones hung from the horns on his mask; one horn was sharp, but the other's tip had been broken off long ago. His arms were both armored with two massive gauntlets, both the size of barrels. Each armored forearm was an ungodly weight and had claimed a disturbing amount of lives. They were cruel weapons made of stone and metal. An unkempt beard covered the lower half of his face; a few braids, with green beads, had been woven in. He was hunched over, nearly resting on his oversized fist like a silverback gorilla. He bore the mark of the Serpent on his chest—an old grimy leather hide hung over his shoulder.

"Interesting, three members of the Order of Eden, all from different clans? The old Stag must be getting desperate." The Bat was shrill and thin; he slowly moved closer to the boys. He continued to drag his bone hatchets across the floor as he crept. "I see you found one of our Seals. You do understand I can't let you leave here alive. Cain will be pleased to hear of your deaths." He spoke with an infuriating arrogance.

Malachi communicated with the other two through the mental link, "All right, I'll take the big guy in the back—you guys distract the Bat until I'm done."

"It would be more effective if I lead the attack because of my superior combat skills," Cyrus commented.

"I don't need help from either of you," Zacharias thought as he drew an arrow. After releasing a fierce roar, the Sabertooth sprinted toward the Ox at full speed. The Ox reared back and drove his massive gauntlet into the much smaller Malachi; he was hit with a thundering clap. The force of the punch sent shrapnel flying through the air. He crashed straight down into the floor; he became a projectile as he ripped down four stories beneath them. The floors gave way under

Malachi like they were made of glass. Malachi had never been hit so hard in his life.

Malachi and his comrades were in for the fight of their lives. Immortals almost always did their hunting in pairs; their skills expertly complemented each other's. They were now facing the Screeching Bat, Kai—a presumptuous intellectual. His partner was the Juggernaut Ox, Mednik. He had incredible strength, but little intelligence. They both served the Serpent's legion without question and without mercy. Kai was known for his brain and, of course, Mednik was known for his brawn; together they were a fearsome duo.

"Foolish boy. He was just crushed with over 20,000 pounds of force. What a fool. And you two might as well surrender now; you are no match for my superior intellect or skill." Kai said as he moved closer to the Wolf and Owl. Behind him, the giant Ox dropped through the hole after Malachi.

Zacharias, still holding an arrow back and pointing it straight at the Bat's skull, said, "Are you the one who killed Fenrir?" He growled in anger. Kai tilted his head and stared straight at Zach.

"Ah, you are the younger sibling of Fenrir, the Wolf. No, that fool did not die by my hand, but I hear he was an unimpressive opponent. He was slain in three moves; I will kill you in two." Zacharias scowled under his mask; anger overwhelmed him. He let his arrow fly; Cyrus also threw two of his feathered throwing blades. Kai twirled and deflected the attacks with his crooked bone hatchets; his form was flawless. Zacharias drew his hand axes and charged the Immortal, Cyrus attacked with him. A ring on Kai's finger spun and glowed emerald; he leaned forward toward the boys. An awful sonic screech came from his open mouth; both Zach and Cyrus were flung backward across the room. All the windows shattered at the sound; Cyrus and Zach crashed into the wall as they frantically tried to cover their ears.

Zacharias flipped back to his feet as soon as the noise ceased—his ears ringing intensely, and his mind disoriented—he bolted at the Bat. He swung both his blades at the Immortal with incredible speed. Each one of the attacks was redirected with the handles of the Bat's weapons with ease; Kai made it look easy. He was fluid and smooth, as if he was in a simple training exercise. This only made Zach more furious; he swung harder and faster, grunting wildly as he drove his axes at the Bat. Kai continued to toy with him; he had not thrown even one offensive attack yet. Zacharias lunged at Kai with both his blades; the Immortal slid his hatchets up Zach's arms and disarmed the Wolf.

"Your speed makes you sloppy, fool. You have no control. I can predict your every movement." He used the ends of his bone hatchets to jab at Zach's shoulders—both his arms fell limp. The jab momentarily removed all feeling from Zach's arms. "You are out of your league, child," the Immortal hissed as he winded up to throw his finishing blow. Zacharias sat defenseless, frustrated beyond comprehension. Despite not having the use of his arms, he flipped away and kicked the Immortal across the chin.

"I won't need arms to kill you. You will have to do better." Zacharias said emotionless, trying to conceal the ferocity burning within him. Kai was impressed with the Wolf's adaptability. He drew his thin axes back and attacked again, this time Cyrus jumped in. He blocked the attack with his elegant blade, then forced Kai back.

"Ah. A Keeper. Maybe you will provide more of a challenge."

"Get out of the way, Cyrus. He is mine." Zacharias was offended he intervened.

"You are incapacitated at the moment; you would only have a fifteen percent chance at surviving." Cyrus said as he raised his blade toward his opponent.

"And what percentage do you have, Owl?" The Immortal asked with a smirk.

"Forty-eight percent, but I shall try and win despite the odds."

"Ha! Truly inspiring." He lowered his hatchets, symbolizing that Cyrus could have the first attack. Cyrus attacked with a swift poke; it was blocked, of course. Their battle involved no power or strength; it was a battle of finesse. Their blades clashed and slid together intricately, neither of them making any mistakes. Swift and well-placed stabs, slashes, and thrusts took the warriors all across the office. To everyone's surprise, Cyrus was actually holding his own. He moved like a coursing river to and fro, swift and smooth. He stayed low to the ground and swayed back and forth like a snake waiting to strike; his blade was like liquid silver. Cyrus rushed forward and slashed with his beautiful silver blade; Kai dodged it and sliced him across the arm with his hatchet. He swung the other hatchet at Cyrus's feet; the Owl did an excellent backhand spring and avoided the attack. As he flipped backward, he let off multiple throwing knives; one sliced across Kai's shoulder, but the others were blocked. Cyrus watched intrigued as the wound on the Bat's shoulder began to heal itself—everything they had heard about these monsters was true. Cyrus remained calm and confident; he took a graceful defensive stance. The Owl parried two quick attacks, then jabbed for the Bat's throat, but the Immortal let out another sonic screech. Again, Cyrus was thrown across the room violently.

The very instant Zach regained the feeling in his arms, he picked up his blades and dove back into the action. He attacked like a rabid dog, spinning and slashing wildly. Zach's speed actually started to overwhelm the Immortal, who was now fighting on his heels.

"You should have stayed out of the fight, fool." Kai said with a confident scowl. The Bat rolled under all of Zach's hurried attacks with ease. In a spinning twirl, Kai swung his thin bone hatchets with precision and grace; the first strike ripped open Zach's torso, the other driving into his hip. Zach cried out in agony, blood spat from his wounds as the Immortal slowly ripped his weapon from the Wolf's hip. With a sinister smirk, the Bat opened his colorless lips. This time his sonic screech was more powerful than before; Zach's cloak and pieces of fur were ripped from his armor. The sonic waves sent him flying backward, straight into Cyrus; they slapped into one another with terrible force, rendering them both unconscious.

While a battle of speed and finesse took place upstairs—four stories down, two behemoths clashed. With a trembling crash, the huge Ox free-fell and landed on the floor where Malachi was waiting. The office floor they were now on was dimly lit and filled with an elaborate maze of cubicles and offices. Malachi dove for cover and slid into one of the cubicles as debris and office supplies shot across the room from the behemoth's fall. The giant Immortal surveyed the dark room and searched for his prey. Malachi took a deep breath and exploded from his hiding place. He used his Solar Stone to create a blinding flash of light; Mednik squinted and shielded his eyes. When he looked back toward Malachi, he received a brutal punch to the jaw. The decorative beads and bones that hung from the Ox's filthy beard rattled and shook as Malachi drove his fist into the Immortal's grizzly face. Malachi thrust his next strike into the Ox's gut. Any other person would have had their intestines burst and been knocked back twenty yards from the blow to the stomach, but the Immortal simply released an un-amused grunt. He only slid a few feet and brushed off the attack as if he had been hit by a measly sparrow flying back to its nest.

Malachi looked at his opponent in disbelief. "Great," he said sarcastically as the Ox moved toward him. The room shook with each step; he swayed his massive arms side to side as he stomped. He wound up and threw an earth-shattering punch at Malachi. Malachi, using both his arms and all of his strength, actually caught the punch. His feet cracked the floor beneath them and it took every ounce of his might to keep the heavy gauntlet from driving him into the ground like it did before. His arms shook desperately, and he growled in frustration as he attempted to push Mednik's gargantuan limb back. While Malachi was occupied with one of the Ox's arms, Mednik's other gauntlet crashed into the defenseless Sabertooth's torso. A terrible force shook the office as Malachi was sent flying through the office, destroying every cubicle in his path. Printers and computers turned to scrap metal as Malachi's body ripped through half the building. Mednik smirked; he thought, without a doubt, Malachi had been pulverized. With a deep chuckle and nod, he looked down the path of wreckage Malachi left behind and admired his work.

To the Immortal's surprise, Malachi came barreling down the path, more furious than ever. Pieces of both his armor and pride missing, he screamed a violent war cry as he ripped through the rubble toward Mednik. Malachi charged in like a cannon ball; he wrapped his arms around the Ox's waist and drove his shoulder into his chest. A grunt and spit sprayed from the Immortal's lips as the tackle sent both of them crashing through a wall into the next room. Malachi began whaling on the Ox, holding nothing back. Malachi exhaled sharply with each furious punch as he crouched over the Immortal and bashed his head with his armored knuckles. The carpeted floor beneath them was torn and destroyed more and more with each one of Malachi's violent punches; each strike sounded like a battering ram slamming into a dense iron wall.

Unfortunately, the massive Ox seemed unfazed by the brutal attacks. Every time Malachi's claws or fist tore open the Immortal's flesh, or snapped his bones, the demon's body repaired itself almost instantly. Mednik threw Malachi off him as he staggered to his feet. He swung his large armored arm at Malachi's head; he rolled under the attack and punched the Ox in the thigh. The strike brought the Ox to his knees. Malachi leaned back and took aim with his own gauntlet, but Mednik head-butted him in the chest with his horned mask. The wind was knocked from Malachi's lungs and sent him rolling backward. The Immortal struck Malachi with his gauntlet sending him into a nearby metal filing cabinet; he let out an inadvertent yelp as the monster's heavy fist slammed into him. The cabinet crumpled like tinfoil as Malachi smashed into it; a few of the young Sabertooth's ribs crunched and splintered from the force.

Malachi attempted to crawl to his feet; the Immortal shook his head. "Just die, boy." Mednik's voice was heavy and lifeless, yet it seemed to shake the building.

"If you want me dead..." Malachi struggled to say as he attempted to ignore the crippling pain in his rib cage. "You will have to hit harder than that, sweetheart..." Malachi replied as he wiped a trail of blood that had trickled over his eye; he could barely stand.

"And—" before Malachi's next smart comment, the Ox landed a devastating uppercut. Malachi's limp body shot up another four stories and broke through the floor where the battle first began. After slamming into the celling, he fell lifeless to the ground just a few feet away from Zach and Cyrus. The Wolf, Owl, and Sabertooth lay there, a bloody mess.

CHAPTER 11

LAMBS TO THE SLAUGHTER

The Immortals of Abaddon crept closer and closer toward their beaten prey. The Bat dragged his blood-soaked hatchets across the floor, creating an eerie grinding noise, the Ox took long and slow stomps toward the boy's limp bodies that shook with every step from the monster. A crimson trail of blood ran from Zach's open gashes and stained Cyrus' snowy-white cloak.

The heavy pounding of Mednik's marching shook Cyrus back into consciousness. The Owl's eyes peeled open under his mask; he saw the demons creeping toward them. His head pounded with a fierce knocking and he struggled to get a wholesome breath to his lungs. He closed his eyes and focused intently.

"Great Stag... Your Grace... We need an immediate extraction..." Cyrus used his Echo Stone to telepathically call out for assistance. Almost immediately, signs of Aldafar surrounded each one of them in a circle of silver light. The Immortals stopped in their tracks and took a defensive stance. With a great flash, Malachi, Cyrus, and Zach vanished.

When Malachi and Zacharias awoke, they were surprised to see the pearly white inner walls of the Aldafarian temple. As they realized what had happened, they were not surprised to see all of their fathers there arguing amongst each other. Shara, Cyrus' father, along with Tarjak and Varden were in the hall with the Great Stag.

"You sent two children to watch the back of a Guardian. Disgraceful," Tarjak bellowed.

"How could you send such slow and inexperienced fools on such an important mission? Zacharias should have gone on his own." Varden scowled as he crossed his arms.

"Inexperienced fool? Malachi is probably the only reason your brat is still alive." Tarjak was furious; his voice was like thunder.

"They would have been successful if they had followed Cyrus's every order. I am sure he had a detailed assessment of the situation." Shara complained as he flipped his silver hair over his shoulder. Malachi and his fallen comrades ignored their squabbling and removed their masks, revealing disappointed and blood-stained faces. Healers dressed in silvers and grays knelt beside the boys and assessed their wounds.

"Enough!" The Great Stag slammed the bottom of his staff to the ground. It sent a small shock wave throughout the whole room; everyone fell silent. "Gentlemen," gesturing toward the younger warriors, "Please head to the healing chambers and have them tend to your wounds. You will spend the night here and rest. I need to have a word with your fathers." The healers all stood and hurried to prepare their healing chambers. Malachi was the first to his feet; his body trembled in pain. He looked to the Wolf who was struggling to rise. Malachi fought back his own pride and offered a hand to help Zacharias up. With a grunt, Zach swatted away his hand and stared at him with his dark eyes. His thick black hair was a mess and covered some of his face; he stood on his own and limped out of the room leaving a thin trail of blood. Cyrus quickly followed, afraid to look at his father, or the Great Stag, and scurried out of the hall toward a healing chamber.

Malachi nodded to Tarjak and slowly trailed behind them—frustration and anger in his eyes.

The Great Elder of Aldafar stood in silence, looking down at his staff. It seemed as if the wisest Knowledge Keeper of the Order of Eden was at a loss for words. "Those three warriors are our only chance." He finally spoke up. "The Owl, Wolf, and Sabertooth are the future leaders of the Order of Eden, and I will not let another generation fall victim to division and pride." Varden, Shara, and Tarjak all looked down at their feet. "Unified, this Order could be unstoppable. Even the members of Abaddon are unified, despite being from different clans, and that is what makes them so dangerous. The Order of Eden will no longer be led by bickering fools, but a single body, with a single purpose. If we continue in our ways, the forces of Abaddon will collect all the Seals and release the Serpent before our very eyes... and a darkness will consume the world." He paused and closed his eyes, "We must all agree with one another in what we say; there can be no divisions among us, but we must be perfectly unified in mind and thought." He turned and left the hall; the other three said nothing to each other. They stood in silence, conviction, and hopelessness.

The following day Malachi awoke in the late afternoon. Although any visible wounds had been healed, he still felt a terrible soreness throughout his body. He sat up slowly, releasing some grunts and moans.

"Good morning, Malachi of Talitha," a thin and matronly woman said quietly from the corner of the room. She had soft silver hair like the rest of her clan; it was tied back tightly so it would not be in the way as she worked on a patient. Malachi nodded respectfully to her as he swung his legs off the table where he was perched.

"I recommend you stay here and rest..." Before the healer could finish, Malachi was already standing and putting on a thin sand-colored shirt.

"I just need some fresh air." Malachi said quietly without his normal charm or spark. He pushed back his wavy-blond hair and grunted a little from the pain of moving his arm. The healer continued her attempts to convince him to stay, but he ignored her pleading and limped out of the palace. He spent the rest of the afternoon relaxing in the temple's pristine garden. The area was landscaped just as elegant as the rest of Aldafar. A wild assortment of rare and beautiful plant life ran along every path; thin vines spread and clung to the gray walls. Rich scents and crisp mountain air floated along the stone paths and filled Malachi's lungs with each relaxing breath. He continued down the path toward a decretive gazebo that sat in the center of the garden. As Malachi moved closer, he realized a hooded woman was sitting in the gazebo alone, writing in a small journal. He spotted a fox pendant pinned to her collar and soon realized it was Skye.

Malachi attempted to turn away silently and head back the way he had come, but stealth had never been one of Malachi's strengths.

"Malachi?" She asked, surprised to see him just before he clumsily tried to turn away. She pulled back her hood slightly to take a better look. Malachi was now pretending to be studying a few white orchids planted alongside the path. He looked up from the flowers and acted surprised to see her.

"Oh. Hi, Skye," he said awkwardly. "I didn't see you there. What are you doing here?" He asked as he moved closer to where she sat. He did not enter the gazebo; he hovered around the entrance. He pulled flowers and leafs nervously off the wooden frame, trying to avoid eye contact.

She closed her journal and set it in her lap. "I wanted to make sure Zacharias was all right. My father said Immortals had ambushed you?" She too avoided looking in his direction. He could tell talking about the Immortals was uncomfortable for her; Fenrir's death still haunted her.

"Well, he's fine. He is stubborn and doesn't listen to orders very well, but he's fine." They both chuckled nervously, Malachi finally started to head into the gazebo. "It is good to see you, Skye. How are you?" She still would not look up at him.

"Fine," her voice was cold and shrill.

"Good, good." Things were becoming awkward once again. He sat on a bench across from the where she sat and looked up at the celling as if he was admiring the structure. Neither of them knew what to say; she hid herself behind a blank stare. Her raven hair was not braided and festive as it usually was; she rested her cheek against her palm. Despite her being in more casual apparel, Malachi still could not take his eyes off her. She wore a thin black hooded top with a light blue trim; it was snug on her womanly figure. Malachi looked around for a moment and built up some courage; he looked her straight in the eyes now. He knew she was not *fine*.

"Let's get out of here," Malachi said with confidence.

"What?"

"Come on. I could use a break from everything." He looked around and shrugged.

"What? Are you crazy?" She scoffed.

Malachi stood up and walked over to her; he held out his hand to her, "Probably a little. What, are you just going to sit around here all night? Let's go." He smiled a reassuring smile, as she reluctantly placed her hand in his.

"Where would we even go?" She was still not fully on board; she kept looking back making sure no one was watching them.

"I know a place." Malachi pulled out his Phoenix Charm and pulled Skye close to his chest. She could not help but blush when touching his muscular torso; he was even bigger than when she saw him almost a year ago. They ported from the gazebo in a large burst of flames.

They burst into a rundown alley; clearly, they were no longer in Aldafar.

"Wow. What a lovely place, Malachi." Skye said sarcastically with a laugh as she kicked an empty bottle at her feet.

"Oh, hush. Just trust me." He took her by the hand and guided her around the corner, "Here, look."

"Where are we?" Skye asked amazed. "Look at all the people."

"New York. Do you like it?"

A bashful grin snuck across Skye's thin lips; she nodded in approval.

"Here, follow me." He guided her through the crowds. Malachi took her down a few side streets to a much less crowded area. The beaten-down neighborhood Malachi and Skye entered was quiet, the streetlights and signs flickered and seemed to struggle to stay lit. They came up to a small, simple establishment, a white sign with cherry-red writing read MARTY'S.

"Marty's?" Skye asked, "Who's Marty?"

"You'll see." They entered the little shop, "Marty!"

"Malachi! How is my favorite customer?" A large African American man reached across the counter to shake Malachi's hand. Marty's white apron was stained with a rainbow of colors across his torso, a joyful grin sat glued to his face. "Well, shoot! Who's this?" Marty asked, impressed by the gorgeous girl Malachi bought in.

"This is my friend, Skye." She too shook the man's pudgy hand.

"Well she is much cuter than those other two knuckleheads you normally bring in."

"Ha! I agree." Malachi laughed. Skye furrowed her brow in confusion; she had no idea Malachi and his cousins were regulars at Marty's Ice Cream Parlor. "All right, I need two scoops of the chocolate fudge explosion, and two scoops of cookie dough crunch." Skye looked at Malachi almost appalled; she had never heard anyone say anything so strange. Malachi snickered when he saw Skye's disapproving glare.

"You got it, buddy." Marty moved over his giant belly as he scooped out their ice cream and handed it to the couple. He winked at Malachi and gestured at Skye. Malachi just rolled his eyes with a smile and took the ice cream. They took their dessert and sat at a little table out behind the restaurant.

"I have to admit, I am a little concerned to eat food from such an unsanitary establishment." She laughed and moved her spoon around timidly in the ice cream.

"Marty's is the best ice cream parlor in New York! It may be in a rough neighborhood, but I love it. Dag, Felix, and I come here whenever we get the chance." She took a bite, and again her eyes lit up.

"This is wonderful." She said as she tilted her head, surprised by the sweet dessert. "How'd you guys find this place?"

"Well actually, Dag did. On accident, really." He took another bite, "He used to steal Uncle Roman's Phoenix Charm and port us places. Obviously, he had no clue how to control it, so we never knew where we might end up. One day, we showed up outside of Marty's and decided to check it out."

"He would steal his father's Phoenix Charm? Did he ever find out?"

"Hell ya, he did. We didn't see Dag for a month. Felix wouldn't even tell me what his punishment was, but he said it was bad. Dag still says it was worth it though, anything for Marty's ice cream I guess." They both chuckled, and locked eyes. He paused for a second and looked down. "Skye, I've been wanting to talk with you. What happened to you?" She shifted her jaw and fidgeted with her plastic spoon.

"I'm sorry I ignored you this last year. We had a lot going on."
"I understand, I just wanted to help."

"I know, but there was nothing you could have done. It was between my family and me. Who weren't much help honestly..." She paused for a while, "I was very much alone this last year. Fenrir's death made my father and Zacharias unapproachable and distant... more so than usual. And I guess it made me that way too, I'm sorry."

"You have nothing to apologize for, and you're not alone." He smiled at her and gently placed his hand on hers.

"I know," she said. She reached into her collar and pulled a necklace from under her top—the necklace Malachi had given her, "I never took it off."

Malachi, who was mid ice-cream bite, was taken by surprise and spit the dessert all over his lap. "Crap! Wow. I'm glad you like the necklace... Um, excuse me for one second." He said flustered and embarrassed, his face became tomato red. She could not tell if he was blushing from the necklace or the ice cream that covered his lap. Skye couldn't help but laugh and roll her eyes at the ice-cream covered warrior, who was running back into Marty's to get some napkins.

Skye continued to enjoy her ice cream; she patiently awaited Malachi's return. Suddenly she heard a frightened yelp come from around the corner. She jumped to her feet and surveyed the area, curious as to find the source of the squeal. Again, someone cried out, but this time it was a desperate cry for help. Skye threw her raven hair over her shoulder and slid over the table dropping her ice cream to the ground; the huntress then took off in the direction of the scuffle.

As Skye rounded the corner of the alleyway, she spotted four large men surrounding a frantic young woman lying in the mud. The unruly dressed men cursed slurs and snarled at the defenseless woman who was being thrown about between them. Her auburn hair was knotted and a mess, her clothes ripped and splattered with filth. Tears filled her eyes as the raggedy thugs beat her and dragged her through the alley.

Skye, filled with rage, came sprinting down the alleyway. She moved with the slyness of a fox, dashing through the shadows as fury filled her bronze eyes. Out of the darkness, Skye dove through the air and drove her knee into the chest of one of the thugs. The man was slammed into a dumpster behind him, forcing the air to shoot from his lungs and a cigarette to fly from his lips. The other men froze, baffled by the wild vixen attacking them. Skye rolled across her back and swept the feet from under the next man, sending him crashing to the ground. As he hit the ground, Skye jammed her foot into the man's crotch, forcing him to let out a sharp whimper.

The next thug attempted to punch Skye in the chin. Skye dodged the blow and caught the man's wrist; she threw her legs up around his arm and forced him down to the mud as she ripped his shoulder from its socket. Two of the attackers were now squirming on the ground in agony. The man, who had been slammed into the dumpster, was struggling to get back to his feet as he drew a knife from his pocket. Skye, like a trained assassin, spun and flung a black dagger—with a violet rose sketched into the blade—from under her coat. The menacing blade drove into the man's knife-wielding hand and pinned it to the metal dumpster behind him; he cried out in pain as his limp fingers released his pocketknife.

Skye smirked from under her hood, pleased with her work. She drew another blade, but a fist slammed into the back of her head; a ruthless punch from the fourth attacker caught the young warrior off guard; everything fell silent and went black.

Malachi came out of Marty's parlor and was surprised to see Skye not at the table—her ice cream cup and its contents splattered across the ground. At first, he feared maybe she had ditched him, but then he surveyed the area. He scratched his head as he looked around the table, and began retracing her movements. Malachi soon realized she had taken off in a hurry; he followed her path down the alley. It did not take long for the young warrior to find where the scuffle had taken place. Malachi slid through the mud and spotted Skye's bloody throwing blade that had clearly been pried from the metal dumpster. His heart raced; he struggled to believe that Skye was in an altercation. Suddenly, rage overcame the skilled tracker as he realized that her body had been dragged off. The Sabertooth of Talitha was overwhelmed with emotion; he had a knot in his stomach. He clenched his fist and shook with frustration. Malachi had never felt such anger. Marty came running around the corner, "Hey, Malachi. Is everything—oh God, I'll call the police Malachi, hold on." Marty said as he realized Skye was gone and saw the blood splattered across the dumpster. Malachi knelt down and grabbed Skye's dagger; he would not take his eyes off it.

"Don't bother." He said quietly. Marty could hear the passion in his voice. "They will all be dead by dawn." Malachi drove his fist into the dumpster, crushing it as if it were made of paper. Marty stepped back in disbelief, then watched nervously as Malachi rose from the ground, clenching the dagger so tightly his knuckles were a cold white. Marty did not know much about Malachi, but by his muscular build and strange clothing, he knew he was no normal young man. He suddenly felt a great deal of pity for whomever took Skye.

"Now hold on, Malachi. These guys are bad news. Let's just let the cops handle it."

Malachi ignored his friend and dashed off in the direction they took her. "Malachi!" Marty yelled after him one last time, but it was pointless, nothing could stop the Sabertooth from hunting his prey now. Malachi was hot on their trail, probably only a few minutes behind them. It was clear they had gotten in a car and Malachi would have to move quickly. He raced at speeds that were thought to be impossible for a Guardian; he ripped straight through any car or dumpster that blocked his path.

The streets began to puddle as rain fell from the dark clouds above; the trail was getting harder to follow. Malachi cut through the rain in a panic, terrified that he might lose them in the storm. He was not himself; his mind was scattered and unfocused. He was being driven by emotion instead of his instincts—he truly felt afraid. This was not the fear he felt when facing the Immortals. This was a new terror he had never felt before. He slid through the mud and followed the trail to a run-down house in the ghetto. The rain fell harder and harder, but all Malachi could hear was the pounding of his own heart.

Inside the building, Skye had just woken up. Blood dripped from the back of her head and her body ached. She was being dragged across the floor of the kitchen toward the living room; trash and bottles were littered across the home. Tarps and sheets covered the windows, and the house reeked of smoke. Skye came to and started kicking and clawing, trying to get away from her kidnappers. There were more than four thugs now; there were at least twelve men in the house—all watching and laughing as Skye panicked. One of the men grabbed Skye and pinned her down on a table; he started ripping away her clothing. The redhead Skye had defended earlier looked to Skye and begged for her to help her once more as men began attacking her as well. Skye screamed and kicked wildly; she begged to wake up from this awful nightmare that had unfolded so quickly.

"Get off her!" Skye screamed violently as the men pinned down the other helpless girl. Skye drove her heel into one man's face, breaking his nose in a swift crunch. Two more men jumped on her to restrain her as she desperately fought back.

Malachi came crashing through the ceiling, soaking wet from the rain. His body shook with anger, and he had not even seen Skye being assaulted yet. The storm had killed the electricity to the house; Malachi could only be seen when the room was lit from the lightning. He was panting like a rabid animal; he couldn't decide who to kill first.

"What the hell?" One of the gang members screeched as he reached for a knife. He grabbed it and lunged at Malachi. Malachi grabbed him by the face and slammed him straight through the wall. His eyes were glowing with anger; his blood began to boil as if his chest was a burning furnace. He entered the next room, and he saw her. She was still fighting off her attackers. She locked eyes with Malachi. Malachi was no more—the Sabertooth took control. His Savage Mark burned and smoked on his forearm. The primal design spread and burned all over his body. The hair on his head grew wildly, and his teeth became like fangs. His muscles rippled and grew; he was twice his original size. His shirt burned away and was torn from his flesh as his muscles tore and reformed. Burning jagged claws emerged from his hands as he let out a terrible dragon-like roar. The thugs looked on in terror at the monster in the dark that was morphing before their eyes. When Malachi's transformation was complete, he stood brooding in silence, not moving a muscle. The monster released a lion-like roar deep from its chest, everyone covered their ears as the whole house shook.

Skye dove for cover as the house turned into a warzone. She tried not to watch the massacre. He showed no mercy; he would butcher them all before the night was through. The lightning left shadows of men scrambling for their lives from the mad creature. Blood splattered the walls of the house as the men fell to their deaths; screeches filled the air as the cowards were torn limb from limb. One man managed to slide under the couch where he thought he would be safe, but he too was ripped in half as the monster dug its claws into the furniture and tore it in two. A refrigerator was thrown through the front of the house, crushing anything and anyone in its path. Bullets and daggers melted if they touched his burning skin, and limp bodies were tossed across the house like rag dolls. They were simply lambs brought to the slaughter.

After the carnage, only muffled moans of agony, the panting of the monster, and the rainfall outside could be heard in the house. The mindless beast tore through the building looking for something else to kill. He spotted the frantic redhead curled up on the ground across the room; he growled and crept toward her. She was hysterical, sobbing uncontrollably as the beast before her approached. She tried to scoot farther away and crawled spastically until she was cornered. The monster slid his claws into the flooring and released a dismal roar as blood and spit from his fangs splattered the defenseless girl. She screamed in terror just as Skye dove between them.

"Malachi...! It's me. Malachi, please," she said quietly as she slowly backed herself into the frightened girl. "Get out of here," Skye whispered sternly to the other girl; she nodded and frantically stumbled for the exit. Sabertooth did not take his eyes off Skye. He did not recognize the beautiful girl in front of him; he continued to snarl at her. Despite her situation, she seemed unafraid and glared back at the monster. Like her brother, she was calm and confident. The blood of his victims dripped from his hands; he growled fiercely, and Skye could feel the intense heat from his body.

"Malachi. It's me, Skye. We're safe now." He was now face to face with her—the Savage Mark still scorching his flesh. She reached out slowly and touched the monster's cheek. "Malachi, it's me." This time, he heard her voice loud and clear; it seemed to awaken him; his eyes began to return to their normal color. The Savage Mark began to retract back to his forearm and his hair returned to its original length. At the sound of Skye's quiet, yet strong voice—the tension left the room and Malachi's body. His body returned to its normal state and he passed out, falling into her arms. She struggled to support the huge young man. She gently laid the Sabertooth on the ground.

The shirtless Malachi looked around the room in confusion. He saw Skye's injuries and the destruction throughout the building.

"What happened? Are you all right?" He asked in a panic as he tried to sit up. His body was weak and terribly sore; every movement hurt.

She brushed his hair back with her hand, "I'm fine, thanks to you. How are you feeling?" Her voice was soft and tired. The smell of blood filled the room and her body shook from exhaustion. The storm had ceased outside, but a gentle sprinkle still fell from the clouds. Malachi's eyes scanned the filthy house and destruction. The dead bodies of the men that attacked Skye littered the room. Those filthy *men*—those cowards that would attack a woman; he felt the rage turn in his stomach once more.

"This is the world we swore to protect?" Malachi muttered as he pushed some trash and a beer bottle away from him.

"Lovely, isn't it?" Skye said as she wiped a drop of blood from her cut chin. Malachi buried his face into his hands, trying to hide from the carnage.

"I feel like I just fought the Ox again," he said as he tried to sit up. "Seriously though, what happened?" As she told him of the events that took place, he began to remember everything. He looked around in horror at the men he slaughtered and was grateful he did not hurt Skye in the chaos. Malachi peered down at his Savage Mark, terrified of its power. He told himself he wished he were rid of the curse, but deep down he was thirsting for the next time he could use it. The transformation made him unstoppable and he knew it—he thought not even the Immortals would be able to challenge him.

"Malachi?" Skye asked, concerned as he drifted off into his fantasies. He slowly lifted his gaze up at her and forced a smile.

"Let's get out of here." Malachi helped her to her feet and then looked deep into her eyes, "Are you sure you're okay? I'm so sorr..."

Before he could finish, Skye pulled him in close and pressed her lips against his. Malachi's eyes opened wide in disbelief as she kissed him. They stood there in the room and held each other for a moment, listening to the peaceful pitter-patter of the rain. They did not say anything to each other the rest of the night; nothing else needed to be said.

When they ported back to the Zaurakian estate, it was late into the night. They appeared in the snow after a quick burst of flames and headed toward the fortress. The doors swung open and Zacharias came marching out, his face scrunched into a fierce scowl. His thick black hair was pulled back tight, and he wore a dense fur coat. When he saw Skye's clothes tattered and ripped, his heart sank.

"Where have you been? What the hell happened to you?" He realized she was with Malachi; he dropped his coat into the snow. "What are you doing with him?" Ferocity rang in his voice and a vein sprung from his neck. He darted toward them like a missile; snow flew up from beneath him and shot out in all directions. He punched the exhausted Malachi straight across the jaw. Malachi was sent crashing through the snow, his body already in great pain.

"No! Zach, stop." Skye tried to push her brother back, but he was too quick and spun around her. He flew at Malachi again. Blood dripped from Malachi's mouth; he would not take another hit. Malachi caught the next punch and flipped him over his shoulder into the snow. Zach slid through the slush and sprung back to his feet.

"What did you do to her?" Zach screamed as Malachi struggled to stay on his feet; he shivered in the frigid winds.

"I didn't hurt her! I would never hurt her." Malachi pleaded. Zach reared back ready to strike again, but Skye jumped in front of Malachi.

"He is telling the truth. Stop." Skye cried out with tears in her eyes. Zacharias saw the pain in his sister's eyes.

"Go inside, Skye. Now." She nodded at her brother and turned to go inside. She brushed Malachi's hand and gave him an empathetic look, but he would not take his eyes off Zach. Once she was inside, Zacharias moved toward Malachi.

"What do you think you're doing?" He asked in anger.

"We were just…" Before Malachi could finish, Zach jumped in.

"Don't ever talk to her again." He was yelling now as he trucked through the snow toward the house and passed Malachi. "I'm serious."

"I would never hurt her. I care about her." Malachi said softly, almost too weak to speak. Zacharias spun around and stared straight at Malachi.

"Care about her? You don't even know her! You know nothing about my sister. She is far too good for you. You hear me? She is far too good for an arrogant ape like you."

Malachi roared in frustration. "You have no idea what you're talking about. This has nothing to do with you!"

"What? This has everything to do with me. She is everything to me." Zach's voice became heavy and he even choked up a little, "She is all I have left—" they stood there in the snow and stared at each other for what felt like an eternity, "—and no one will take her from me. Never talk to her again." He turned away and headed back to his home. Zacharias slammed the door behind him and smashed his fist against it; he was furious. Skye wept in her room, certain she would never get to see him again. Malachi was left weak and shivering in the snow, drops of his own crimson blood dripping into the icy powder beneath him. His body was in impossible pain, but it felt nothing like the scalding-hot daggers tearing into his heart.

CHAPTER 12

FEATHERS

The sun crawled over the canyon side and took away the morning shade, the sweat glimmered on Felix's shirtless torso as he pushed through the valley.

"Drive, Felix. Drive." Dag growled, motivating his brother. Felix was strapped to a leather harness that was chained to a large wooden sled. Four enormous and solid clay plates sat on the wooden sled that was being dragged through the dirt by Felix. He let out an exhausted grunt as his shaking body crossed the finish line; he collapsed in the dirt. Sweat dripped from his face and his long hair was tied back in a bun behind his head.

"Well done, brother." Dag said as he held out his fist toward Felix. "I think that's the most weight you've ever done."

Felix, still lying on his back in the dirt, lifted his shaking arm and bumped his brother's waiting fist. "Ya, felt good," Felix panted, as he tried to catch his breath. He had just dragged the sled more than two football fields and his body resented him for it. Felix removed the leather harness and dropped it in the sand beneath him as he rose to his feet. Malachi scooped it up almost immediately and slid his arms in. Felix and Dag exchanged confused glances.

"Hey, we're done for the morning. Let's go take a break," Dag said as he watched Malachi spin the sled around.

"I want one more," Malachi grumbled quietly.

"You already went twice. Let's get some water." Dag said with a chuckle, thinking maybe Malachi was joking.

"Go ahead," Malachi said as he took a ready position and crouched down.

"Are you that worried I'm getting stronger than you, cousin?" Felix joked. "Worried I might actually beat you in our challenge one day?" Malachi did not respond; he began pulling the sled toward the other finish line. Dag and Felix shrugged and followed alongside the sled.

After a few yards, Malachi grunted, "Another." Dag and Felix hurried off to the side of the trail and grabbed one more clay plate to add to the sled. Malachi pulled viciously and was moving at an impressive speed.

"Pace yourself, cousin. You still have a long way to go." Dag reminded Malachi who was stomping across the trail.

"Another," Malachi responded. Dag and Felix grabbed more and threw it on the sled. Malachi continued to press forward, slower now, because the added weight, but he showed no signs of stopping. About half way through, the Sabertooth grunted, "Another."

"You already have too much and—"

"Another!" Malachi screamed. The brother's shook their heads and grabbed one more. The sled was now leaving behind a deep divot in the clay as Malachi dragged it farther and farther. Not even two oxen could pull this load the way Malachi was. He drew closer to the finish line.

"Another," Malachi barely managed to say. Dag and Felix reluctantly rolled a clay disk over and had to lift together to get in on the stack. Malachi was barely moving now, but still pressing forward. He inched closer to the finish line, every muscle in his body shaking wildly. New veins sprung from his neck and across his forehead as he pressed closer and closer. Dag and Felix, against their will, put a new plate on the sled.

Malachi was now on all fours, literally crawling toward the finish line. He released a rage-filled grunt with each step he forced his body to take. His cousins watched in disbelief as Malachi drug an impossible weight through the valley. "A-Another," Malachi struggled to say.

"Malachi let's—"

"Another!" he screamed. Spit and sweat sprayed from his chapped lips.

"Mal…"

"Another!" Ferocity and frustration filled his scream.

"There're no more plates, Mal…"

"Another!" He bellowed once more, only a few inches from dragging himself across the line. Malachi's face was a fiery red, every vein in his body looked as if it were going to explode. He dug his fingers into the ground, and his eyes began to water. He tore his hands through the clay and pushed with great force with his massive thighs. "A-Another!" His voice cracked with emotion as tears streamed down his filthy cheeks. Felix and Dag glanced at each other in confusion and concern.

"Malachi," Felix said softly as he knelt beside his cousin. Vomit spewed from Malachi's lips and he was now nearly weeping, but he would not stop.

"Another!" He cried out like a mad man, sweat and vomit running down his chin. He was maybe a centimeter from crossing his hand over the line, but the sled would not budge. Malachi bore down and pushed with all his might, he let out a ferocious roar. The chain on the harness snapped. Malachi was sent tumbling forward through the clay. He lay in the dirt and wept, his body nearly shaking from the intense pain.

"Dag, go grab some fresh water." Felix said quietly to his brother. Dag gave a nervous nod and trotted off.

Felix sat next to Malachi in the dirt and placed a hand on his throbbing back. He sat silently alongside the Sabertooth until he ceased crying.

"It's that Zaurakian girl isn't it?" Felix asked cautiously, staring up into the cloudless sky. Malachi spit into the dirt and rolled over onto his back.

"Why did it have to be her?" Malachi said, his voice weak and shaky. He covered his eyes with his hand. They sat in the peaceful silence of the morning while Malachi regained his breath.

"Come on, let's meet Dag at the stream." Felix said as he helped Malachi to his feet.

Felix and Malachi limped down the canyon path to a patch of wild palms growing by a small oasis where Dag was still fetching water. An assortment of desert plants and flowers sprouted from the red clay rocks surrounding the tiny water source. The shade hid them from the scorching sun above; the crisp blue water of the watering hole kept their sore feet cool.

"I think you need to go talk to her." Felix said right before he took a swig of water from a leather pouch. He flipped back his long, sweat-drenched hair.

"It's been two weeks since I've heard from her. She doesn't wanna talk to me, Felix. Zacharias probably told Varden... She will be lucky to ever see daylight again." Malachi sighed and washed off his face in the water. The young Sabertooth then lay down across the sand, his bare toes just hardly skimming the top of the water.

"All the more reason to go see her. She has to be bored out of her mind sitting locked up in that fortress. Besides, you need to do something other than training yourself to death," Felix said as he handed Dag the water. Dag poured some of the water across his Mohawk after taking a sip.

"I'm the reason she is locked up, remember? I'm telling you, she doesn't wanna see me." Malachi watched a crimson and gold banner strung to one of the clay towers of the fortress across the canyon dance in the wind.

"I don't blame her," Dag jumped in and teased Malachi. "She probably wants me to come rescue her. A *real* man." Malachi could not help but laugh as he wiped some sweat from his brow. "Come on though, what's the big deal? What is so special about her anyways? There are plenty of girls in Talitha lined up to be with you, and they aren't the sister of your worst enemy."

Malachi laughed again as he shook his head, his cousins got quiet. They were genuinely interested in Malachi's answer. "I'm not sure. She is not like anyone I've ever met." He looked down and ran his hand across his Savage Mark, remembering what he was willing to do to keep her safe. "It's her spirit; she's tough. She's brave. She's wicked smart. She's got this fire in her; she's just different?"

"And I'm sure her figure has nothing to do with it," Dag butted in with a whimsical wink.

Malachi threw a swift jab at Dag's ribs; all of them laughed. As they joked, a winged shadow ran over the oasis and caught the boy's attention. A large red hawk swooped down from the sky and landed by their feet, kicking up dust and sand as it touched down. They looked at each other in confusion. The bird was much bigger than any hawk they had ever seen. It had thin, leather Talithan armor on his breast and head. It bore a symbol on its breast that Malachi was not familiar with, but it was clearly a Talithan design. Malachi, now sitting upright, slowly slid closer to the handsome bird. It twitched its head back and forth as Malachi approached.

"What do we have here?" Malachi asked curiously. There was a small leather sack tied to the hawk's leg. Malachi reached out his hand gingerly toward the bird's head. It pulled its sharp beak back and took a few steps away from Malachi.

"Don't touch it," Dag said in disgust as if it were a rabid rodent. Malachi ignored his cousin and slowly moved his hand toward the hawk once more. The bird's yellow eyes watched Malachi intently.

"It's all right. I won't hurt ya." Malachi reassured the bird, it let the young warrior inch a little closer. Soon, Malachi was close enough to gently brush his hand across the bird's head. Once Malachi felt the hawk was comfortable, he untied the leather sack from the bird's leg. He opened it and a small paper note was inside that read, "TO THE SABERTOOTH OF TALITHA."

"Who is it from, Malachi?" Felix asked curiously.

"It doesn't say," Malachi flipped the bag into his palm and a tiny oval stone fell into his burly hand. It was a dark, blood red. Black streaks danced through the stone and swirled against the ruby's colors.

"Is that a Scorch Stone?" Dag asked, jealousy in his voice.

"I think it is a Lava Stone." Felix answered as they both hurried over to Malachi, making the bird jump back a few paces.

"I think you're right, Felix! I have never seen one before!" Malachi said enthusiastically.

"Me either. You can melt through anything with one of those can't you?"

"That's what they say," Malachi said, unsure of himself as he held the stone up to the sunlight. "Where is Cyrus when you need him?" Malachi thought to himself, missing the human encyclopedia.

"Well, go on then. Try it out." Dag yelled at Malachi. Malachi nodded and placed it in front of one of his vacant Legacy Rings. Almost immediately, the ring morphed and shifted around the stone and merged with it. All three boys *ooh'd* and *aah'd* at the intricate process. The hawk, still standing in front of them—watching, unimpressed by the immature young men. Malachi addressed the bird once more, surprised it was still there.

"Where did you come from? Who is this from?" Malachi confidently asked the bird.

"It's a bloody bird, Malachi, you idiot. It's not gonna talk to you." Dag said rudely to his cousin. The hawk nodded at Malachi, spread its massive wings, and took off. The boys watched helplessly as the messenger hawk disappeared just as quickly as it had come.

"Well hell, Malachi. Go melt something already." Dag barked impatiently.

"All right. All right. No need to get pissy, Dag." Malachi Jumped to his feet and headed toward the entrance of the fortress, his cousins followed closely behind.

"Maybe not destroy an ancient part of our ancestry?" Felix advised as Malachi headed toward an old banner post.

"Ah, zip it Felix. Go ahead Malachi." Dag gestured to a large wooden post sporting a Talithan flag at the top. Malachi nodded and placed his hand against the dark wood of the post, nothing happened. Dag giggled a little at his cousin's failed attempt, making Malachi furrow his brow in frustration. This time, Malachi closed his eyes and truly focused; he took a few deep breaths and then the stone began to glow. The gold ring shifted and moved as Malachi's eyes changed into a sharp canary yellow. His cousins stood and watched, anticipating the destruction of the post, but nothing happened.

"Well, this is just thrilling," Dag said as he crossed his muscular arms across his chest and tilted his head back in boredom.

"What do you mean?" Malachi yelled out as if he was a great distance from them. "I'm flying!" Malachi cried out, smiling from ear to ear. Felix and Dag turned to each other, then spat and snorted as they busted up in a mad laughter. Malachi was still leaning against the post; he had not moved a muscle, and he was certainly not flying.

"The fool has lost it," Dag said as he laughed deeper and deeper, pressing his hand against his gut.

"Malachi, what the hell are you talking about?" Felix was becoming concerned for his cousin. He scratched at his wavy-brown hair and pushed it out of his face.

"Look. I'm flying!" Malachi was yelling again, and he was fully convinced he was soaring through the sky. "I can see the fortress. Oh, look, I can see you and Dag. Look up." Felix and Dag both looked up, actually very curious as to what he was talking about.

"Well, I see the hawk." Dag said confused; he blocked his eyes from the sunlight and squinted.

"The hawk? What? No, it's me. I see both of you. And... I see myself? I see myself against the post?" Malachi now too was baffled.

"Wait," Felix was the first to figure it out. "Stop using the stone, Malachi." Felix exclaimed. Malachi had forgotten all about the stone; he relaxed, and it stopped glowing and his eyes returned to their normal color. Malachi looked around and back at his hands; he smooshed his lips together, trying desperately to solve the mystery. The Guardians were clearly not well known for their detective skills. The hawk swooped down and landed by Malachi once more.

"This definitely isn't a Lava Stone." Malachi knelt in front of the bird, and once again activated the stone. His eyes morphed back to a golden yellow. "I'll be damned," Malachi muttered to himself.

"What is it? What's going on?" Dag asked, still very much confused by all the excitement.

"The stone lets me control the hawk, I think. Or create some kind of mental link, maybe?" The bird spread its massive wings again and took off.

"Is that you Malachi? Or is it just flying away again?" Felix asked.

"It's me. This is amazing. I can see everything he sees. I can control his every movement. It's like our minds are fused together as one." Malachi used the hawk to dart down the cliff-side at incredible speeds. He soared over the valley and dipped down the steep clay rocks with great finesse. The bird weaved its way in-between palm trees and the thin crashing waterfalls that surrounded their home.

"This is incredible. I will be able to survey areas for miles. I could sneak past enemy lines without any chance of being seen."

"I have never even heard of a stone that can do anything like that. It has to be very rare," Felix said in excitement. Dag, more jealous than ever, just shrugged and tried to act unimpressed as he kicked at a stone beneath his bare feet. Malachi deactivated the ring, and to everyone's surprise, the bird came and landed on his forearm.

"What should I name him?" Malachi asked as he scratched his new friend under the beak.

"How about, Hawky? Or Feathers?" Dag asked.

"You're a fool, brother." Felix said as he slapped his burly hand against his own face. "I'm not sure. He is pretty fierce looking. He needs a warrior's name." Felix moved closer to better observe the Hawk. Malachi studied the hawk for a while; it was a beautiful bird. His feathers were a dark reddish color, and random streaks of copper ran down his tail feathers and wings. It had a sleek build, but a strong chest. Its talons wrapped around Malachi's thick forearm; the bird could probably carry off a small goat with ease. His eyes were focused, and his beak appeared as sharp as any dagger. He looked as if he could wreak havoc on any enemy that challenged him. Suddenly, Malachi's eyes lit up and a smirk shot across his lips.

"I think I will call him Havik." Malachi was very pleased with his new companion; his cousins nodded in agreement. "Maybe my father will know who sent him. Let's go ask him." Felix and Dag agreed that was a reasonable idea and headed toward their home.

When they entered the fortress, they saw Tarjak and Ravor standing by the front entrance; they were not alone. A thin scrappy-looking Zaurakian messenger stood in the front room with them. His totem mask was that of a Crow. A narrow bow was strung to his back; his cloak was covered in charcoal feathers and he wore very little armor. Purple beads and tassels decorated his uniform and he sported the Zaurakian crest under the left eye of his mask. His name was Siren; he was Varden's most-trusted messenger.

"Hello, boys. We have company." Tarjak gestured for the boys to greet the Crow. All three of them bowed respectfully; he too bowed in return.

Ravor couldn't help but notice the large bird sitting on Malachi's arm. "What's with the bird?" The Ox of Talitha asked.

"It's kind of a long story." Malachi was more curious as to why Siren was there. Tarjak gestured at everyone to remind them they had a guest.

"My apologizes, how can we help you, Siren?" Tarjak asked politely.

"I bring a message from Aldafar." The Crow spoke quickly. The Talithan Guardians looked at each other nervously. There must be an emergency if they sent the Order's fastest messenger. "Our spies have discovered another Seal. The Great Stag requests that Malachi reports to Aldafar to be debriefed for his mission." Malachi's eyes fell to the ground and his stomach sank, the extraction of a Seal most likely meant facing the forces of Abaddon once again.

"We will all go. I don't want my nephew going on another mission without another Guardian. You Shade Runners and Keepers almost got him killed last time!" Roman, who appeared at the top of the staircase barked. All of them nodded in agreement.

"I apologize, but the Great Stag only asked for Malachi. It will be hot where you are going boy, dress accordingly." In a great gush of wind and smoke, Siren had vanished from the room.

"Great, Malachi probably has to get paired up with those weaklings again." Roman growled and slammed his fists together as he descended the staircase.

"We may disagree with his ways brother, but the Great Stag has not misled us yet. Malachi, gear up, you have a mission. Never the hunted..."

"Always the hunter," Malachi replied with a fearless grin, hiding his true nervousness. He headed to his quarters to dawn the mask of the Sabertooth once more. As he got ready to leave, he realized he probably could not bring Havik with him.

"Sorry, friend. I don't think I can carry you around on my mission. You will have to stay here for now." Havik turned his head to the side and gave Malachi a confused look. Suddenly, Malachi's Legacy Ring began to glow and shift. In a rapid swirling flash, Havik was absorbed into the stone. Malachi's jaw dropped in admiration and for a moment, he sat in awe of his new feathered friend and all of his hidden tricks.

CHAPTER 13

A BROKEN CITY

Malachi ported onto the front steps of the Temple of Aldafar in a ball of flame. He put away his Phoenix Charm and headed inside. As he slid the massive wooden doors of the temple open, he looked around, surprised not to see Zacharias or Cyrus.

"Your Grace?" Malachi yelled out.

"Ah, Malachi. Please come in." The Great Stag's voice came from a room around the corner. He was sitting in a large throne-like chair made from twisting, aged branches. The walls behind him were covered in shelves overflowing with ancient scrolls. At the center of the wall, directly behind the Stag, the great Elder's armor and totem mask were artfully displayed across twisting vines and branches that formed a tee shape. "How are you my boy? Is that a new ring I see?"

"Oh, yes. Were you the one who sent it?" Malachi asked, thinking he had just solved the mystery.

"No, I was not. You don't know who gave it to you?" The Stag asked, surprised by the news.

"No, I have no clue." Malachi laughed, he took off his mask and rested in a seat across from the old man.

"And not to mention, a Hunter Stone. That is a very rare jewel. Take good care of it." Malachi looked down at the Hunter Stone and smiled. "Whomever sent you the stone will reveal themselves when the time is right I imagine; that is very peculiar, my boy. Another mystery for you to solve on your own, I suppose." Malachi nodded and looked around the room. Something about the Great Stag's staff really caught his eye today. He studied it for a moment: all the markings, its crooked shape. It looked fragile, as if the ancient white wood could snap at any moment. "Something the matter, Malachi?"

"Your staff. It's one of the Seals isn't it?" The old man's face wrinkled as he smiled at Malachi.

"Indeed, it is. Why do you ask?"

"I'm not sure. It reminded me of the Spear of Golgotha we tried to recover in Los Angeles a few weeks ago. They have similar markings."

"Impressive. Yes, this is the Staff of Exodus." The Stag picked it up and examined it. "Incredible healing abilities…and has the power to split time and space down the middle. That is how I am able to port as many people as needed, wherever I may choose." He put the staff down and looked at Malachi for a moment, "Speaking of Seals, why don't you tell me what went wrong the other night?"

Malachi looked down in embarrassment, then grunted. "Where do I even begin? I was hotheaded and charged into battle, as usual. Cyrus constantly wants to take charge with these overly analytical strategies, and Zacharias doesn't listen to anyone and thinks he is a one-man army." Malachi was getting frustrated just talking about it. He clenched his fist. "We are all great warriors separately, but together—we are useless. We are all so different. I was taught to charge in headfirst. Cyrus was taught to prepare every moment, every move. Zacharias was taught to be fast, unseen, and efficient and then get out, no questions asked. None of us respect each other and it almost got us killed. I don't know what to do. I don't want to work with them ever again." Malachi stared at the ground, embarrassed and angry.

"Many years ago, I fought alongside your grandfather, Malachi." Malachi looked up at the old man and raised a surprised eyebrow toward him. "That's right. We were assigned a mission together once in secret, and we hated every second of it. He was brash and stubborn, and I was snobby and entitled. We constantly clashed, but we attempted it, because the Elders before me thought it could unite the Order of Eden." His voice became soft and quiet, "And I failed. We couldn't set aside our egos for the good of the Order. We lost a Seal to the Immortals, and your grandfather lost his arm."

Malachi's eyes widened, and his lips parted. "You were there that night? I had no idea. He never told us that story."

"Ha! I don't blame him. That was no glorious victory; that was a complete and utter disaster." Malachi had a hard time picturing those two legendary warriors being beaten in battle. "We failed Malachi, but you will not." He walked around his desk and knelt before Malachi. "You will bring them together. You will bring our families together. One man's path fades with time, but a family can chisel a rode that no man can brush away. It won't be easy, but with this, and this, you can do it." The Stag gestured to Malachi's blade, Tiger Fang, and to Malachi's heart. "Be selfless, fearless, and compassionate, Malachi, and they will follow. One act of selflessness is all it may take." Malachi hung his head and stared at his hands; his mind shifted to what he saw the other night when Skye was attacked.

"I saw something the other night," Malachi said, cautiously. The Old Stag looked back at Malachi, his gentle gray eyes watching patiently. "I saw a side of the humans I have never seen before." Malachi clenched his fist and his jaw; he shook his head slowly. "I don't know if some of them are worth protecting." The Sabertooth shifted his gaze up at the Stag, his eyes shaking with pain.

The old man nodded his head steadily. He gripped his staff firmly in his hands and used it to prop himself up and get to his feet. He moved to the doorway and looked over his shoulder back at Malachi, "None of us deserve to be saved, Malachi. And it is truly the least deserving who need it the most." The great Elder started out of the room. "Selflessness, young Guardian."

The old man headed out of the room, leaving Malachi with his thoughts for a moment. Cyrus and Zach were waiting in the hall now, in an uncomfortable silence. After some time, Malachi donned his Sabertooth mask around his chiseled jaw and headed out to join them. Zacharias clenched his fist as Malachi entered the main hall; he stared straight ahead and refused to look at him.

"Zacharias, Cyrus," Malachi addressed them both. Naturally, Zach said nothing back. All three warriors were not dressed in their usual attire. Instead of their warm fur pelts and thick cloaks, they wore much thinner garments. No longer looking like Norse conquers, they now looked like Middle Eastern warlords from an ancient world. They, of course, still had their same weapons and armor, but were now dressed for a desert environment. Cyrus was not wearing his heavy feathered cloak and hood. Instead, he wore a turban-like wrap that covered the edges of his mask and the back of his head. The cloths and drabs that were wrapped around him were clean and unworn, crisp whites and silvers. Zacharias left behind his thick wolf pelts and wore a large scarf-like wrap around his neck that covered his jaw line and draped down his chest. Malachi too, had shed his pelts and heavy hood for thinner wraps; he still wore the red and golds of Talitha. No longer wearing thicker garments, one could see Malachi's true girth. His broad shoulders plated with battle-damaged armor, his square chest wrapped snug behind a leather chest plate. A dark-red cape, with a gold Talithan crest, hung over just his left shoulder, and Tiger Fang was strapped firmly off to his right.

"Greetings Malachi, the Sabertooth of Talitha," Cyrus nodded. "I hope that this mission is more successful than our last." His voice was optimistic and friendly; he obviously had no idea about the drama between his two comrades.

"No kidding," is what Malachi thought to himself, but he remembered the old Stag's words. "Yes, me too, Cyrus", he said kindly through the snarling fangs of his bronze mask. Malachi hardly listened to the Great Stag as he described the details of their mission, his mind wandered. He was lost; he had no idea how to unify the three of them.

His mind wrestled with his pride. Did he need to humble himself and let the Owl or the Wolf lead? Or did he need to follow his instincts and hope that the other two would simply follow? The stress grew in Malachi's stomach. He wanted to quit. For the first time in his life, he felt like giving up. He knew Zacharias would not listen to him, and Cyrus would want to be in charge of the mission. Malachi wanted to make the Stag—and his clan—proud, but these two were serious barricades in his path to success. He soon realized the situation was out of his hands; he closed his eyes and whispered, "Give me strength. Give me wisdom." He exhaled long and slow, and for a moment, he felt at peace.

"Malachi?" The Great Stag asked, he noticed he seemed unfocused. "Is everything all right?"

Malachi snapped out of his daze to find all three of them starring at him, "What? Oh, yes, I'm fine. Sorry."

"No problem, son. So, gentlemen, are you ready?" The old man asked confidently.

Malachi looked at Cyrus and then at Zach. He took another deep breath, and then answered, "Yes, your Grace. We are ready." Malachi was still not entirely sure where their destination was, but it was too late.

"As I have said before, many people will fight in this war..." the Stag said, "but only a few will change it. I believe you three are those few." The Great Stag's staff slammed into the ground, and in a blinding flash, they were gone.

Dust and sand kicked up into the air as the three warriors ported into a desert wasteland. They were now deep in the deserts of Saudi Arabia, hundreds of miles away from any civilization. The raging sun beat down on them from up above, and the sand burned beneath their feet.

"Which way, Cyrus?" Malachi asked the Owl. Cyrus spun around and gestured behind him.

"We need to head east," Cyrus said confidently. Malachi nodded and headed in that direction, trudging through the mounds of soft sand that seemed to stretch on forever in front of them. After hiking through the dunes for some time, Malachi finally spotted their destination. Made of clay and stone, the ruins of an ancient civilization were hiding perfectly behind the dunes of sand and rock. This once-great city had been slowly decaying from the elements and was now crumbling and weak. At the north end of the city, a massive temple sat alone. A long path of high steps led all the way to the main entrance, guarded by a few towering stone pillars that were still standing. Great sandstone and rock formations surrounded the north and east sides of the city; the trio hid behind them for cover.

"This is it. The Seal is somewhere in that temple. Cyrus, can you scan the city? See if there is anyone else here." Malachi looked over at Cyrus.

"I apologize, but I cannot from this range. My Sight Stone is not effective from such a great distance."

"Don't worry, I can handle it." Malachi said smirking under his mask. He activated his Hunter Stone, and Havik came spiraling out of the ring. Cyrus and Zach watched in confusion. "All right, Havik," Malachi said as he scratched the great bird under the beak. "I need your help." Malachi activated the stone once more and his eyes became like those of a hawk as they did before. "Let's see what we can find." Havik spread his wings and took off; sand and dust sprayed the three of them.

"Impressive, Malachi. Tell us what you see." Cyrus said, interested in Malachi's tactic.

"Nothing yet." Havik flew high above the city, like a vulture circling its prey. "I'm going to get a better look at the temple." Havik folded his wings and swooped down just above the ruins as he made his way toward the temple. Zacharias ignored the whole process and seemed un-amused with the large bird. Havik landed on a building just across from the temple steps and studied the area. "Dammit," Malachi said quietly.

"What is it? What do you see?" Cyrus asked concerned by Malachi's expression. Zach now sat up and finally looked interested.

"Vipers," Malachi's voice was stern and serious. Three Vipers stood twitching and shaking in front of the temple entrance. The hawk's eyes could see every detail of the creatures from where he was perched—their pale white flesh with the green veins running through their bodies, and their bone hatchets and swords they clenched tightly in their rotting fists. Malachi took a deep breath; he knew that Immortals were inside that temple searching for the Seal. "All right, we need a plan of attack." Malachi said, still observing the temple using his feathered friend. Suddenly, a black arrow zipped through the air and impaled one of the Vipers through the head. Before the other two could react, they too were picked off by the Zaurkian archer. Havik and Malachi watched helplessly as Zacharias charged up the stairs to the temple—alone.

"That fool is going to get himself killed," Malachi growled.

Zacharias, consumed with revenge, bolted the moment he realized Immortals were possibly in the temple. He prayed it had been the Immortals that had taken Fenrir's life; he hoped to avenge his brother on this day. Malachi discontinued his connection with Havik and spun around looking for Zacharias.

"Why didn't you stop him?" Malachi barked at Cyrus.

"I too was oblivious to his disappearance. My apologizes Malachi, Son of—"

"Oh, shut up! It's fine. Let's go." Malachi interrupted him knowing that the apology would be long and dragged out. They both slid down the rocky cliff-side and down the sand dunes as fast as they could. "Cyrus, I think something's wrong."

"What do you mean?" They talked as they dashed through the ruins of the city like professional acrobats, tumbling and twisting over every obstacle.

"I think the Order has a mole."

"Like a spy? A traitor?" Cyrus asked, appalled.

"How else are the Immortals always one step ahead of us? They know all of our leads and anywhere we think a Seal might be. Only members of the Order know that information. Someone is tipping them off." Cyrus said nothing; he was clearly disturbed by Malachi's accusations, mostly because they made sense. "But for now, let's just worry about the mission at hand. Create a link between us and try to contact Zacharias." Cyrus activated his Echo Stone and did as Malachi asked.

"Zacharias, son of Varden, and Wolf of the Shade Runners. Please report your location?" Cyrus asked politely as they reached the steps of the temple.

"Go home. I don't need your help."

Malachi clenched his fist, "Zach. Please, we need to work together on this one. Where are you?" Zacharias ignored Malachi's plea. Malachi now spoke aloud to just Cyrus, "If the Immortals don't kill him, I will." He shook his head in frustration, then raised his hand and Havik swooped down to him and was returned to the ring. They continued up the stairs quietly, but it was too late. The Vipers inside the temple noticed their dead comrades and were now spewing out of the main entrance. "Cyrus, how many?"

Cyrus scanned the incoming horde with his Sight Stone, "Twenty-Six Vipers, and two other hostiles in the temple, possibly Immortals."

Malachi drew Tiger Fang from his back and prepared for battle. "Let's do this together, Cyru—" Before he could finish, Cyrus was already engaging the Vipers on his own. Malachi took all the frustration he had for Cyrus and Zach and channeled it into killing the monsters in front of him. He climbed the stairs like a colossal Titan, fearless of the oncoming horde. He swung his blade violently, cutting down multiple enemies at a time. Malachi was fighting recklessly and hacked away at the Vipers blindly. Soon, the Vipers surrounded him; they snarled and hissed as they tried to overpower him. With every slithering opponent he tore down, it seemed as if two more took their place. Malachi, suddenly finding himself on the defensive side of battle, began to feel his Savage Mark burn. His body lusted for the uncontrollable power that hid inside him. It called out to him; it begged him to release it.

As desperately as he wanted to unleash the power, he knew he had no control of it and he could jeopardize the whole mission.

Cyrus, unaware Malachi was in trouble, was elegantly cutting down his foes. He parried any attack thrown at him and responded with a swift counter. His thin sword spun and danced across enemies—first across their chests, and then across their spines. He twirled through the air and released a flurry of silver throwing darts. Each knife always hit its mark, and each one was thrown more dramatically than the last. He jabbed and poked at the Vipers vital ligaments and would watch them crumble to the floor. A silver-haired assassin, the Owl was as fluid and dangerous as ever.

Malachi blocked attacks and tried to spin away from the action, but he was surrounded. A sword cut Malachi across the arm; he kicked his attacker in the chest, then tore through him with his claws. Warm blood trailed down Malachi's chiseled bicep from his wound. His Talithan anger was starting to take control, but he tried to recall the Great Stag's words. He knew he had to keep it together for the sake of the mission—and truly, for the sake of the Order. Again, Malachi took a deep breath, and then regained control of his body and the battle. His eyes became focused and fierce; he smirked under his mask. He threw a swiping backhand with his heavy gauntlet; it sent three of the Vipers spiraling through the air. Their limp bodies crashed into the stone beneath them as they flopped down the stairs. He slammed his elbow into another, crushing its bandaged face with a gruesome *cracking.* Two hatchets came swinging down toward him from two different directions. He dove to the side, dodging both; then, with a single thrust, he ran through both attackers with his sword. Malachi ripped both the Vipers open as he removed his blade from their chests; he was now on a rampage. His punches crushed bone and stone and launched enemies through the air. He wielded his sword like a feather, but the damage was that of an oversized battle-axe. The Owl and the Sabertooth made quick work of their slithering enemies.

"Cyrus, can you patch me up?" Malachi asked the Knowledge Keeper through their mental link.

"Certainly," Cyrus hustled over to Malachi and placed his hand on his arm. Strands of light spun from his Healing Stone and closed Malachi's wound.

While Malachi and Cyrus were fighting off the Vipers, Zacharias lurked in the shadows of the temple. He dashed from cover to cover as silent as a mouse, his bow in hand. As he crept deeper into the temple, he realized he was no longer there for the Seal—his mission was simply revenge. His brother's un-avenged death haunted him. Fenrir was his closest friend, and he wanted answers. Zach would fight all six Immortals by himself if he had to; he had nothing to lose. His heart felt heavy. Rage was flowing through him as he moved deeper and deeper into the labyrinth. Finally, Zacharias found his prey. He entered a large open room. A single cloaked figure stood in the middle with his back to Zacharias. At the opposite side of the room, a narrow stone bridge led to an isolated altar, a twenty-foot drop was under the bridge on either side. The altar was clearly designed to display a small item, but nothing sat upon it. Gigantic stone statues of warriors sat on each side of the altar—their curved blades dawned proudly in their hands.

Zacharias emerged from the shadows, an arrow drawn back tight in his hand. "Turn around," he growled at the hooded man in front of him. The man was clearly surprised to hear Zach, but he did not turn. "I said turn around!" Zacharias shouted angrily.

Without turning, he held up a small leather sack. "Is this what you're looking for, boy?" His voice was shrill and cold. It echoed through the temple like a whisper.

"I'm not here for that. I'm here for you; now, turn around." Zacharias ordered. The man removed his hood and slowly turned to face Zach. Zacharias realized who it was, and his stomach knotted with anger. Grinding his teeth, he scowled, like a snarling wolf.

"What? Not who you were looking for? It is good to see you again. This time, I will not let you live though." Kai, the Screeching Bat hissed at Zach with a chuckle.

Zacharias let his arrow fly; it spun straight for Kai's head. With ease, the Bat slapped it out of the air with his bone hatchet—but

Zacharias had learned from his failures the last time they fought. The moment Zacharias released his arrow, he drew his own axes and followed close behind the projectile. Just as Kai blocked the arrow, Zacharias was on top of him with another attack. The Bat blocked one hatchet, but the other sliced across his chest and tore open his cloak. Kai was caught off guard by the Shade Runner's speed and was now fighting on his heels.

"Impressive, boy. But your speed still makes you sloppy." Kai bobbed and swayed, avoiding the angry Wolf's attacks as his chest wound healed itself. He landed a spinning kick across Zach's jaw, but it hardly slowed him down; he kept attacking with no signs of stopping. Kai used his hooked hatchets to disarm him and sent the Wolf's axes sliding across the temple floor. Zacharias countered with five or six wicked-fast punches to Kai's torso and face. Zach got in close and used his forearms to slap away any attacks from the Bat's hatchets—any opening he had, he threw another quick jab. The Shade Runner had never moved faster; Kai began getting nervous. The Screech Stone on Kai's ring rose and began to shift. Zacharias yelped as he was sent flying backward from the Bat's terrible sonic scream. Kai's bone totem mask hung tightly to his face, its piercing eyes glared back at Zach.

"I may not be the one you were looking for, but what about him?" The Bat asked as he gestured to Zach's left.

Zach looked over, but it was too late, Mednik, the Ox of the Immortals was already upon him. Mednik's massive gauntlet slammed into the unsuspecting Wolf like a freight train. The force of the blow sent him flying across the room; a large stone pillar cracked as he crashed into it. He flopped to the ground where his hatchets had been dropped earlier; his head and body ached with pain. The Wolf moaned in agony as blood sprayed from his lips. Zach's body was still functioning, but his will was destroyed. He knew he had no chance at victory, and he accepted that he might never avenge his brother's death. He closed his eyes; he listened to the heavy stomps as Mednik slowly inched closer to his limp body. The great Ox lifted his heavy gauntlet and prepared to crush Zacharias. Kai's prideful laughter echoed through the temple. Mednik brought his armored fist down with all of his might. Only two sounds were heard in the ancient ruins; the sound of armor being crushed, and the snapping of bone. Zacharias screamed out in terror. Zacharias looked up from where he cowered, baffled by what he saw above him. The Sabertooth of Talitha dove under the attack and caught the Ox's gauntlet. The blocked attack sent a shock wave throughout the temple, making the ancient building shake and moan. Some of Malachi's armor broke under the blow and his wrist was snapped in two. As much as Malachi would have enjoyed seeing Zacharias get pulverized from his own reckless behavior, Malachi replayed the Great Stag's words over in his mind. "One act of selflessness is all it may take."

"I don't need your help," Zacharias said, his voice weak and shaky as blood spat from his lips.

"I don't care. Fight with me," Malachi growled back. "Please, Zacharias," his voice was genuine and strong, "set aside your pride. Set aside our differences... fight *with* me. Together we can win. Together, the three of us could be unstoppable." The agony of his broken wrist shot through his entire arm. Malachi's arms and legs were shaking; he was using every ounce of his strength to hold back Mednik.

A desperate and savage cry, Malachi roared, "ZACHARIAS! We can't bring your brother back... but we can avenge him... *together.* Fight with me!" Chills ran down Zacharias's spine as Malachi's command echoed through the temple like heavy thunder. A new energy rushed to him and he picked up his blades.

"Push back, now." Zacharias demanded through the mental link, Malachi pushed back as hard as he could with a mighty roar and threw Mednik off balance. In a blur, Zacharias slashed away at Mednik's right hip as he wobbled backward. The great Ox released a gritty moan. Although the wound Zach inflicted was deep and gushing blood, the Immortal's pale skin started to heal itself right away. Mednik went to kick Zach, but two silver throwing knives drove into his leg through his armor, again making him grimace in pain. Cyrus dropped from his perch ready to join his comrades. Zacharias ran up the huge man like he was a great oak tree and kicked him in the mouth; Malachi drove his shoulder into his gut and forced him across to the other side of the room.

The three warriors of the Order regrouped across from the Immortals—a new fire was lit inside them all. Malachi flipped backward, landing with a thud and cracking the stone floor beneath him. Cyrus twirled beside him on his left, landing on his pointed toes without a sound. Zacharias kicked up dirt and debris as he dashed to Malachi's right. In unison, the three drew their weapons and struck a fierce stance ready for battle. Kai and Mednik exchanged glances, not sure of what to make of their new foes.

"What's the plan, Malachi?" Zacharias asked through their telepathic link.

"What is our best chance of winning, Cyrus?" Malachi asked, gripping his broken wrist.

"We have a sixty-five percent chance of victory if we fight them one at a time, three on one."

"I'll take it. So, let's separate them."

"How?" Zacharias asked.

"See that drop-off under the bridge behind them? Let's try and put the Ox down there for starters." Malachi said with a smirk. "Cyrus, flank him and disable one of his legs; I will do the rest."

"Very well," the Owl nodded and prepared. "Your wrist, Malachi?"

"It's fine." Malachi said quickly with a scoff.

"What about me?" Zach asked eagerly.

"You have to keep the Bat off us; pin him down until we're done," Malachi ordered. Zacharias nodded and drew an arrow back. "Go. Now." Zacharias shot arrow after arrow at Kai as fast as he could. Malachi lunged at Mednik; he slashed at him with his heavy sword. As Mednik blocked the attacks, he did not notice the silver Owl slyly sneaking behind him. Cyrus poked three precise jabs with his palms into Mednik's thigh, making him fall to one knee. As he struggled to get back to his feet, Malachi landed a punch with his own gauntlet that even Mednik was shocked by. Some of the Ox's bone armor splintered under Malachi's fist, and the stone temple shook from the force. Mednik was violently thrown back and slid into the chasm behind him.

"Malachi, Zacharias, we have exactly forty-six seconds until the Ox climbs back out."

"Then let's make it count," Malachi said proudly as he scowled over at Kai who was watching in terror as his partner fell.

"Cain, my Lord, we are in need of assistance. Send him now." Kai whispered aloud, frantically.

"How do we kill the Bat?" Zacharias said to his comrades with a smile.

"Simple. We make him screech," Malachi said with confidence. Cyrus grabbed Malachi's good hand, and they both spun. Then was Cyrus launched across the room straight at the Bat. The Owl flipped at Kai and elegantly slashed at him with his thin silver blade. Malachi jumped in the air and came down with incredible force right in front of the Bat. He slammed his fist into the ground; it shattered like ice—cracking and shooting in every direction and sending Kai flying across the room. Before Kai even touched the ground, the Owl and Sabertooth were upon him once more. Kai was being overtaken and he was beginning to panic. He activated his Screech Stone, but this time, Zacharias was ready. As Kai opened his mouth to release a sonic screech, the Wolf of Zaurak released an arrow. The arrow shot straight into Kai's mouth and pierced through the back of his throat. The Immortal fell to his knees with the arrow lodged in his gullet, baffled at what had happened. No screech was released, only a muffled gargling and a fountain of black blood came from the Immortal's throat. A new confidence came over the boys; they knew together they could stand against a foe they once deemed invincible.

"He will heal," Cyrus said to his comrades. "Let's get the Seal and leave now."

"Right. One down." Malachi said, kicking Kai over. As the Bat hit the ground, a dense puff of smoke was forming in the air behind

Malachi. The smoke was green and thick; a dark figure was emerging from the cloud.

"What is that?" Zacharias asked.

"It is a Toxic Charm—the Immortals's port charm. Another member of the Six has arrived," Cyrus declared frantically, taking a step back. A tall well-built man emerged from the smoke; he was hooded with a bow and quiver on his back. The bow was dark and demonic looking; the arrow tips were chiseled from bones. His black cloak had the insignia of the Immortals in green on his shoulder; his totem mask was hidden under his hood. A complex bone necklace dangled around his neck and swayed as he moved. His hands were swift as shadows; they struck Cyrus before any of them could even react.

First, he punched the Keeper in the gut twice, Cyrus bent over in pain. The Immortal kneed Cyrus in the side of the head, sending him crashing to the ground. Malachi threw a heavy roundhouse kick at the cloaked creature's head; he dodged it with incredible speed. He chopped Malachi in the throat, then elbowed him in the face; he too hit the ground with a *thud*. Malachi struggled to regain his breath from the attack. The mystery man reached down and removed the leather sack hidden in Kai's cloak and darted for the exit.

Mednik was out of the hole and now charging for the warriors. "Zacharias, GO. You are the only one who can catch him. We will take care of the Ox. Go!" Malachi yelled as he hurried back to his feet.

"Right." Zacharias agreed as he took off after the new Immortal. The chase was on. The man he pursued was clearly once a member of Zaurak; his speed was overwhelming even for Zacharias. It did not stop the young Wolf though. He pushed harder and harder, slowly gaining on him. They raced out of the temple and into the ruins of the city. The sun had now set, and a chilling darkness ran across the ruins. The Immortal rolled and flipped over every obstacle in his path: he knew Zach was hot on his heels. The Wolf hunted his prey, focused and fierce. They ripped through the sand faster and faster. Zach's heart was racing; he felt that familiar anger for the Immortals taking over him once again. The anger gave Zach the speed he needed to close in on the monster; he ripped the leather bag from his cloak and kicked him across the chest as he flipped away. The Immortal stopped and slid across the sand.

Zacharias drew back an arrow and pointed it at his foe. He let it fly, but the Immortal snatched it out of the air, centimeters from his hooded face.

The Immortal spoke quiet and dark, almost charming. "You have gotten fast... little brother." Zacharias knew that voice; he knew it well. Zach's heart stopped; his mouth became dry, and his chest ached. Everything seemed to go dark. Zacharias was trapped in a fog; he struggled to breath. He shook his head in confusion; his very breath had been stolen from his lungs. The Immortal removed his hood to reveal a wolf skull mask—an ancient green mark was carved into the forehead of the skull; scruffy black fur ran behind the edges of his mask. The canine fangs on the skull were long and sharp—others were chipped and cracked. The mask, just like Zach's, covered the top half of his face, but exposed his mouth and jaw. Zacharias looked deep into the Immortal's eyes—one was a poisonous emerald and the other was a soft gray.

"Fenrir?" Zach asked, praying he was wrong. His voice shook with fear. He fell to his knees and clenched his bow.

Fenrir said nothing; he pulled his bow off his back and drew an arrow. Zacharias sat motionless with tears in his eyes as, with an eerie smirk, Fenrir raised his bow at his baby brother.

"Zach? What are you doing? Run. Zacharias!" Zach could not hear Malachi screaming his name from behind. Cyrus followed closely behind Malachi. They too were horrified to see Fenrir alive. Zacharias heard and felt nothing—in that moment, it was as if he were dead inside. He watched as Fenrir released his arrow. Zach closed his eyes. When he opened them, he was staring face to face with Malachi. Fenrir's arrow was driven deep into Malachi's back. Fenrir shot another; again, it speared Malachi's flesh. The Guardian grunted in agony, but he would not move.

Malachi spoke softly to Zacharias, "That is not your brother, not anymore. I'm sorry, but I need you to focus. We have to go." Zacharias said nothing. He sat motionless, his mind in another world. A third arrow was shot and headed for Malachi, but Cyrus jumped in the way and redirected it, using his sword with great finesse.

"Cyrus, get us out of here. Now," Malachi called out to the Owl through their telepathic link. He was in great pain from the arrows protruding from his back. "Hang in there Zach, we're going home." Malachi said, still kneeling in front of Zacharias. In a white flash, they vanished from the desert.

Fenrir stood alone in the ruins of the city—a once-incredible civilization destroyed by a lustful inner struggle for power—now an empty, lifeless, and broken city...a broken city that could not be rebuilt...a broken city scarred by corruption and death.

CHAPTER 14

SEVEN SEALS

Malachi's body clenched in pain as Cyrus pulled the arrows from his back. The white stone floor of the temple began to puddle from Malachi's blood. The Great Stag hurried to his side and began healing him immediately.

"What happened?" The old man asked in shock as he studied the jagged arrows that had been ripped from the Sabertooth's flesh. Zacharias was still kneeling, staring off into the distance, motionless.

"Fenrir," Malachi grunted as his wounds began to heal; he tore off his mask and spit blood from his mouth. "It was Fenrir. That's how the Immortals new all of our leads and plans. Fenrir is an Immortal." Malachi's words rattled the old man; he was just as taken aback as the rest of them. He stopped healing Malachi for a moment. He was at a loss for words. The Stag looked over at Zacharias, his pain obvious.

"The mission was not a complete failure, your Grace." Cyrus broke the silence as he removed his totem mask. "We retrieved the object." He picked up the leather sack and presented it to the Elder.

"Malachi, I need to get you to a healing chamber, and I am going to need my staff. Cyrus, bring that with you and help me move Malachi." He placed his hand on Zach's shoulder, "I'm sorry son; you made the Order proud tonight." Zacharias did not react. He could not hear the Knowledge Keeper's words. They flopped Malachi's heavy body onto a table in the nearest healing chamber down the hall. "Cyrus, go get my staff."

"Yes, your Grace." Cyrus hurried from the room.

"Malachi, what happened?"

"Fenrir knew all of our plans and has been feeding them intel since he disappeared." Malachi said with a groan.

"That explains why they ambushed you in Los Angeles. Fenrir told them that we knew about the Spear's location," the old man said, shaking his head. "So, what happened at the temple?"

"The Bat, Ox, and Vipers beat us there. We were forced to engage head-on. Honestly, things were going great." He clenched his jaw and winced as the old man applied pressure to his wounds. "We finally came together; we fought as a team." Malachi said proudly with a smirk. "It just all went to hell when Fenrir showed up."

"Malachi is an adequate leader, your Grace," Cyrus reentered the room, holding the Stag's staff. He pushed his long silver hair out of his face and took a seat next to Malachi. "He led with wisdom and strength. It was an honor to fight alongside him." Malachi nodded at his new friend, looking rather flattered.

"I did not doubt you three for a second. Still, how did you retrieve the object?" The Stag asked.

"We killed the Bat," Malachi became very serious. "Zacharias put an arrow straight through his throat."

"Very impressive. But, as you know, that will not kill an Immortal of Abaddon—any wound they receive will heal almost immediately. Unless, of course, you disembody them completely like Tarjak did the night of the ceremony. I'm afraid you will probably see the Bat again. You cannot technically kill that which is already dead." The Stag was now using his staff to heal Malachi at a rapid pace; angelic symbols spiraled and hugged the Sabertooth's back.

"Your wrist, Malachi." The Stag said gesturing for Malachi to give him his broken arm. The old man gently took the Sabertooth's wrist and ran his staff above it. Rings of white light encased Malachi's arm and slowly rotated around it.

"Already dead? Are you saying Fenrir is dead?" Zacharias was now standing in the doorway; his mask was off, his long black hair wild and unkempt. The thick mess had not been cut in years; it ran all the way down his back. There was a moment of silence; they were all surprised to see Zacharias joining the conversation.

"Ya, is he? And why would Fenrir join them?" Malachi asked.

"I am afraid so. In order to become an Immortal, they first must destroy your body and spirit. Becoming an Immortal promises you immense power and eternal life. Fenrir must have allowed the forces of Abaddon to kill him...*willingly*. When the Immortals revived him, using a dark and ancient technique, he was reborn stronger than any of us can imagine by being injected with the Serpent's venom." There was a long pause; everyone watched as the last of Malachi's wounds closed. "There are always six Immortals that serve Abaddon. I knew that after Tarjak killed the Boar on the night of the ceremony that they would try and recruit someone new to replace him, but I thought it would be years before that day came. Honestly, I thought that they would come for one of you when you were older." All three of them looked at each other—curious if any of them would have taken the offer. "They only recruit the strongest of the Order. Fenrir was no exception." Bitterness fell over the room; everyone felt betrayed. The Stag tried to lighten the mood, "Well, Malachi, you are all patched up, my boy. You will be sore for a few days, but you should be fine." The old man put down the staff and picked up the leather sack. Malachi sat up, the best he could, and watched closely. Zacharias moved a little deeper into the room.

The Stag pulled the object from the sack; a thick iron key sat in the old man's frail fingers. The key was ancient, grimy, rugged, and heavy.

"I don't remember a key being one of the Seals. What is that?" Malachi asked, confused.

"It is not a Seal, but a key to a Seal," Cyrus interrupted, before the Stag could answer. "It is the only object that can unlock the Chains of

Samson—the Seal that can restrain any living creature." Malachi still looked confused; so Cyrus elaborated.

"There are Seven Seals, all infused with power by the Angels to subdue the Serpent. The Great Stag has in his possession the Staff of Exodus. The Club of Cain is said to be the ultimate combat weapon. The Blade of Isaac can reanimate a corpse. The Pendant of Esther is a powerful teleportation relic and the first port charm. The Coins of Judas can control the mind of any man. The Spear of Golgotha can pierce any material, and as I said, the Chains of Samson can restrain any creature."

"Ya Cyrus, I learned all of that when I was like twelve. I just didn't know the Chains of Samson needed a key. So, what? We have one and a half Seals? And…Abaddon has three? We are still so far behind," Malachi said in a frustrated tone, moving his sore shoulder blades back and forth.

"No, sadly they have four. The Club, the Blade, the Spear, and the Coins. The Spear, as you know, they just acquired, but the other three they have had for thousands of years. The King—Cain—has the Club. Mixed with the Serpent's venom, they use the Blade of Isaac to create the Vipers. And they use the Coins to control the minds of humans, and even members of the Order at times," the Stag reminded Malachi. The young Guardian's head hurt from the elaborate history lesson. Malachi had learned all these things many years ago, but the Guardians did not study the information like the Knowledge Keepers did. Zacharias just continued to listen in silence and said nothing.

"Cain, the King? King of what?"

"Cain was the first Immortal—the first to be recruited from the Order of Eden to serve the Serpent. He is the King of the Immortals and the Vipers, the King of Abaddon."

"Correct. He is not someone you want to engage in combat," Cyrus added. Malachi smiled at the thought of going head-to-head with the King of the Immortals.

"Maybe one day I will be up for the challenge," Malachi thought to himself. "The King defeated by the Sabertooth—the Order of Eden would talk of that battle until the end of time." Malachi began to day-dream; he was feeling quite confident after their mission earlier that day. He ran his hand across his Savage Mark.

"None of the Immortals are men you want to engage in combat; they are wicked and merciless creatures. Demons." The Stag said, forgetting that it was now a sensitive subject for Zach.

Zacharias clenched his fist and turned to leave the room, but he stopped briefly and looked at Malachi and Cyrus. "Thank you. Both of you." Malachi and Cyrus nodded, then looked at each other surprised by the comment. Zacharias slowly left the room. Malachi jumped up to chase after him—moving stiff and sore.

"Zacharias. Wait up," Malachi yelled out as he hobbled down the hall after him. Zach turned and waited for him. Malachi kept his eyes down, and ran his hand through his hair nervously. "We make a great team. I'm looking forward to our next mission. The Immortals will grow to fear the Wolf and Sabertooth." Malachi held out his hand. Zacharias hesitated for a moment, but then grabbed Malachi by the forearm. "If you ever need anything, just ask." Malachi playfully punched Zach in the shoulder. Zacharias' face remained expression-less and cold; he nodded respectfully and continued on his way out of the temple. Malachi leaned against the wall and watched in pity as his new comrade sluggishly walked out of the hall.

Zach felt as if he were drowning as he tried to gasp for air; his frustration was almost as overwhelming as his confusion. Fenrir's dead pale face, hidden under the bone mask, haunted his every thought. He finally received the answers he was looking for, but they left him feeling emptier than ever. He kicked the temple doors open with great force and screamed in agony. He fell to his knees once more as he fought back tears, biting hard on his lower lip. He read the words that had been etched into his gauntlet—the last words his brother had ever said to him:

NO BLADE, NO ARROW, CAN MATCH THE FANG OF THE WOLF

He tore of the gauntlet with his claws and threw it down the steps. Zach lay out on the Temple steps all night; he did not move until the sun crept over the mountainside the next morning.

That same morning, Malachi and his cousins hiked around the perimeter of the Talithan estate to get some fresh air. Havik flew overhead, enjoying the open blue skies. Malachi told them of his eventful mission that unraveled the day before.

"I knew it!" Dag yelled out as they walked across the canyon ridge. Dag was shirtless, as he almost always was when they were home. He spun a wooden staff in his hands as they walked.

"You did not," Felix yelled back, his hair tied back behind his face. The Eagle of Talitha wore a loose and flowing scarlet shirt.

"I did too. I have always said he was Zaurakian trash—a piece of filth. How could anyone turn their back on the Order and join Abaddon?" Dag said, snarling and panting. He always hated Fenrir. He snapped the wooden staff over his knee and threw the pieces down the canyon side in frustration.

"Sure, but you had no idea that he joined Abaddon." Felix said, unconvinced. All three boys pulled to the side of the trail so an ox drawn cart could pass. They all nodded respectfully to the old farmer driving the cart.

"Well, I ain't surprised. Let's go after him. We should be the ones to take him down." Dag said as he punched a nearby palm tree; it splintered and came crashing down. Felix and Malachi had to spin out of the way as the tree slammed to earth.

"Hey. Relax, would ya?" Malachi rolled to his feet; dust and dirt clouded the air. "We will get him when the time is right. We have to be patient."

"Patient?" Felix asked with a smirk, surprised at Malachi's sudden maturity.

"Whatever," Dag grumbled. He ran his hand through his Mohawk, then kept marching ahead.

"Ignore him," Felix said to Malachi once Dag was far enough ahead. "You know, he hates Fenrir." Malachi nodded in agreement and followed Dag.

"Who doesn't hate Fenrir?" Malachi said with a chuckle as they continued across a great stone bridge leading deeper into the valley away from their home. "He was going to kill Zacharias. I saw it in his eyes. He didn't hesitate at all. His own brother." Malachi tossed a small stone off the massive bridge down to a wiry blue stream below. The bridge was handsomely carved from the cliff-side and surrounding red clay like the rest of the Talithan fortress. Decretive desert plant life and vines ran atop the thick stone side rails.

"Good thing you were there. Sounds like you were the hero, again."

"Ha, no. Without those two—I would probably be dead on the floor of a dusty old desert temple. If there is one thing I've learned, it's fighting an Immortal one-on-one is an easy way to get yourself killed." Malachi looked out over the canyon and watched Havik floating leisurely above the oasis. "We had the Immortals on their heels. We were actually fighting as a team." Malachi said quietly, passion in his voice. Felix hung his head and said nothing. Malachi noticed Felix was being uncharacteristically quiet, "What's the matter with you?"

"Nothing," he said. Then, after a few more steps, he stopped and looked out over the bridge. "Well, I don't know. We have trained together since we could walk." He looked around, "We trained on these very cliffs. It's hard to see you have to fight alongside these strangers. We were raised under the impression that we would be fighting beside you on every mission—and you alongside us. We just don't trust Zacharias or Cyrus; I don't think they are willing to lay their lives on the line for you like we would. We are blood, the three of us." The warm morning air drifted through the valley as the cousins continued down the path. They moved deeper into the valley; Havik floated above them making sure never to stray too far. Malachi nodded in agreement with his cousin; he understood his concerns.

"As much as I love fighting with you and Dag, there was something powerful that took hold of me when I was fighting with them yesterday. Sure, as Guardians, our combined strength is unchallenged, but I am learning so much by fighting with the other clans. Yesterday, on that mission, I truly felt unstoppable when we fought together as a single body. I honestly think that if the clans fight together, we could change this war. Maybe even end it." Malachi paused for a moment and looked over at his cousin, "I'm sorry, I know that's probably not what you wanted to hear. You and Dag will always be my most trusted comrades; I promise you that."

"No, I know. You are leading the Order in a way Dag and I never could. We just wish we were out there with you. That's all," Felix said with a smile, returning to his normal supportive attitude. Malachi jokingly punched Felix in the arm, an attempt to feel manly after their vulnerable conversation.

"So, tell that scrawny bookworm and that bitchy archer I will kill them if anything happens to you." Dag yelled from up ahead of them; he had clearly been eavesdropping. Malachi and Felix laughed and picked up the pace so they could catch up with him.

"So, what is Fenrir?" Dag asked once they caught up to him.

"What do you mean?" Malachi asked.

Dag explained, "Well, Cain is the King of Abaddon, right? And they all have a title, don't they? So, if the Ox is the juggernaut, the Bat is the genius, the Vulture is the spy, and the Hyena is the lunatic..."

"Then what is Fenrir?" Felix interrupted his brother and looked over at Malachi.

"Oh, I'm not sure. I hadn't really thought about it. They usually just embrace the role they had while they were a part of the Order, don't they?" Malachi replied as he scratched his head.

"So, an assassin?" Dag snarled in a disgusted tone.

"I guess so. The Wolf, the assassin." Malachi said quietly. A cold silence fell over the canyon. They reached the end of the bridge; they now walked along a faint path that led straight down the center of the canyon.

"You have to be the youngest Guardian in history to have already faced three of the six Immortals. Four, if you count the Boar," Felix declared, impressed.

"Gee, lucky me." Malachi said with a chuckle, "Hopefully I don't run into the other three anytime soon."

"Ah, just send them over to me if you get scared, cousin." Dag growled confidently. Malachi and Felix rolled their eyes. Without warning Havik swooped down and landed on Malachi's forearm.

"What's wrong, Havik?" Malachi asked the hawk, confused by his sudden interruption. Havik peered up into the branches of a nearby barren tree; Malachi and Felix looked over to investigate.

"Someone's watching us," Dag said as he stepped closer to his cousin and brother. "There, in the tree." A hawk, even larger than Havik, sat perched on a branch watching the three of them. Unlike Havik, this hawk had a gray and gritty appearance. Its feathers were scraggily, and it looked as if it had been seen many battles. It was armored like Havik, and bore the same Symbol on its chest.

"Think it belongs to whomever sent you Havik, Malachi?" Felix asked his cousin.

"That would make sense," Malachi said as he studied the gray bird across the way. The hawk spread its large wings and glided down to the ground in front of the Guardians. They all spun around in hopes of seeing its master. It was carrying a small scroll tied above its right talon. Malachi knelt and untied the rolled piece of paper from its claws.

"Get away from that bird!" Roman leapt over a boulder as he yelled out to his nephew. He carried one of his smaller axes; his eyes were red with rage as he tore through the gravel toward them. The hawk, startled by the angry Guardian, spread its wings and took off in a panic. "Kill that ugly feathered traitor!" Roman cursed as he chucked his axe at the hawk. It spiraled through the air and just barely missed the bird; the axe drove into the body of the tree and cracked the bark straight down the middle. The hawk flapped its wings vigorously and vanished over the canyon ridge. Roman screamed after it, "Ya you better run! And tell your filthy master I'll be coming for him too!"

"What the hell?" Malachi and his cousins were baffled by the strange events that just unfolded. "What just happened? Why did you do that?" Malachi asked in frustration.

"Because that messenger hawk belongs to the enemy," Tarjak said from behind them, startling everyone—they had been unaware of his presence. "And I fear the bird on your arm may as well."

"Father? What do you mean *the enemy*? You know who sent the bird?" Malachi asked Tarjak.

"Many years ago, when Roman and I were just young men, a Guardian betrayed the Order of Eden." Tarjak perched himself on a nearby rock and got comfortable. He stroked his scruffy beard as his son and nephews moved closer to hear the story. "He was a highly respected Guardian, and even bore a Savage Mark. But the Order became suspicious of him; his lust for power became worrisome. It was no secret he wanted to be the head of Talitha, but he knew he could not beat your grandfather in combat if he were to challenge him. He would send out his messenger hawks in the middle of the night—in secret—and they would return a few days later.

"When the Order confronted him and asked where he sent his hawks, he had no believable answer. The Order had reason to suspect he was sharing knowledge with the forces of Abaddon in hopes of gaining favor with them. They feared he craved the Serpent's venom, everlasting life, and the incredible power that comes with it. The Order sent the Stag to apprehend him, but they were too late—he had deserted the house of Talitha and hasn't been seen since."

"The traitor lives out in the wilderness somewhere, just rotting away with his nasty birds," Roman added in, as he pulled his axe from the tree. "I'd love to be the one to find him. I'd carve him to pieces." Roman was showcasing where Dag got his temper.

Tarjak would not take his eyes of Havik, still standing proudly on Malachi's arm. "He probably spies on us now. We should kill that bird." Tarjak muttered. Roman nodded in agreement.

"You won't lay a hand on Havik. Besides, only I can see into his mind; we are linked." Malachi brought an open hand in front of Havik and took a step back.

"You are a fool nephew. That hawk would be better off with a spear in its chest," Roman grunted.

"He has proven himself useful in battle and a loyal comrade. Even if he is from this traitor, he isn't anymore. He is mine." Malachi absorbed Havik back into his ring just in case his uncle tried anything.

"Fine," Tarjak said, un-amused. "What did the other bird want?"

"I don't know. Uncle Roman scared it off before I could get the message from it." Malachi said in a frustrated tone. Dag and Felix exchanged glances; they both knew Malachi had extracted the scroll and slid it into his belt before their father had intervened.

"Very well then. Let's head back. We should alert the Keepers that he is active again." Tarjak rose to his feet and moved close to Malachi. "And next time you see one of those hawks, you better kill it. Understand? And if your bird gives me any reason to think it is not on our side, I will be roastin' it over an open flame." Malachi nodded, but Tarjak still swatted him across the head. He turned and headed back toward the fortress; Roman followed him. Once they felt like they were a safe distance from Roman and Tarjak, Felix whispered to his cousin.

"Why didn't you show them the scroll?"

"Because they probably would have taken it before I had a chance to read it."

"Well, what does it say?" Dag asked. Malachi reached into his belt and pulled out the tiny piece of paper. It read;

TO THE SABERTOOTH OF TALITHA:

THE SMALLEST SEAL IS WHAT THEY PLAN TO STEAL.

"Who is going to steal it? The Immortals?" Dag asked as he snatched the paper from his cousin.

"I'm guessing," Malachi replied as he reached for it back.

"Which Seal is that? Does the Order even have the smallest Seal?" Felix questioned as he stole the paper.

"I don't think so."

"How could they steal something we don't even have?" Dag asked as he took it back from Felix, "and how would this guy know that anyway?"

"I said, I don't know." Malachi blurted out. He tore the paper away from his cousins and studied it once again. "We don't even know if we can trust anything this guy says—according to my father. Let's just relax until we get some answers." Malachi stormed back toward the Talithan estate.

CHAPTER 15

THE SMALLEST SEAL

The next day Malachi was awoken by a fully armored Tarjak, the Lion of Talitha. He was prepared for battle; the red and bronze fanged mask, the clawed gauntlets, the massive long sword, and his thick golden mane were all pristinely in place.

"Get up, boy." Tarjak growled sternly behind his mask.

"Is everything all right?" Malachi asked. He was half awake and startled to see his father in his armor.

"Your uncle and I have a mission. I want you to come and hear the briefing with the Stag. Get dressed."

"Yes sir," Malachi hurried and got ready, jealous that his father had an assignment. When Malachi came down from his room, the Tiger and the Bull of Talitha were also suited for war. "They need all of you?"

"Apparently," Tarjak answered as he greeted Ravor, the mighty Bull.

"Do they want Dag, Felix, and me? Should I suit up?"

"No. The Stag is just sending out the veterans today." Tarjak pulled out his Phoenix Charm and sizzled from the room; everyone else followed him to Aldafar. When they entered the temple, Malachi was surprised to see many of the veteran warriors of the Order all dressed for war. Varden was there with all of his Crows and Ravens. Zacharias stood behind them. Like Malachi, he was not suited for battle. Even the great Stag had dawned his antlered mask. Koji the Bear and Cyrus's father, Shara the Crane, accompanied him. It was very rare to see even one—let alone three of the Elders—armored for a mission. Malachi realized this must be a serious situation.

"Gentlemen," the Stag called out to all the men, "thank you for coming so quickly. Let me explain the circumstances. Our trusty Shade Runner scouts have spotted three different Immortals in three different locations. We have reason to believe they are either searching for Seals or have already located them. Therefore, I am sending out three response units to engage the Immortals. The Hyena was spotted in Brazil; the Shade Runners of Zaurak will be stationed there. The Ox was spotted in Japan; the Guardians of Talitha will go there. And lastly, the Vulture was spotted in the United States—myself and two other Knowledge Keepers will be heading there. You all know the rules. If Cain is there for any reason, retreat. Do not engage." The warriors looked around and puffed out their chests, all pretending they did not fear the King of the Immortals. "Fight for your clan. Fight for your brother next to you. Fight for the Order of Eden, and fight for the Creator." Every warrior, except Varden, howled and roared making quite a ruckus. The clans huddled together with their comrades and began to talk strategy.

Zach approached Varden, "Father, are you sure you don't want me to come?"

Varden scowled at his son's interruption from behind his dark wolf mask. "We can't afford to lose another Seal." Varden said in his usual bitter tone, "You and your *friends* are too much of a risk. The Stag is sending me because I do not fail, and he is sending Tarjak simply because I cannot be two places at once. Hopefully, that oaf and the Guardians can actually pull their weight for once. Besides, if Fenrir is there, I am the only one who can put him down." Zacharias looked down and said nothing.

"All right, boy. I will be back. Never the hunted..." Tarjak said to Malachi.

"Always the hunter," Malachi responded proudly. "Good luck," Malachi said farewell to his uncle and Ravor, and they were off.

"Looks like we are going to miss out on all the excitement, huh?" Malachi said to Zach who was sulking by himself, as usual. He wore a dense, black-fur floor-length trench coat. Zacharias removed his hands from under his cloak, turned, and grabbed Malachi by the forearm, nodding.

"It would appear so," Zach said quietly as they watched the Shade Runners and Knowledge Keepers port out of the temple.

"Should have sent us. We're better than all of those washed-up old men," Malachi said jokingly as he nudged Zach.

Zacharias smirked and shook his head at Malachi. "Well, I definitely am, but I don't know about you." Malachi was surprised by Zach's playful banter, even if he remained emotionless and stoic.

"Did you just... make a joke?" Malachi said with a grin. Zach ignored him. "Come on, let's see if we can't find our favorite nerd studying somewhere." Malachi headed up the stairs of the temple, hopeful to find Cyrus. Zacharias slowly followed him. They reached a long stretch of hallway; it seemed as if it went on forever. The hall was decorated with sleek Aldafarian weapons and masks of retired or deceased warriors. There was a clean scratch in one of the many marble pillars filling the hall. Suddenly, Zach's face became more gloomy and serious than usual; he rubbed his finger over the scratch.

"Is everything all right?" Malachi asked, noticing Zach suddenly stopped.

Zacharias looked around, then down at his feet—something was clearly bothering him. He gazed up again at the scratch but avoided making eye contact with Malachi.

"When I was younger, and my father was in meetings with the Keepers, Fenrir and I used to race each other down these halls. Sometimes, my father would be in there arguing with the Elders for hours. Fenrir and I would race as many times as we could until he came out. I never won. Well, except once. I think he let me win." He pointed over at another pillar, directly across from the one where he stood. This pillar had hundreds of similar tiny scratches. "Skye would sit there and watch. This was the finish line. Every time he won a race, Skye would put a scratch in that post with a dagger." He ran his finger over the single scratch one more time.

"And she made that scratch for when you finally won?" Malachi commented. Zacharias said nothing; he just continued to observe the mark. Cyrus emerged from one of the many doors in the hallway. His silver hair braided neatly all the way down his back.

"Greetings Malachi of Talitha and Zacharias of Zaurak. What a pleasant surprise. How can I help you?" Cyrus announced cheerfully. Malachi was happy that Cyrus interrupted the increasingly depressing conversation he was having with Zach.

Malachi gestured to both of them, "Come on. Let's go get something to eat; I'm starving." Malachi said in an effort to distract Zacharias from his memories of Fenrir.

"It would be an honor to consume food with you two," Cyrus said as he bowed gracefully. Malachi tried to hold back his laughter and Zacharias rolled his eyes in annoyance.

"You're lucky you're pretty, Cyrus." Malachi said as he turned away and headed for the exit with Zach.

"What do you mean, Malachi?" Cyrus asked sounding very concerned as he raced after them.

After the meal, the three headed through the great city of Aldafar back toward the temple. Zacharias twirled a dagger in his hand as they walked; he watched as the blade flipped in and out of his hand.

"Why would they split up?" He asked Malachi and Cyrus without looking up from the spinning knife.

"What do you mean?" Malachi asked.

"The Immortals. They always run in pairs. So why did the Hyena and Vulture split up? And why was the Ox spotted alone too?" Malachi and Cyrus looked at each other interested in Zach's question.

"You bring up an interesting point, Zacharias. Ninety-eight percent of Abaddon's missions over the last two thousand years were conducted in teams of two. I wonder what Seals they are searching for," Cyrus informed Zach and Malachi. Malachi halted suddenly and looked ahead as if he was thinking truly hard. An idea clearly came to him.

"What's the matter?" Zacharias stopped a few steps down from Malachi and looked back at him.

Malachi turned his gaze toward the Knowledge Keeper, "Cyrus, what is the smallest Seal?"

"I suppose the Pendant of Esther would be considered the smallest in size."

"Do you have a scroll or something with all the Seals on it? Something where I could see what they look like?"

"Yes, but I am sure Lady Winslow has one in her shop. It is right around the corner. It would take far less time to go to her than all the way back to the temple and search the archives."

"Perfect. Let's go."

Malachi hurried and headed toward Lady Winslow's shop; his friends followed closely behind him. They barged into the shop, almost giving Lady Winslow a heart attack.

"Awk! Surely to God! What are you kooks doing?" Lady Winslow nearly fell from the chair she was sitting in. Malachi hurried over to her side to comfort her, laughing at her startled reaction.

"I am so sorry, Lady Winslow, but we need your help." She gathered herself and fanned her face.

"Oh, it's quite all right, my boy. What do you need, sweetheart?" She asked kindly.

Cyrus stepped forward and respectfully bowed in front of the elderly woman, "Forgive us, Lady Winslow of Aldafar; we are in need of a document that displays the Seven Scripture Seals."

"Oh, sure. There is one in the back; you are welcome to fetch it."

Cyrus bowed once more, "Thank you, my Lady." Cyrus headed into the other room; Zacharias went with him.

"It is good to see you, my boy." Lady Winslow wrapped her arms around Malachi for a quick hug, then pinched his cheek. "I have heard some great tales of you on your recent missions. I knew you would be a thing of legend!" She grabbed his cheek once more and shook him proudly.

"Ha! I don't know about a legend, but I have had some tough fights. Thanks to those two, I am alive to tell the tales." He gestured to the Owl and Wolf in the back.

"I'm glad, sweetheart. You three are changing the Order of Eden for the best. I'm proud of you boys."

"Thank you, Lady Winslow." Malachi patted her on the shoulder.

"Oh! How did your lady like the necklace?" She asked excitedly.

"Ah, she loved it. I can't thank you enough."

"Oh, Malachi, that's just wonderful. I hope she deserves you. And, I'm glad I saved it for you—that Zaurakian boy was very interested in it. I had to tell him about a hundred times that it wasn't for sale." Lady Winslow's comment interested Malachi. He leaned in close.

"Which Zaurakian boy?"

"Your friend's brother," she gestured at Zacharias.

"Fenrir? Why would he have wanted it?"

"I'm not sure, but he was very persistent. Bout' had to fight the boy out of the shop right before you came in that day. And later that night, I caught him in here again; he snuck in here in his full armor and everything. He was snooping around, but when he saw the necklace was gone, he just left. I truly think that fool was going to try and steal it."

"Malachi!" Zacharias called out from the other room; it sounded urgent. Malachi hurried into their corridor.

"What's wrong? Did you find something?" Malachi asked. Cyrus and Zach had a scroll rolled out across the table. An image of each Seal was hand drawn on the ancient scroll. The drawings were simple, and time had weathered away the more intricate details of the sketches.

"I recognize this image. Why do I know this Seal?" Zacharias was pointing at the silhouette drawing of a small amulet. Malachi's heart stopped; his stomach turned, and he felt as if all the air had been sucked from his chest.

"Because it's around your sister's neck," Malachi said quietly; his voice shook with fear. Zach's eyes widened; he frantically shot up from his seat. Malachi recalled the words written on the note he had received;

THE SMALLEST SEAL IS WHAT THEY PLAN TO STEAL.

"I need to get home, now." He stormed out of the shop with a zip. If Fenrir knew about the Seal, which he did, Skye was in terrible danger. Malachi and Cyrus hurried out of the shop as well—suddenly, everything felt rushed.

"What do you advise we do, Malachi?" Cyrus asked.

"Suit up. I think we are going to have a fight on our hands. I think the Hyena and Vulture were just a diversion to pull away some warriors from the Immortals real target: Skye. When you're ready, meet me at the Zaurakian fortress." Malachi hurried outside and pulled out his Phoenix Charm; he burst into flames and vanished.

He ported into the Talithan estate and found his cousins. "Hey! Gear up *now*. I think Skye is in trouble. Let's go." Without question, Felix and Dag jumped to their feet and hurried to get ready. The Leopard came down first, ready for a battle. A leopard skin draped over his right shoulder, three spears strapped to his back, and too many accessories to count. His armor was thick and mainly comprised of shades of red and copper. The Eagle came down quickly after him, his beaked mask looking sharp as ever. His twin straight swords hung from his back, both parallel to his spine. His feathered cloak and armor shimmered with gold and bronze—the red mark of Talitha worn proudly on his chest. Malachi hurried into the main lobby behind them, "Good, you are ready. Follow me." The three heavily armored tanks marched outside. Felix could tell Malachi was frazzled; sweat was pouring down his face, and he seemed to be shaking anxiously. Felix placed his armored hand on his cousin's burly shoulder.

"Hey. She will be fine. We won't let anything happen to her; you have my word." Felix said steadily from under his beak. Malachi nodded and recollected, his breath steadying. They all ported out of their home, unaware of the dangers they were pursuing.

When they ported to the Zaurakian fortress, Cyrus, in his Owl armor was waiting outside the front door of the estate for Malachi. He greeted the Guardians, then followed them inside.

"Zacharias?" Malachi shouted as he entered the building.

"Up here!" Zacharias responded, shouting from Skye's bedroom. Everyone hurried up the stairs. Skye's room was littered with books and scrolls. She had her own library of facts and research, probably to entertain herself when Varden had her on house arrest. Zacharias was fully in armor as well, but was not wearing his mask. "She's not here. I have no idea where she is."

"Dag, see what you can find," Malachi ordered his cousin. Dag activated a ring on his finger; it spun and shifted.

"What is he doing?" Zacharias asked.

"Dag is an excellent hunter. He uses a Blood Stone in order to see scents and trails." Malachi explained.

Dag sniffed around and studied the room for a moment. "She definitely was in here recently, but she ported out. Here, this is the last thing she touched." Dag tossed a small journal to Zacharias. He opened it up and frantically flipped through the pages.

"What is this?" Zach said aloud. The journal had list upon list of random locations all around the world—some crossed off, some circled, and some underlined.

Malachi grabbed the book from Zach. "I've seen her writing in this before. She once told me she wanted to see everything, the whole world. Maybe she is using the Seal to port to as many places as she can? The ones crossed off must be the places she has already been."

"So, she could be at any of these locations? How the hell are we supposed to find her?" Zacharias asked sounding more and more frustrated.

"It would be effective to split them up," Cyrus said as he memorized the locations in the journal. "Zacharias, you and I can take the first half of the list. Malachi, Dag, and Felix can take the second half. Since she is clearly visiting each location, in no particular order, we may just have to guess and check each place until we locate her."

"I agree," Malachi added, "and if anyone finds her, call for backup immediately."

"Fine. Cyrus and I will check the Roman coliseum first."

"Okay. Be careful. Do not start a fight without us," Malachi advised.

"You too," Zacharias said as he reached out his arm. Malachi grabbed him by the forearm; they both nodded at one another; Zach and Cyrus took off.

Malachi released Havik out front of the manor, "Havik, stay here. Alert me if Skye returns. Felix, where is our first stop?"

Felix looked down at the list. "Um. A place called San Clemente in America, I suppose?" They removed their Phoenix Charms and ported to their first destination. Each location would bring them closer and closer to a battle that the Order of Eden would tell tales of until the end of time.

CHAPTER 16

FAMILY REUNION

In the Peruvian Andes Skye sat alone on the stones of an ancient fortress known as *Sacsayhuamán*. The ruins were crafted from enormous stones and set in a strategic alignment down the green hillside. Some of the great gray stones were over twenty feet tall and ran all the way down the valley. As the sun began to set, the stacked stone walls cast heavy shadows across the hills where the ruins hid. Skye took in the beauty of it all and forgot the worries that normally swirled around her head. She was dressed for adventure; a dagger was strapped to her thigh and the Pendant of Esther hung around her neck. A sudden chill fell over the hillside, and Skye had a feeling of uneasiness creep inside her. She turned and looked slowly over her shoulder. Two hooded men, dressed in all black, stood a few hundred yards behind her.

Without hesitation, she sprung to her feet and tried to run, but she was too late. Before she even took a few steps—like a phantom sliding across a shadow—one of the hooded men was upon her. He wrapped his bone claws around her neck and picked her off the ground. He pinned her against the walls of the ruin, her feet dangling beneath her. Her attacker slowly removed his hood; the man wore a bone wolf mask; it was Fenrir.

"B-Brother?" Skye asked, appalled, and struggling to speak. She had heard the rumors, but she refused to believe them; she chose to convince herself that he was still dead. As tears filled her eyes, she slid the dagger from its sheath and cut him across the arm. It startled the Immortal enough to drop her back to her feet. She bolted away as fast as she could; Fenrir's wound healed almost instantly. Skye darted for a stone archway in the fortress, but with ease, Fenrir used his incredible speed to cut her off.

"Come now, sister. Give us the necklace and you will die a quick death. You have my word." His voice was like poison, and still he carried his notorious charm. He leaned against the wall, relaxed, and stuck out his hand as if they were playing a game. Skye had never seen such evil. His bone armor and weapons looked as if they were out of an incredibly dark and twisted fantasy. His mask—now the skull of a wolf—was forged from bone, stones, and iron; it stared back at her with dead eyes.

"How could you? How could you?" She cried out at him as she raised her knife in a defensive position. "How could you leave us?" She kept inching slowly away from him, her hands shaking with fear and anger. Fenrir took a step closer. He ran his vile tongue across his lips with a grin. The Immortal seemed overjoyed - almost giddy. Suddenly, dust sprayed over Fenrir's black boots, forcing him to move back.

A spear had been thrown from behind Skye and drove into the ground between them. Dag and Felix dropped down almost immediately after, "Sorry to interrupt, traitor." Dag said as he pulled the spear out of the ground and twirled it. Malachi ran up behind Skye.

"Come on, let's get you out of here," Malachi said as he gently placed his hand on her back. The overwhelming rage and terror that was racing through her chest finally began to fade upon seeing the Guardians. Malachi turned to run with Skye, but the second hooded man appeared in front of them. They were now sandwiched between two Immortals. Malachi stepped in front of Skye and growled at the second Immortal. "Skye, port out of here, NOW." Malachi barked. She nodded in agreement then fumbled to grab her necklace.

The hooded Immortal raised his hand, a Legacy Ring shined and shifted on his finger. A forceful shock wave, green in color, shot across the whole fortress.

"No one can port until I do," his voice shook Malachi to the core. It was gruesome and powerful—as if the mountains would crumble if he simply told them to. Malachi's heart raced; his nerves were swallowing him whole. Skye tried frantically to port, and suddenly she seemed to evaporate into the sky. Malachi nodded to reassure himself of her safety and released a tension filled sigh.

Just as quickly as Skye had vanished… She reappeared in an emerald flash. Skye stood in front of the hooded monster, clenching the necklace that had failed her.

"What? No." Malachi's voice cracked and rose as he pulled her behind him once more.

"Malachi, take your cousins and get out of here! Please. They just want the pendant." Skye whispered to Malachi in desperation. "Please."

Malachi looked over his shoulder and winked, "Not likely." Whatever fear once claimed Malachi's spirit was being driven away.

As the Immortal stepped forward, darkness seemed to sweep over the earth; his very presence was that of a demonic god.

"Cain," Malachi said confidently. The hooded Immortal tore off his cloak and threw it into the wind. He revealed a bone mask, very similar to Malachi's. It covered his nose and mouth, leaving his pitch-black eyes to be seen in all their terror. A black and gray mane covered his head, neck, and shoulders. Bone jewelry and stones were braided throughout the knotted mess. His arms were un-armored; his biceps were shaped like bowling balls and covered with scars. Two bone and iron clawed gauntlets covered his forearms and hands; they were not big and heavy like Mednik's, but were more sleek and sharp like Malachi's. He wore no armor or clothing across his torso, just elaborate jewelry hung from his neck, all of it made from the bones of his many victims. Any skin that he showed was tattooed with the green markings of the Serpent; they slithered all around his body. The Club of Cain hung from his back. It was a primitive weapon with a jagged stone running down the middle of the bone handle to the end. Its narrow, yet top-heavy, design made it the ultimate blunt-force weapon—able to crush any foe. Alongside it was a bone machete, the mark of the Serpent carved into the grimy blade. Malachi stood strong in front of Cain, trying to prepare for what was to come. He faced the black Lion, the General of the Serpent's forces, the King of the Immortals, Cain…the Author of Death.

Fenrir drew his long and thin bone sword from his belt. Dag and Felix, side by side, took defensive positions. "I have been waiting a long time to run you through." Dag said with a smirk hidden behind his fanged mask.

"You two stood no chance against me when I was simply a Shade Runner, and now you want to fight me as an Immortal? I knew you were dumb, boys, but this is a new low even for you two." Fenrir joked as he confidently paced back and forth in front of the Eagle and Leopard. Dag, offended by Fenrir's comments, attacked first with great ferocity. He leapt in the air and thrust his spear at the Wolf's chest. Fenrir dodged it with his quickness and watched the spear turn a stone to rubble as it drove into it. Felix attacked with both his swords and covered Dag as he regained his position after his missed attack. A spinning kick sent Felix rolling down the hillside. In the blink of an eye, Fenrir put away his sword and drew back an arrow; he took aim for Felix. Dag, using his heavy spear like a bow staff, slammed it into Fenrir's arm and made him miss his target. Fenrir answered with three swift punches to Dag's head and forced him down the hill.

Malachi watched for a moment and hoped his cousins could fend off Fenrir. Then he looked back at his opponent and suddenly only felt pity for himself.

"I have heard whispers of you, boy," the wind carried his oozing voice to Malachi. "My spies tell me that the Sabertooth is the strongest of the Order. They say the Order thinks you will lead them to victory—that you will carry the Order of Eden on your shoulders if you must. You may be strong child, but you have barely brushed the surface of your true power. I can show you true strength; you could be a conqueror, a god. You could live forever as the most fearsome creature to walk this earth. If one of my Immortals ever falls, you have a place by my side in the forces of Abaddon, child." Cain said in his dark and dreadful voice.

"Is that the same horseshit you sold to Fenrir? Well, I am sorry Cain, but I am in my place. Right between you and the Seals." Malachi roared at the King of Death. Cain tilted his head in curiosity, surprised by the young warrior's fearlessness. "And no Immortal, or the Serpent himself, can drag me from that place. You may break my body. You may shatter my armor. But I promise you, I will not move. I will not move!"

"Hm. Then, you choose death," his voice dragged into an echo and sliced into a whisper. "Very well. Send my regards to the Creator. And ask him how many more of his puppets must die in order to keep his once most-valued servant locked away?"

"Ask him yourself," Malachi whispered through the snarling fangs of his mask.

"Well then, come child. Let me see the infamous strength of the Sabertooth of Talitha."

"Be careful what you ask for," Malachi whispered once more. "Father, give me strength." Malachi charged like a crazed bull. With the back of his hand, he swatted a boulder blocking his path; it turned to dust and debris. Malachi pounced in the air, and as he came down, he threw a straight jab at Cain's chest. Cain did nothing. The force of the strike sounded like a train crashing into a mountainside, but Cain did not flinch. Malachi looked up at the monster he had just struck and regretted his decision, but it was too late to turn back now. He flipped away before Cain could strike back and got ready to attack again.

"They said you were strong, boy. Show me." Cain's voice ripped through the hillside. Malachi came in again and struck the same spot, this time Cain hunched over slightly from the force of the blow. Malachi followed with a heavy uppercut from his gauntlet, then threw a fierce kick toward the side of Cain's head. Cain caught it like he was catching a stick thrown by a child; he flung Malachi aside like he was the very child who threw it. Malachi slid through the dirt but rolled to his feet.

"I said show me, boy!" The dark Immortal cried again.

"Dammit," Malachi cursed, then let out an angry roar as he charged in once more. Malachi unloaded punches, kicks, and elbows. Cain blocked them all showing he too was a master of combat.

"That's it, child. Let your anger fuel you. Let it take control. Show me your strength." Malachi's attacks became more and more powerful; eventually, he landed a vicious blow. Malachi reared back his fist and drove it across Cain's armored chin, making him stumble backward. "Good, Sabertooth. Now I will show you why I have never lost a battle." Malachi ignored his words and came in with another punch. Cain avoided it and kicked Malachi across the torso. Malachi released a muffled *yelp* from deep in his chest. Pieces of Malachi's armor and pride shot from his body as he became a projectile across the ancient fortress. He slammed into one of the stone walls and quickly staggered to his feet. His chest pounded; he sucked in the crisp air that his lungs so desperately needed. Dark rain clouds rolled overhead; the sun barely shined over the hill. Thunder and lightning roared across the sky.

"All right, he just got lucky," Malachi whispered to himself as he brushed himself off. "You have been hit harder," he hadn't. "You can take this guy," he couldn't. Just as Malachi was about to charge in for another bout, Cyrus and Zach ported in.

"Took you long enough," Malachi yelled over at his friends.

"My apologizes, Malachi of Talitha," Cyrus said.

"What's the matter? You look like you have things under control," Zach said sarcastically.

"Oh ya, I got this." Malachi joked. "But you should go handle your brother." Malachi pointed down at his cousins and Fenrir who were still fighting. Zacharias stared in disgust at the Immortal whom he once called a brother. He growled with anger, then jolted down the hill with his incredible speed. Like a missile, he slammed into Fenrir with all his might. Fenrir rolled through the grass and flipped back to his feet with grace.

"Cyrus, I could use your help up here, my friend." Malachi said. Cyrus created a telepathic link between them.

"Certainly, Malachi, I would be glad to assist you..." Cyrus hesitated. "Is that Cain? The black Lion and King of the Immortals?" Cyrus asked sounding worried.

"Unfortunately," Malachi informed the Owl.

"We were advised never to engage in combat with..."

"I know. But we can't port out of here. Our only option is to fight."

Cyrus nervously crunched his face under his totem mask. "Very well. Did he use some sort of stone to block long-distance porting?" Cyrus asked reluctantly as he drew his blade and curled it back behind his body like a crane preparing to strike.

"Apparently," Malachi said as he coughed under his mask.

"I shall attempt to inform the Stag of our situation."

"Good."

The Owl, thin and sleek, was not an ideal match for the beast known as Cain. The silver linings of his feathered cloak shimmered as raindrops trickled down his back. He looked to Malachi and nodded, reassuring him that he would fight with him.

"Together then?" Cyrus asked.

"Together," Malachi said proudly.

As the Sabertooth charged Cain, Cyrus slid and rolled, flipping and hopping around Malachi in hopes of distracting the Immortal. The Owl ran up Cain's torso as light as a feather, then spun over the black Lion. As Cain watched Cyrus twirl over him, Malachi continued to charge with great force. The Sabertooth jumped through the air and drove his knee into the Lion's chiseled, stone-like chest. Cain was launched backward, but never left his feet. He backhanded Malachi away as if he were swatting a fly. Cyrus jabbed his talons deeply into Cain's side, and he slashed at him with his thin sword. Cain swung his boned gauntlets at the Owl, but Cyrus showed his flexibility and mobility as he slyly avoided each attack.

"It has been many years since I killed a Keeper," Cain's deep voice snarled beneath his bone fangs, echoing with the thunder overhead. The ancient Immortal's armor was battle-damaged from countless brawls and murders.

"Well, let's keep it that way," Malachi cursed as he blocked Cain's punches from reaching the Owl. Malachi grabbed both of the Immortal's immense fists and tried to hold him back. Cyrus hopped in the air and ran down Malachi's arm as if he weighed nothing at all and headed straight for the Lion. Cyrus was simply serving as a decoy in hopes of creating space for Malachi to land an effective blow. The Owl cracked swift kick across Cain's face, then whirled out of the way as Malachi threw another punch. Malachi landed the strike, but again, it had no effect on Cain. Cain stopped and stared down his two opponents who took defensive positions. As lightning lit up the sky behind him, he slowly reached for the weapon strapped to his back. Both Cyrus and Malachi's hearts began to race with terror as Cain, the ultimate killer, removed his instrument of death from his back. The Club of Cain hung in his hand and seemed to whisper with all the voices of its victims.

Cain pulled it back behind him and swung it parallel to the ground. Malachi rolled under the attack while Cyrus danced over it. The force of the swing sent vibrations and heavy winds smashing throughout the air; the shock wave from the swing alone was enough to send a legion of men flying. The Sabertooth took shelter against a nearby stone wall; Cyrus fell on top of it just above him. Malachi had never seen such brute strength; Cain's power was inconceivable. Cain swung the Club again, this time from the bottom up. Malachi dove to the side, and the Club smashed into the wall. The great wall disintegrated into debris and dust from the blow; Cyrus barely escaped the destruction. The Owl was sent flying through the air, but landed with incredible grace alongside falling shrapnel.

"Malachi," Cyrus contacted through the telepathic link, "I recommend avoiding Cain's attacks when he uses that relic."

"I think that's a great idea, buddy," Malachi said as he looked on in amazement at the power of the Club. "Zach, I hope you are doing better than us down there," Malachi reached out to Zacharias through the link.

Zacharias ignored Malachi; he was in the heat of battle. Dag drove his spear at Fenrir, and Felix kicked at his head. Although outnumbered three to one, Fenrir remained his cool-and-cocky self. The Immortal blocked the kick with his forearm and redirected the spear with his sword. Fenrir, spinning through the air, kicked both Dag and Felix in the head and sent them crashing to the ground. Suddenly, an arrow from Zach's bow pounded into the Immortal's chest. The Immortal looked down at the arrow and smirked as he ripped it from his flesh and threw it to the dirt.

"You will need much more than a few arrows to stop me, little brother," Fenrir said as he drew an arrow of his own. A ring on the Immortal's hand began to shift and glow; his bone-marrow tips began smoldering in a poisonous smoke. The Venom Stone upon Fenrir's ring riddled with toxins any weapon he wielded. He let it fly straight for Zacharias; the young Wolf spun out of the way and Fenrir drew another arrow. It became a battle of speed and archery—the two wolves hunted one another across the hillside. Toxic arrows and Zaurakian arrows cut through the air from every direction. Zach ran across the stone walls like a spider and shot his arrows with impressive precision, but Fenrir matched his every move. They slid and spun, dodging each other's shots with incredible speed. Neither of them could land a clean shot, both the Wolves were two fast and agile.

Zacharias drew his hatchets and attacked head on. "I trusted you!" he screamed as he crashed into Fenrir. Tears and anger filled his eyes—each slash from his blades becoming more and more fierce "You were my best friend!" His words were barely audible behind the grunts and sheer rage. Zach had lost all control and was now fighting with a wild ferocity. Fenrir kept his composure and dodged or parried all of his brother's attacks. Skye watched nervously from a distance, praying neither of them would be hurt. The Immortal blocked a strike and elbowed Zach in the teeth; blood sprayed from his lips and ran down his chin. Fenrir threw six or seven rocket-like punches to his brother's torso and smirked at the sound of his ribs cracking beneath the blows. He completed the combo by bashing the bone handle of his sword into the side of Zach's head. The young Wolf's legs gave out beneath him and he fell to his knees. Fenrir raised his blade and angled it toward his brother's head. In his downward swing, small shimmering fragments of what appeared to be glass or crystal swirled to his right.

The fragments came together and, piece-by-piece, formed a figure: Skye. She swatted Fenrir's sword away with her dagger. The Pendant of Esther around her neck allowed her to disintegrate into microscopic fragments of light in order to port to different locations. She may not have been able to port out of the barrier Cain created, but she could port small distances within the perimeter. Skye grabbed Zach by the shoulder and helped him back to his feet.

"Get out of here, Skye." Zacharias scoffed at his sister.

"Not without you," Skye said as she flipped the dagger in her hand to a more comfortable position.

"How sweet," Fenrir said with a cold laugh. Zach jumped in the air and came down spinning in a furious double-axe attack. Fenrir parried the blades away with his own and jabbed at Skye. Skye, to his surprise, rolled away from his attack. She spun right off his blade, her raven hair twirling viciously as she spun and slashed at him with her dagger. The blade ripped his cheek open and Fenrir grunted in disbelief. In anger, the Immortal swung his blade at her neck. Just as Fenrir's attack was about to decapitate her, she activated the Seal and shattered into millions of pieces. The bone blade slid through where she once stood but struck nothing but air. The millions of shining crystal-like shards danced through the air together like a school of fish, then reformed directly behind Fenrir. Once Skye was whole again, she drove her dagger into Fenrir's back. Fenrir growled and arched as her cold blade slid into his undead flesh. Zacharias then brought down his two hatchets into Fenrir's chest and stomach. The family stayed there, locked together, with blades in their flesh and tears in their eyes.

"Look at us. One big happy family again," Fenrir joked as he ripped the blades from his body and his wounds began to heal themselves. The Immortal's mind was truly lost; he had no remorse or compassion for his once-beloved family members. He kicked Zach away and turned to slash at Skye with his claws. She did a back-handspring-like move to avoid the first attack, but he kept after her. As he clawed at her once more, again, she shattered into fragments and ported to safety. Annoyed with her tactics, he turned to thrust his blade into his brother. Zacharias blocked his next attack and kicked the Immortal in the chest, then twice in the ribs. Fenrir released muffled grunts after each blow, but kept his multi-colored eyes on his attacker. He used his bone sword to shield himself from Zach's blades. With a swift slide of his sword, he pushed his baby brother's axes up away from him.

"You have much to learn, little brother." Fenrir whispered with a smirk. The Immortal released an explosive frenzy of attacks—too fast for any mortal eye to see. Each strike hit its mark and Zacharias was trapped in a hurricane of blades, punches, and kicks. As Zach stumbled backward and wobbled on his heels, Fenrir spun and kicked him across the face. The Shade Runner's Wolf mask ripped from his face and twirled through the air. Zach's limp body rolled down the hillside of the fortress. Warm blood bubbled from his lips as he fought to stay conscious.

"Zach!" Skye screamed, fear swelling in her eyes. As she ran to his side, Fenrir intercepted her. He grabbed her by her thick hair, held her high in the air, then slammed her into the ground. The impact knocked her out instantly.

Fenrir drew an arrow from his quiver and used his Venom Stone to drench the tip with toxins. As he pulled the thin and frayed string of his bow back, Zach's body shook, struggling to get up. Without warning, Felix tackled the Immortal with great force, making him drop the arrow. Fenrir lay on his armored spine. Felix raised his fist. The undead Wolf moved his head just as the Eagle's knuckles came crashing down. The punch cracked the earth and made a great *thud*, but the Wolf kicked Felix off him with haste. Both warriors were now back on their feet; the Eagle threw two quick jabs, but missed both due to the Immortal's ungodly agility. Dag hurried in to help his brother, but he was too late... The Immortal drew his bone blade once more and with deadly speed slashed it at Felix. The attack was so swift, not even Felix realized what had happened.

Felix fell to his knees. Dag watched in horror as blood ran down his brother's neck from a jagged gash across his throat.

"Felix!" Dag screamed under his mask; his heart shook with fear. Felix ripped off his Eagle mask and dropped it to the ground as he coughed up blood violently. His eyes turned red and began to fade; he fell to the dirt, grasping his neck. He tried to stop the blood with his shaking hands, but it spat uncontrollably from between his fingers.

Zacharias had gathered himself and made it back up the hill; he too was frightened to see the carnage.

"No!" He thought to himself, forgetting he was still linked to Malachi and Cyrus.

"What's wrong Zach?" Malachi asked as he dodged another swing from Cain's club.

"Cyrus, we need you here now." The intensity of Zach's voice frightened Cyrus and Malachi.

"Well I—" Cyrus was nervous to leave Malachi with Cain.

"Now!" Zacharias said as he charged in to protect Dag.

"Who is it, Zach? Who's hurt?" A panicked Malachi asked. Zacharias did not answer.

"How bad is…" Before Malachi could finish the question, Cain's fist slammed into Malachi's chest with terrible force.

CHAPTER 17

THE KING AND THE MONSTER

Malachi slid through the dirt, clenching his now-cracked chest plate. He had become distracted; he knew one of his cousins, or maybe Skye, was down. His stomach turned in agony over the stress; he no longer was concerned with his battle with Cain. The King of the Immortals was upon the Sabertooth once more. The bone claws of his gauntlet dug into Malachi's shoulder and tore through his flesh. Malachi groaned as he was lifted into the air, his blood trailed down Cain's arm.

"I'm unimpressed, child." Cain said with a growl as he threw Malachi to the ground in a violent crash. From where Malachi landed, he could see Felix. Malachi clenched his fist in anger as he looked upon his blood-drenched cousin clawing at his open throat. A furious rage consumed Malachi. The rain began to fall heavily. Malachi's chest felt as if it was going to explode; he slammed his fist into the ground, shaking the earth. His Savage Mark burned intensely; Malachi did not fight the sensation as all of its power screamed to be released. In a deep growl, then a sigh of relief, Malachi unleashed the monster hiding within him.

The roar Malachi released shook the whole fortress and even rang louder than the cracking thunder from the storm. His muscles doubled in size and the primitive Savage Mark spread over his body. He steamed and sparked as the raindrops hit his burning body. His armor smoldered and morphed into his flesh; the fangs on his mask grew and seemed to become part of his own teeth. His dirty-blond hair grew and knotted itself as it fell over his shoulders and back. Magma-drenched claws ripped from his hands as the Savage Mark finally covered the rest of his body. He stood hunched over in the pouring rain, a huge smoldering beast.

"Good, I was growing bored with this battle." Cain said coldly as he approached Malachi from behind, showing no fear of the creature. Malachi backhanded Cain without even turning to look at him. Cain was launched through the air and skipped across the ground like a pebble over a lake. He slammed into the cliff-side of the fortress and dug deep into the rock face; the force of the impact released a rattling *thud* more powerful than the initial explosion of a nuclear warhead. Malachi had no idea what he was truly capable of in this form, but he intended to find out.

Cain tore himself free from the mountainside and grinned under his bone mask. Malachi charged him like a rogue torpedo crashing across the surface of the cliffs. With the force of a tidal wave, he swung his giant clawed arm like a falling redwood at Cain's torso. Cain calmly ducked under the attack and carried himself as if they were in a simple training exercise. Cain thrust his armored fist into Malachi's ribs and forced a deep snarling grunt from his throat. With Cain's other hand, he brought his Club slamming into the burly chest of the monster. It was a direct hit and, for a split second, the world seemed to cease moving. Then, in a massive release of energy, time unfroze, and Malachi was sent flipping and tumbling through the hillside. Boulders and stones were turned to rubble as the monster flopped uncontrollably through the fortress.

A silence fell over the battlefield. Malachi was surely dead after taking such a devastating blow, but the hulking monster released another thunderous roar of wrath, shattering the silence, and springing from the destruction his body had left behind. The Savage Marks running across his body were now smoldering even hotter than before; the creature's eyes lusted for war. He shot up into the air hundreds of feet above Cain and came down with the force of an imploding star, leveling the mountainside. The Immortal King crumpled under the force. All the other warriors took cover from the incredible destruction and chaos as earth and debris shot in every direction.

Malachi emerged from the dust, his rage-filled eyes hunting frantically for his next target. Zacharias and Dag both stopped to look up at the creature glaring down at Fenrir—who did not seem to be oozing his usual confidence.

Cyrus, who was knelt over Felix's blood-soaked body, realized he needed to warn his comrades, "I recommend we remove ourselves from this area." Zacharias nodded and grabbed his sister.

Malachi came ripping down the cliff-side like an avalanche, destroying everything in his path. His throat released deep and rabid panting as he charged. Cyrus and Dag dragged Felix away from the action and continued to try to heal his wound. Fenrir zipped away from the monster slamming into the ground where he once stood. The force of Malachi's landing left a gigantic crater in the earth and sent force waves and dust slapping through the air. Fenrir had to tap into incredible speeds and all of his Immortal powers to evade Malachi's mindless attacks. For the first time, Fenrir was not his confident and cocky self; he actually seemed panicked. Every attack left behind extreme destruction and sent Fenrir diving for cover. The power and rage in Malachi's eyes made it clear he we would not stop pursuing Fenrir until he had torn him limb from limb.

Fenrir was pinned against the cliff-side. Malachi dove at him and ripped his claws at the Wolf. He flipped over the attack, the claws swiping Fenrir's cloak and leaving melting claw marks in the stone. The Immortal ran up the wall trying to escape the Sabertooth. Malachi clawed the wall like a grizzly behemoth snarling and growling wildly. Fenrir again dashed away, but Malachi pursued him, relentlessly.

Suddenly, to everyone's surprise, Fenrir dropped and slid across the dirt, leaving himself defenseless. Malachi dove upon him like a lion pouncing upon its prey, but Cain appeared from the darkness of the rainfall and grabbed Malachi by the throat, stopping the giant creature in its tracks. Cain's arm was locked and straight; he did not even flinch as he stopped the speeding freight train.

"Your fight is with me, child." Cain said fearlessly as he stared into the monster's burning eyes. Malachi responded by releasing a dragon-like roar. Cain shut him up by driving his fist into Malachi's fanged face. Malachi came upon him like a raging demon, clawing, biting, and striking with no mercy. Cain was able to block some strikes, but even he was no match for Malachi's power. Cain kicked the monster in the chest, sending him back a few feet, but Malachi returned fiercer than ever. It was truly a battle of Titans; the earth shook with every strike. Malachi drove his massive fist into the King of the Immortals; his body buckled under the force of the attack and Cain crumbled. Malachi snapped the Immortal's femur, concaved his chest, and ripped open his spine. Blood and bone shot from the King's body. The moment Malachi was free from Cain's grasp, he continued his hunt for Fenrir.

Zacharias was now pursuing Malachi and his brother. Cain's body was repairing itself from the encounter with the Sabertooth, and Zach noticed something as he sped by him. A Savage Mark—identical to Malachi's—sat on his spine just below his neck. Cain was already the most powerful warrior in existence, and he had the hidden power of the Savage Mark as well; Zacharias' heart sank at the sight. Cain rose from ground and smirked beneath his bone muzzle as his once-destroyed body finished the healing process. He wanted to see Malachi's true power; he was satisfied for now.

In an angelic glow, the center of the battle field was illuminated by Aldafarian markings. Everyone, except the Sabertooth, shielded their eyes from the light. The Great Stag, armored from head to toe, appeared at the heart of the shinning designs. The rain briefly halted, and a feeling of warmth swept across the fortress. His platinum sword sat in his wrinkled fingers and the Staff of Exodus was held high above his antlered mask.

"Your Grace!" Cyrus called out to the head Elder of Aldafar.

The black Lion and Great Stag stared fearlessly at one another from across the field. Cain's ancient voice spoke, "Wolf, we are leaving. Let the Sabertooth deal with the other children and the old man." A cloud of thick green smoke and shadows began to consume Cain. "Do you feel it, Stag?" His dreadful voice slithered across the hills. "Your death is coming. *He* will be freed." The great Lion of the Serpent's army faded as suddenly as he had come—the air seemed lighter with his absence.

The Stag turned and hurried over to Cyrus and Felix.

"It's been a pleasure, boys." Fenrir said smugly as he was still desperately trying to avoid Malachi. Zacharias released an arrow, but Fenrir vanished into smoke. The Sabertooth tore into the smoke Fenrir left behind and swung about wildly in confusion. He whipped around violently trying to locate the undead Wolf that had wounded his cousin. A sort of peace fell over the valley once the Immortals had ported from the land. Zacharias let out a great sigh as he wiped blood from an open cut across his cheek; the rain forced it to run all the way down his neck and under his armor. He put away his bow and stood in the rain contemplating all that had happened. His heart felt heavy, and his body was riddled with soreness from the battle. They had done well though; they had kept the Seal and Skye out of the hands of their greatest enemy.

Zacharias, who was lost in his thoughts, was awoken by the roars of his comrade. This battle was not over. Malachi, having no control over his own body, locked eyes with Zacharias.

"You saved us, Malachi, well done." Zach said as he spit more blood from his lips. The monster—who was once Malachi—twitched and snarled as he eyed the Wolf. Zacharias expected Malachi to return to normal now that the battle was over, but he quickly realized he was not out of harm's way yet. The burning monster panted wildly as he stepped closer.

Zach slowly took a step backward and whispered, "Malachi... It's me... Zac—" Before he could finish, Malachi darted toward him. Water and mud shot up behind him as he pounced. Zacharias took off in a flurry and ignored the fear gripping his chest. He had never been trained to face such a creature. The storm raged on, and the hillside was slick and dangerous, especially for someone moving at such great speeds. Zacharias flipped over a nearby wall, which was then pulverized by Malachi's steaming armored body. As Zach slid down the hill, he had no clue how to stop the crazed monster, "If Cain couldn't stop him, how will I?" Zach thought to himself. His feet slipped from under him upon the wet grass; he crashed into a large boulder. Malachi drove his claws into his chest and tore at him like a piece of meat. The Wolf screamed out in pain as he was pinned to the stone.

Zacharias watched as Malachi tore off his armor and ripped away the Zaurakian emblem form his torso. He screamed in agony as blood spilled across the ground and covered the monster's claws.

"Malachi?" Zach pleaded in terror, praying he would recognize his voice. Malachi did not. His burning claws carved into Zach as he tore at him—the Wolf could not even scream anymore. Everything went silent; Zach could no longer hear the rainfall or the terrible sounds coming from his armor being ripped from his body. Zacharias tried to call to Cyrus for help, but his mind was consumed with pain, which blinded his focus. The young Wolf of Zaurak released a faint moan that rolled off his bloody lips as the monster raised his claw and aimed for Zach's face.

"Malachi," a strong, yet gentle, voice cut through the air. Skye was drenched from the rain. Despite all the chaos, she seemed elegantly calm. Malachi immediately ceased his attack. Her voice, a soft whisper, struck Malachi's heart like an arrow. Her caramel eyes, framed by long black lashes, locked with Malachi's and crushed him like a war hammer. Her touch on his massive neck released every tension from his body, and he fell to his knees. Not Fenrir, Zacharias, or even Cain, could slow Malachi down—apparently, Skye was the most powerful warrior of all. As Malachi watched her gentle movements, darkness crept in from every direction until he saw only black.

CHAPTER 18

SUNRISE

When Malachi awoke, his body ached, and he struggled to breath. He peeled open his eyes and shook as he tried to sit up. The rain had ceased, and Malachi had been moved into a more sheltered area of the fortress. What was left of his armor and mask had been removed.

"How do you feel?" Cyrus asked very quietly.

"Where's Felix?" Malachi asked without hesitation, fear in his eyes. Cyrus gestured to Malachi's left. Felix lay a few feet beside him, a terrible wound running across his throat. Dag was sitting next to him, emptiness in his eyes. The Great Stag knelt by Felix's head, he quietly prayed over the Eagle of Talitha.

"Dag?" Malachi asked, his voice shaking with anguish. Dag said nothing; he slowly lifted the blood-soaked totem mask of his brother, his hands shook uncontrollably. An expressionless peril ran over Dag's face. Tears filled Malachi's eyes as he slid over to Felix's lifeless body. Malachi fought back a growing sickness in his stomach and tried desperately not to weep. Malachi gently closed his cousin's lifeless eyes and placed a hand on his stiff chest. Dag looked down at his brother once more; something within him broke. He collapsed over the corpse and wept uncontrollably like a child. The fortress echoed with Dag's cries for his fallen brother.

"Fenrir will die," Dag finally said, still clenching his brother's Eagle mask. A stream of tears had cleaned off the dirt and blood in a line down his face. Malachi looked down at Dag, his eyes tear-soaked and red; he bit his lip and nodded. "Fenrir will die. He took my brother. My baby brother!" Dag bellowed, screaming wildly. Malachi slid over to Dag and wrapped his arms around him.

"He was my brother too..." Malachi said as he pressed his face against Dag's; he averted his eyes from the corpse, still in disbelief. "T-Take him home, cousin." Malachi struggled to say. Dag nodded, his hands shaking as he fumbled with his Phoenix Charm.

The Stag gently placed his hand over Dag's. "Allow me." The old man's voice was kind and graceful. "I will send you both to the Talithan fortress." The Staff of Exodus was driven into the mud beneath them, in a flash of light, Dag and Felix were gone.

Malachi stood slowly, agony gripping his chest. "Why him?" Malachi struggled to say. "He was the best man I knew. He was... good."

"Do not pity Felix. He is at peace now, Malachi." The Elder rested his palm on the side of Malachi's face. "Paradise welcomes him. The angels sing his name. He is wrapped in the Creator's arms. Someone so pure and just will be celebrated beyond our comprehension, Malachi." Malachi responded with a weak nod. "The Order will honor the Eagle for all of eternity... and Abaddon will regret challenging us."

Malachi clenched his fist, "Abaddon will burn." The Stag removed his hand from Malachi face and gave him a hopeful glance.

The old man changed the subject. "The other Immortals were only serving as a distraction. From my understanding they all fled after only a few minutes of combat. The other Guardians, Shade Runners and Knowledge Keepers of the Order should have all returned to their homes by now. Your fathers are safe."

"Good." Malachi whispered.

"I am going to the fortress of Talitha. Join me when you are ready." Again, the Stag jammed his staff into the earth. A celestial flash lit up the night sky and the old man vanished.

"M-Malachi, I'm so sorry. I did everything I could. Maybe, if I had gotten to him sooner…" Cyrus's voice was quiet and weak, but before he could finish, Malachi grabbed the back of his neck. Malachi pushed his forehead against the Owl's and he could no longer hold back the tears.

"Thank you," Malachi said weakly as he wiped away smeared teardrops from his eyes. Snot, blood, and tears drenched his face as he fought to stay in control of his emotions. Cyrus stood before him awkwardly, clueless of how to comfort Malachi.

"I'm sorry," Cyrus whispered again. "I'm sorry." Malachi shook his head as he wiped away his tears.

"Where is Zach? And Skye?" He asked as he released Cyrus; he tried to clear his voice and cease crying.

"Zacharias is recovering. Skye is with him." Cyrus answered.

"Recovering?" Malachi asked as he stumbled backward. Cyrus looked away; he did not want to answer.

"It does not matter," Cyrus said softly looking out over the dark hillside. "He is alive. That is all that matters." Malachi was confused, but he simply nodded in agreement; he did not have the energy to dig the answers from him. "I did the best I could." Cyrus said as he gestured for Malachi to leave their small shelter. Malachi slowly wobbled out; he found Zach and Skye lying in the wet grass.

"Zach, are you all right?" Malachi asked sincerely, "What happened?" Malachi activated his Solar Stone to better see through the darkness and was appalled by the massive scars slashed across Zach's torso. Zacharias opened one eye and pushed his luscious black hair from his face, revealing two jagged claw marks that ran over his right eye.

Skye and Zach exchanged glances, "You don't remember?" Zach asked amazed, his voice grumbled with pain.

"No?" Malachi said, almost frustrated with himself.

"It was you," Zacharias said quietly as he closed his eyes. Skye averted her eyes and looked down. "You did what had to be done," Zach added after a long pause.

In quick flashes, the events came rushing back to Malachi. He looked down at his hands and began to shake as he recalled every gruesome attack on his friend. His stomach turned, and he felt nauseous.

"Zach... I'm so sorry." The words barley dribbled from Malachi's lips. He was at a loss for words; he never could have forgiven himself if he had killed Zacharias. "I'm—" He tried to speak again, but nothing audible came out.

Zacharias, with the help of Skye, slowly rose to his feet. "We would all be dead if you didn't use the Mark, Malachi. You kept my sister and me alive. I can never repay you." Zacharias held out his hand. The sun began to creep over the hills from the east. Malachi proudly took Zacharias by the forearm. "I look forward to our next battle, Malachi, Sabertooth of Talitha."

Malachi tried to force a smile, "As do I, Zacharias, Wolf of Zaurak." The sun sat right between the two boys and gave them a glorious warriors glow; they had fought well and represented their clans with honor.

Zacharias pulled Malachi in close, "The Eagle was a brave warrior. I was honored to fight alongside him." Zach whispered to his friend. Malachi nodded and again held back tears. Zach looked over to his little sister, then back at Malachi. "And... I was wrong... wrong, about you two." A small flutter of hope filled Malachi's chest, a glimmer of joy in a seemingly hopeless and tragic night. Zacharias headed over to Cyrus for another healing session and left Malachi and Skye alone.

Malachi ungracefully and stiff, dropped his sore body next to Skye's on the grassy hillside. The sunset created a gorgeous orange sky that warmed the whole countryside after the terrible storm.

"Thank you," Malachi said softly as he looked out over the fortress, "for stopping me when you did. No one else could have."

She nodded, but did not smile. Skye's hair was a knotted, wet mess. Her clothes were ripped and covered in filth; her eyes were red and joyless.

"Felix seemed like a great man, Malachi. He defended Zach and me both." Skye said as she gently placed her hand on his knee. Malachi said nothing; he simply nodded his head in agreement.

"He would have been great," Malachi said quietly as he watched the sun continue to rise. Skye looked at Malachi and tilted her head.

"Great at what?" She asked softly.

"A great leader of our clan. He was going to challenge me when the time came." A single tear ran down the side of Malachi's face; he continued to stare ahead. He brushed away the tear and smiled as Skye took his hand. "So, where to next?" Malachi asked, trying to get his mind off the subject.

"What do you mean?" Skye finally looked at him.

"Well, you still have a lot of places to visit," he said with a weak smile.

She finally cracked one of her beautiful smiles that Malachi was waiting for; it brought warmth to the hillside. "I suppose I do. But I don't think I should travel alone anymore." She said, looking around at all the carnage and destruction.

"I agree. You will need an escort," Malachi said.

"Agreed," she said with a gentle smile as she pulled herself in close and rested against him.

"What about you? What's next for you?" Skye asked seriously. Malachi thought for a while. He held up his totem mask and studied its square and proud Talithan design.

"This war is just the beginning for me," he paused as she nestled her head farther into his muscular shoulder. "I still have a lot of unanswered questions." Malachi observed the dark Hunter Stone on his finger and thought about the origin of the curious hawk he now called Havik.

"There are still many Seals to be found. And, more importantly, Seals to be taken back from Abaddon." He clenched his fist in the dirt. "Felix's death won't be in vain. His sacrifice brought us one step closer to winning this war."

He reached over and examined the Seal around Skye's neck—the Seal his cousin gave his life defending. Tears began to rush back to his eyes; he fought them back and bit down hard on his lip. "I won't let anyone else die. I want to be the one to end this war. I want to be the one to win this war, for Felix. For the Order. And with them by my side," he looked over at Cyrus and Zacharias, "I think we can do it. The Order of Eden will end this war."

They sat in silence the rest of the morning and simply enjoyed the sunrise. A rare moment of peace, something they both knew would be scarce in the days to come... For they knew, the fuse had been lit.

Ephesians 3:20

a B**oo**k's Mind

Whether you want to purchase bulk copies of
Order of Eden
or buy another book for a friend, get it now at:
www.abooksmart.com

If you have a book that you would like to publish,
contact Floyd Orfield, Publisher, at A Book's Mind:
floyd@abooksmind.com.

www.abooksmind.com

Made in the USA
Middletown, DE
27 November 2018